HER BLUE-EYED SERGEANT

Soldiers of Swing: Book One

By
Linda Ellen

Reviews

This story takes place in Louisville, Kentucky during WWII. It's a love story with substance and real life experiences that everyone can relate to. This book is about two young women who join a club that entertains servicemen, and of course, our heroine meets Mr. Right there, but that's just the beginning. Ms. Ellen takes us through their personal trials and family surprises with humor and sentimentality. Sometimes while reading I laughed and sometimes I had to wipe away a tear.

The book is well written and the characters were well developed. It was romantic, included some Kentucky history, and it had a happy ending. What more could a reader ask for? I was pleased to discover book two will be about her friend Mary June. Linda Ellen is a talented author and I thoroughly enjoyed her last series: The Cherished Memories.

~ Christian Western Historical Romance Author Barbara Goss

Her Blue-Eyed Sergeant
Soldiers of Swing Series, Book 1
Written by Linda Ellen

Copyright © 2016 by Linda Ellen
Trade Paperback Release: December 2016
Electronic Release: December 2016
lindaellenbooks.weebly.com
ISBN: 978-0-9909044-6-5
Print Edition

Names, characters and incidents depicted in this book are products of the author's imagination or are used fictitiously. Although this book is a work of fiction, real locales, streets, and places were used. Brands are used respectfully. Details regarding Louisville, Ft. Knox, and the surrounding areas during WWII were taken from the memories of those who lived then, as well as photographs and information found online.

The following story contains themes of real life, but is suitable for all ages, as it contains no illicit sex or profanity.

Cover design by Samantha Fury
Editing by Venessa Vargas
Proofreading by Kathryn Lockwood
Formatting by BB eBooks

Chapters

HER BLUE-EYED SERGEANT

Soldiers of Swing, Book One

By

Linda Ellen

There have been many great WWII romance novels written featuring soldiers serving overseas, with detailed fighting and battles in their storylines. This is a bit different, in that it is a light-hearted story about soldiers and civilians who are contributing to the war effort back home, not a part of the monumental battles fought "Over there." Soldiers on the home front were just as important to the war effort.

CHAPTER 1

Home Federal Savings & Loan, Main Branch
Louisville, Kentucky
April 1942

I
T HAD STARTED out as a normal day for Vivian Powell. So normal, in fact, that she could not have imagined it would hold the power to change the rest of her life…

On duty at her job as a teller in the main branch of Home Federal Savings & Loan, Vivian smiled at one of her Friday regulars as her hands hovered over the smooth black granite counter of her station.

Snapping the crisp tens, fives, and ones, she quickly and expertly counted the bills from customer Frank Allison's cashed paycheck where he could see her actions. Then, she gently pushed the money through the slot under the teller window's shiny metal bars.

"There you go, Mr. Allison. Did you want to purchase a Defense Savings Bond today?" she asked, mindful of the bank manager listening from a few feet away. It was one of his strictest rules that the tellers push the bonds hard.

"No ma'am, I can't today…but I plan to at the first of the month," he promised with a sheepish look.

"All right, then. See you next Friday," she grinned. An attractive girl with wavy, honey-blonde hair that fell just past her shoulders, smooth skin, and beautiful light brown eyes framed with long, thick dark brown lashes, Viv was a favorite among the customers.

This one was not immune to her beauty. He grinned back at her as he scooped up the bills and placed them carefully in his wallet.

"Thanks, Miss Viv. You have a good weekend, now, you hear? You work too hard. You should go out and have fun. Young, pretty girl like you shouldn't spend all her time behind these cold steel bars like she was in jail or something," he added, chuckling at his own joke.

"Look who's talking," she shot back in their customary friendly banter. She knew he worked hard all week at his job as a longshoreman down at the Louisville wharf, and he had the calluses and muscles to prove it. "You go home and tell your wife you're going to take her out on the town. I bet she'd love that."

He smiled shyly at her and almost looked as if he were blushing. "Aww, my Alma knows I've got two left feet when it comes to dancing – but thank the Lord, she married me anyway."

Vivian chuckled and shooed him on his way, her eyes following him with a sparkle of affection as he ambled out the door.

"He's right about you spending all your time behind these cold steel bars," a voice piped up beside her, belonging to her best friend, twenty-two year old Mary June Harriman. "You do need to get out and enjoy life."

Vivian rolled her eyes and cast her gaze over at her friend, a pleasant looking girl with dark brown hair and blue eyes, a bit taller than Vivian's 5'2", and saw she was busy counting out her cash drawer for the end-of-day tally. "You know why…" she paused thoughtfully.

"Yes, I know why," Mary June jumped in. "And it's about time you forgot that creep and got on with the business of living! Just because one guy hurt you doesn't mean they *all* will."

Vivian drew in a large breath and released it in a slow sigh. The two girls had had this same discussion more times than

Vivian cared to remember. But, it seemed she was stuck in quicksand, her emotions frozen in time when she thought about trying to actually *trust* a man again. Her last boyfriend, Walter Guernsey, had lied and cheated, scorching her emotions so badly, the mental scar tissue made her wonder if she would ever get completely over it.

"I really wish you'd think about joining the club with me. It's so much fun, and so many cute guys, it's hard to pick just one," Mary June giggled as she shot a grin over her shoulder.

Vivian grinned back as she began counting her drawer. Both girls were silent for a few minutes as they completed the task and took the day's transactions and money over to Mr. Gates, the bank manager.

Mary June took up the conversation where she'd left off. "Dang it Viv, you're just the kind of girl they're looking for! They tell us all the time they need to recruit more junior hostesses. You fit the requirements – you're single, between 18 and 25, and you're what the men would call *perky, cute, and sweet*, the 'girl next door'. And we need *help*, there are so many soldiers – why last weekend, they decided to keep count of the servicemen visiting the club from noon on Saturday to 6 p.m. on Sunday and do you know how many signed in? *Forty thousand!*"

Vivian's mouth dropped open in amazement. She turned her head, piercing her friend's gaze to see if she were exaggerating – but the clear veracity in the blue eyes staring back at her spoke volumes.

"*Forty thousand?* How is that even *possible?*" Vivian shook her head in bewilderment.

"It's called 'organized chaos', that's how," her friend quipped. "I about danced my feet off Saturday night. The place was packed like sardines – wall to wall uniforms of every size, type, and rank. At times my ever-changing dance partners and I could barely move on the dance floor. But it was still the bee's knees," she added, flashing Vivian a silly grin as she reached into the bottom drawer of her station and retrieved her pocketbook.

Vivian lapsed into thought as she gathered her own things to go home for the day. Her co-worker and best friend had been trying for the past six months to persuade Vivian to join her in the ranks of junior hostesses who helped entertain service men at the USO on the weekends and "reminded them of their girls back home." Vivian remembered the excuses she had given her friend, one after the other…first she begged off because she was dating a young man she had gone to school with and he had insisted he wanted her nowhere near "hundreds of lonely G.I.'s with roaming hands and rushing fingers." Then, when their romance had, as they say, "crashed and burned", Vivian had spent several months nursing her broken heart and keeping strictly away from anything resembling an eligible man.

However, Vivian acknowledged, lately she had begun to realize she had made it through the heartbroken stage and might finally be ready to, as her grandmother used to say, "Take off her scarf and shake her hair loose in the wind." To have fun again, like the twenty-one-year-old that she was, for heaven's sake. To take a chance, stretch forth a foot, and stick one toe into the proverbial "warm waters" again. That thought made her chuckle as she retrieved her own pocketbook and began to make her way to the swinging gate in the half wall that separated the lobby from the tellers.

Changing direction after only a few strides, she decided to make a quick trip to the bank's luxurious employee restroom before sitting on the bus for fourteen grueling, bouncing miles – all the way from Fifth Street to Cooper Chapel Road. Her friend had the same thought, and veered in the direction of the restroom as well.

After finishing their business, the two girls stood at the identical marble sinks washing their hands and freshening up their hair and lipstick for their respective trips home. As Mary June liked to say, *"You never know when you might bump into Mr. Right, and you sure don't wanna look like Miss Wrong!"*

Focusing on her friend's image in the mirror, Vivian casually asked, "So…now, I'm not saying I'm going to, but…*hypothetically* speaking…do I just show up at the club, or…?"

Mary June let out a squeal of excitement and spun to grab Vivian in a quick hug. "You'll come? Oh Viv, you won't regret it. I promise, you'll love it, really!"

"But…"

Mary June forged right on, not allowing her friend to skitter back from that infamous water's edge. "First, you'll need to get a recommendation letter and bring it to an interview with Miss Warren, the club's Recreation Director." At Vivian's look of concern, Mary June hastened, "The letter's just a formality. It's a way to help them make sure they are signing up decent girls, and not floosies or girls that would try to fleece the G.I.'s out of their hard-earned pay," she added with a wink.

Vivian laughed at her vivacious friend. "Well, I sure wouldn't do th—"

The other girl interrupted again, "Of course you wouldn't! Now, you can ask Pastor Rodgers at church on Sunday if he'll write the letter for you – and you know he will, heck he's known you since you were born – and then on Monday, call the club's office and make an appointment to go see Miss Warren. You can do it on your lunch hour, since the club's not far from here. I'll go with you. Okay?" she prompted, eyebrows raised in hopeful expectation as she grasped Vivian's arms. "Oh Viv, I can't wait for you to go to the first dance – you'll be wondering why you waited so long!"

Vivian shook her head and chuckled at her madcap companion. She knew it would do no good to say she had not actually agreed to join her as a USO Junior Hostess. Her co-worker drew her into another quick hug, and then suddenly squealed, "Eeek! We'd better hurry or we'll miss the 4:15!" Vivian laughed again and allowed her friend to scurry her from the room, down the hall, across the cool, elegantly marbled lobby, out the door, and miraculously onto the bus just as it stopped at the corner.

Together, they plopped into the last available seat and smoothed their skirts and hair from their mad dash down the street. Like the good friends that they were, they comfortably chatted about various topics until Mary June got off at her stop on Loretta Street.

Vivian spent the rest of her ride in silence, contemplating what could be big changes in the near future.

TUESDAY AFTERNOON, DURING their lunch hour, Vivian and Mary June sat together in front of a meticulous mahogany desk that held a black telephone, bright green lamp, writing pad, and several metal trays for paperwork. Off to one side was a large Remington typewriter. Vivian allowed her gaze to scan the small room, noting pictures with pleasant nature scenes on the walls, a large green metal file cabinet by the door, and a tall window overlooking Fifth Street. The window was open a little, allowing a bit of the fresh spring breeze to filter in.

A woman sat behind the desk dressed in the popular business style of the day, a dark blue ladies tailored wool skirt suit, and for a moment, Vivian felt a bit out of place in her simple work dress of blue and green plaid cotton with a starched white collar. She unconsciously reached up with one hand and smoothed the waves of her hair, which she was sure were askew from her and Mary June's dash down the windy street. The girls met one another's eyes and Mary June raised her eyebrows for a second as they waited for Miss Warren to finish a telephone call.

Finally, she said goodbye and hung up the receiver.

"I apologize for the interruption," she addressed the girls as she stood and held out one hand. "Miss Powell, I'm Elizabeth Warren, Recreation Director for the USO-Louisville Service club.

I'm in charge of screening junior hostess candidates, as well as a hundred other duties," she added with a warm smile as she shook Vivian's hand.

"Nice to meet you, ma'am," Vivian responded politely.

"Miss Harriman," the woman acknowledged Mary June with an upturned curl of the lips that the younger woman returned.

Sitting back down, the director picked up Vivian's application and reference letter, and then took a moment to peruse them both. Satisfied, she glanced up and smiled at Vivian in a cordial, matronly way.

"Your references seem to be in order, dear. Now then, let me tell you a little about this organization," she began. "Sometime in late 1940, certain businessmen in the city saw the need of a place for our boys in the service to go for clean, wholesome entertainment; a place to relax and feel safe and comfortable when they are off duty. Most of them, you know, will be shipped out to places unknown and more than likely face injury or death," she paused as the girls nodded solemnly.

"Therefore, it is our patriotic duty to see that they have a pleasant time until they are deployed. As a result, this facility was opened on March 7 last year, nine months to the day before Pearl Harbor. We have the honor of being the first soldiers' club in the United States – and we served as a model for the national United Service Organizations' clubs that began to spring up once America joined the war."

Vivian, wide-eyed and suitably impressed, cast a quick glance at her friend, who grinned back at her – she had heard the same spiel when she had first joined.

Miss Warren smiled, pleased with Vivian's reaction. "We are quite proud of what we have accomplished here in a little over a year, Miss Powell. Within two months of our grand opening, we had registered six thousand soldiers and signed up twelve hundred girls to be our junior hostesses."

"Twelve hundred!" Vivian exclaimed, surprised at the scope

of the organization. For some reason, in spite of details Mary June had shared over the months, she had been picturing a room in a basement somewhere with a few dozen people dancing.

"That may seem like a lot, but it really isn't, as the need just keeps growing. Our doors are open seven days a week, 365 days a year, and we welcome all servicemen. And they come – from Bowman Field, the Charlestown Powder Plant, the Louisville Army Medical Depot and the Naval Ordnance Plant, as well as, of course, Fort Knox. More are added out at Knox every week."

"My goodness...I feel as if I've been hiding under a rock or something...I didn't realize," Vivian murmured.

The director nodded as she sat back to continue, warming to the subject so close to her heart. "Many are away from home for the first time, and are nervous about an unknown future, which is totally understandable. The boys were coming to Louisville and prowling the streets, looking for something to do – and at times getting themselves in some kind of trouble. Many would get drunk and miss the bus back to their base, and some would wind up sleeping in the park!" She shook her head, her concern for her "boys" evident in her expression.

"Well, now they have a safe place to come. The club is here to make sure that soldiers are surrounded by good, moral influences, so alcohol is not served, but we provide plenty of hot coffee, doughnuts, sandwiches and soft drinks at all times. We have a good group of matrons and grandmothers who volunteer – our senior hostesses. They provide a shoulder to lean on, a reminder of their mothers. They sew and bake for the soldiers and sailors. Then, our junior hostesses remind the boys of girls back home. They chat with the fellows, play cards, ping pong, board games, and other wholesome fun that keeps our service men out of trouble and away from the bars and..." she cleared her throat and added, "houses of ill repute." Vivian felt her face redden a bit at the director's forthrightness.

"All right, then," Miss Warren handed a piece of paper to

Vivian and then folded her hands in front of her on the desk. "That is a sheet stating our rules, Miss Powell. You will need to learn and follow them at all times. Please sign there at the bottom that you have read it and agree. As you can see, we require that our girls never wear sweaters or evening dresses, just pretty afternoon frocks. You must wear stockings, and keep them *on*, and you must not allow soldiers to escort you home."

Vivian's eyes widened for a moment as she wondered about the rule to keep her stockings on...what could have prompted that? Had some of the girls at first actually stripped that part of their clothing off during a dance? Good heavens!

Miss Warren seemed not to notice Vivian startle, but glanced down at the new volunteer's paperwork as she continued, "Since you work a full-time job, you probably won't be available during the week, is that correct?"

"Yes. Mr. Gates," she motioned between her and Mary June, "our manager at the bank, is...very strict about employees not missing work." *That's putting it mildly; he throws a fit if we're five minutes late from lunch.*

Miss Warren inclined her head, "That's fine. We need the most help in the evenings and for dances anyway. The dances last from 8:00 to 11:30 pm and we ask that you stay the entire time and try to dance with any serviceman who asks. Our boys are looking for home-away-from-camp fun, to have a good time while they're here, so I'm afraid we frown on girls who sit around and act choosey, and pass up poor dancers for good ones. We want our hostesses to be friendly to all. Is that agreeable to you?"

Vivian moistened her lips as she signed the paper, and murmured with a nod, "Yes, Ma'am." She wondered about some of the rules – especially the one about stockings – worrying that she only had one wearable pair and they were quite worn. She had stopped wearing them to work months ago, resulting in going barelegged in the cold winter. Oh, how she hated the rationings and shortages of this war!

As she sat trying to figure out where she could scrounge up a decent pair to wear to the dances, Miss Warren finished, "Our Saturday-night dances feature a regular orchestra and the soldiers must pay a 25-cent admission on those nights. So, shall we see you, then, this Saturday night?"

Vivian once again met her friend's eyes as Mary June nodded enthusiastically. She looked back at the director and answered, "Yes, Ma'am. I'll be here."

The woman smiled happily and stood up, indicating the interview was over. Surprising Vivian, Miss Warren moved around the desk and leaned forward to give both girls a quick hug before intoning, "Welcome to the club!"

Somehow, Vivian felt she had just made a decision that would impact the rest of her life, not just the immediate future.

Oh my…should I be scared? Or excited…

CHAPTER 2

Fort Knox Army Base, NCO Quarters
Fort Knox, Kentucky
The following Saturday night...

S TAFF SERGEANT EUGENE Banks glanced over at the door to his quarters and then back to the mirror over his dresser as he tied his uniform's necktie, giving a grunt of greeting to his roommate, fellow Staff Sergeant Blake Hendricks.

Hendricks, a stocky-built man a few inches shorter than Gene, with dishwater blond hair and green eyes, returned the grunt as he sauntered in, stopping to raise a foot onto the end of his cot as he began to unlace his service shoes. With a scowl, he gave Gene a disdainful glare.

"Don't tell me *Buzzkill Banks* is going prowling tonight."

In the small mirror, Gene's gaze flickered to the other man's for a moment, and then he immediately averted his eyes as he completed adjustments to the collar of his khaki poplin shirt and then tucked the necktie securely between the middle buttons, as dictated by regulations. "I don't know if I'd classify it as *prowling*, but I'm going out with a few of the fellas in my unit, yes. Something wrong with that?" he raised an eyebrow at the inherently inhospitable man.

The ongoing current of controlled animosity between the two men hummed for a moment, and then Hendricks shrugged and continued removing his shoes. "Nope. It's just not something you usually do, that's all. You're not the…*socializing* type," he added, sneering out the statement with the force of a smack-down insult. "You're more the type to sneak around in the shadows and stick your nose where it don't belong."

The two men had been over this ground before, and Gene knew if he asked what the oafish sergeant meant by such a statement, he'd get no answer. This time, he didn't rise to the bait, but tamped his aggravation down and merely placed his dress visor cap on his head at just the precise angle. Always meticulous in his attire, he had spent time earlier cleaning the dark green woolen body and leather brim of the hat, as well as shining the American eagle badge on the front. He leaned over to grasp his jacket off the back of the chair where he kept it, as the other man murmured sarcastically, "Oh be *careful*, can't leave a speck of dust on that wool."

Banks slipped into the olive green wool jacket and began fastening the brass buttons as he glanced over at the man who shared his quarters. Not for the first time, he wondered why they seemed to always rub one another the wrong way, as if they were adversaries, instead of on the same side in this man's war. Well, for him, Gene knew why he wasn't his fellow sergeant's biggest fan – the man was a slob, rude to everyone except superior officers, and in general a swine and a brute. He was exactly the kind of sergeant that the lower ranks hated. In general, he gave sergeants a bad name. But Gene hadn't yet figured out why Hendricks seemed to have formed such an instant aversion to *him* from the moment the man had dropped his duffle in the room, which was a month before, when Hendricks had first arrived at Knox. The arrangement was supposed to have been temporary while more living quarters were built to house the ever-expanding population at the base.

Banks stared down at the shoes that had been dropped haphazardly on the floor. They didn't appear to have had a shine in some time.

"I'd say *your* uniform could benefit from some dust removal of its own, but hey, it's no skin off my nose," he remarked with a nonchalant shrug before making his way to the door. "And if you're planning on catching the bus into town, you haven't got much time."

"Don't need the bus tonight. Got use of a jeep for the weekend," Hendricks bragged as he stripped off the uniform shirt he had worn all day before gathering items in preparation of taking a shower.

Gene didn't answer, but he wondered how the man had managed that feat. Jeeps were in short supply around the base – despite the fact that there was a Ford plant in Louisville that turned them out by the hundreds, most of those were shipped overseas – and high-ranking officers were always the first to snap up the ones that managed to end up at Knox. *Oh well, I don't care what he's got up his sleeve. Makes no diff to me. If he's planning something against protocol, it'll be his butt in a sling, not mine.*

Without a backward glance, Gene continued on down the hall and out of the non-com's quarters to join the guys in his unit for a night at one of their favorite places for entertainment and good clean fun – Louisville's USO Service Club.

GENE CLIMBED INTO the bus for the 30-mile trip from the post to downtown Louisville, grinning as the privates and corporals under his command called out teasing comments and slapped him on the back as he found a seat. He knew it was unusual for them to feel friendly toward a superior, and he was proud of the fact that he had the knack for commanding his men with respect and not intimidation. The thought crossed his mind that he probably should call them down for not showing the proper respect for his higher rank, but he shook his head and decided to let it ride. They were all off duty, and they were all enlisted men. It wasn't like he was a stuffed-shirt lieutenant.

Although not much older than the majority of his men, he nevertheless felt he had to maintain an air of maturity, especially since he was the only sergeant on the bus. However, after a difficult and stressful week, he decided that unless something was to take place that necessitated him taking charge or pulling rank, he would just relax and forget responsibilities for a while. Greeting a few of the guys, he settled into a seat near the back.

Grudgingly, he acknowledged that his foul-tempered room-mate was right about one thing – he wasn't, for the most part, a "socializing" type of guy – and he pondered for a minute how he had been talked into tonight's festivities. He had only visited the USO club in Louisville a handful of times, and he'd not had a particularly good time, usually preferring to stay in the back-ground and watch the others have fun, or he'd head upstairs and play a few games of pool.

The bus got underway and once the driver made the turn onto US 31W, Gene soon tuned out his bus mates' conversations, choosing to turn his attention to the passing scenery outside the grimy window.

For some reason, maybe it was the setting sun; this ride re-minded him of another bus ride he'd taken years before. One conversation, just one tiny piece of information, had rocked his very foundations and shaken his world...

The passing landscape faded and images began to swim by like a newsreel in his head. He had struck out blindly and just ran, hopped a bus, and headed into Louisville to the home of a beloved aunt and uncle. Days later, he was stranded in the city when the rains wouldn't let up and the river began to rise – resulting in the flood of '37. He was days from turning twenty years old. Matter of fact, while working to rescue stranded victims with a jovial group of guys whom he would thereafter call friends, he had, indeed, turned twenty. The guys on the boat affectionately named the "Mary Lou" had sung Happy Birthday to him...albeit, a bit off key.

Gene shifted on the hard seat, trying to get comfortable and ignore the banter of his men as he thought back on those days and the other guys. A soft snort escaped his lips as he pictured a crazy goon named Gerald Gutterman. Always cracking jokes, Gerald was nonetheless a hard worker and a good guy to have along when the going got tough. Then there had been Phil Drexler, just eighteen, and scared of his own shadow. But the one who stood out the most, and who had forever impacted Gene's life, had been their rescue boat captain, Vic Matthews.

The quiet, responsible sergeant's lips now turned up in a slight smile as he pictured Captain Vic – or "Chief" as they had called him. All through those cold, wet hours and days as they transported people to safety, like when they saved the lives of a doctor and his family, and later when they worked day in and day out bringing supplies to those who had remained in their second-story abodes, Gene's respect for Matthews had grown rock solid. Vic had dreams of making something of himself – what did he used to call it? His Big…no, his Bold Venture. Gene had known even then that if anyone in this crazy world could beat the odds and succeed, it would be Vic.

Eugene Banks had decided then and there that he would emulate his one time boss, and that's exactly what he had done. Some months later, Vic had unexpectedly left town and joined the CCC – the Civilian Conservation Corps. Within a matter of days, Gene had given up looking for that ever-elusive job and had sought out Doc Latham, their larger-than-life B-13 Flood Rescue Station director, to see if he would help Gene the way he had given a leg up to Vic.

Doc hadn't let him down. He had contacted a friend at a camp in Illinois and pulled some strings to get him a spot there. Then, determined to prove he was worth something, Gene had never looked back. He had knuckled down, worked hard, made the grade – and then some. Rising to the highest point an enrollee could – Camp Leader – he had earned a whopping fifteen dollars a month in addition to the thirty he had signed up for. He'd been proud of his accomplishments then...although relations with his family back home had been strained. Eventually, he had become a foreman of the machine shop at a forest service camp in the Shawnee, Illinois area. Later, he had transferred to Camp Glenn, to oversee their machine shop.

Those were happy, settled, satisfying days, he mused thoughtfully as he felt the bus pick up a bit of speed going down Muldraugh Hill. He had been good at his job and had enjoyed the work and the challenge. Then, once the draft had begun in 1940, his number had come up and he transitioned straight into the army – but as a CCC alumni, he entered as a technical sergeant, pay grade Four. He chuckled softly as he remembered his swearing in ceremony – he sure was walking in high cotton. Then, after the required number of months, he was promoted again...

"Hey Sarge, don't you want in on this?" a voice interrupted his reminiscing.

Gene shook off his memories and turned to one of the men in his unit, Corporal James Evans.

"In on what, Evans?"

"We're takin' bets on who'll snag the most dances, Mack or Rooster," the soldier explained as the others nearby continued to joke and laugh with one another.

A soldier called from four seats up, "I say if it's as packed out as it was last week, we'll be lucky if *any* of us get more than one." The corporal next to him gave him a friendly backhand as his comment caused a chorus of moans and groans.

Gene set eyes on the objects of the bet, and his gaze settled on Private First Class Archie Makowski, a.k.a Mack, whom they all acknowledged resembled a young Tyrone Power and was usually in the sites of every female within aiming distance. The other guy, Private Conrad Deal, a.k.a. Rooster, was a tall drink of water with a stubborn cowlick in his red hair – hence the nickname. He could really cut a rug and thought he was cock of the walk when it came to the ladies. In Gene's opinion, however, if either of them could rack up multiple dances tonight with young, pretty junior hostesses, it would be Mack.

"I'd say my money'd have to be on Makowski." Gene chuckled and shook his head with a half grin as the men hooted and hollered, and reached to slap the young private on the back. Pfc. Makowski just grinned and stood up to take a quick bow, laughing and bending over to retrieve his cap after someone teasingly cuffed it off his head.

"What's the ante?" Gene asked, reaching for his wallet and pulling out the required dollar bill to chip in with the others. "Who's holding the pot?"

That job had immediately gone to the group's usual instigator of shenanigans, Private Red Ackerman, a tall, lanky, sandy-haired recruit from Tennessee who always seemed to be starting up a wager of some kind or another.

"Here you go, Ackerman," Gene murmured as he stretched to hand his money to the private. Then focusing again on Pfc. Makowski, he pointed a finger at him and affected his sternest *staff sergeant* scowl as he growled, "Don't let me down, Private, or you'll be on KP for a week."

Everyone on the bus roared with laughter, even the bus driver up front. Gene joined in as the wheels kept rolling, taking them on to their destination – and their "dates" with Louisville's best and prettiest young women.

For the first time in a long time, Eugene Banks felt something he couldn't define…something deep down in his gut told him that this night would change the rest of his life.

But, in a good way…or a bad?

IT WAS JUST after 8:00 p.m. when the bus pulled to a stop in front of the large three-story stone and brick building already teaming with servicemen of every branch – but mostly army. From the open windows of the bus, the men could hear music playing inside – a rousing rendition of Glenn Miller's *Chattanooga Choo Choo*.

Gene rose from his seat and shuffled along in line with the others as they disembarked. Standing for a moment on the sidewalk, he gazed up at the large blue-lettered sign above the marble-columned entryway at the front, and a curious shiver of anticipation rippled from the nape of his neck all the way down his back. Vaguely, he wondered at the sensation, knowing that had not happened the other times he had visited the club.

Pvt. Ackerman nudged him with an elbow. "C'mon Sarge, the sooner we get in there, the sooner we'll be Cookin' with Helium." Gene shook his head and chuckled at the silly term for dancing the young "hepcats" used, as he and the others made their way up the steps of the building and inside.

A pretty girl with short dark hair, stationed at a table inside the door, smiled at the newcomers. "Welcome to the Louisville Service Club, gentlemen. That'll be twenty-five cents each, please."

The soldiers all began to dig in their pockets for a quarter, eagerly placing it in her hand and signing their names to the register.

"Have a good time. There's plenty of food, soda, and coffee…and we've got some new girls to dance with tonight," she added with a shy smile as Pfc. Makowski flashed his pearly whites and gave her one of his trademark winks.

"That's swell, honey, 'cause I'm planning on knockin' it out 'till the cows come home," he declared with teasing assurance as he turned to make his way toward the large open room used as a dance hall.

"Cows is right, since you dance like a bull in a china shop," Rooster called after him with good-natured teasing. Mack spun around, raised his hands to his forehead to resemble bull's horns and let out a loud snort, before turning back around with a laugh and heading into the fun.

Gene watched him go and then met the girl's eyes and grinned at the look on her face. "A man with a plan," he needlessly qualified. Pvt. Ackerman snorted and mumbled, "Yeah, hope the showboat don't crash and burn. My money's riding on him, too."

They made their way to the door of the dance hall as Gene laid an arm over Red's shoulder. In a jovial mood, the serious sergeant teased, "Relax Ackerman, those new girls will be breaking their own rules and lining up to cut a rug with our Mack. It's as good as in the bag."

The private grinned over at him as the guys threaded their way to a spot near the wall where they could observe the action. The dance floor was packed with G.I.'s of all sizes and uniforms, dancing with girls in dresses of every color. The press of so many bodies was already making the room hot and the dance had just barely started. Gene reached up and hooked two fingers under his collar as the song ended and the band on the raised platform immediately launched into another Glenn Miller hit, *In The Mood.*

Within the first eight bars, Pfc. Makowski had a cute redhead in his arms and was sashaying to beat the band. Ackerman nudged Gene and leaned closer to shout over the music and noise, "Our boy's off and running!" Gene nodded with a laugh as he watched the young, good-looking private really going to town, and perfectly in sync with the distinctive rhythm of the song. The girl in his arms was gazing up at him, totally enraptured as she followed his every lead. The look on her face suggested she thought he might be Tyrone Power's younger brother.

After a few moments, Gene turned his attention to the band, watching as they mimicked the back and forth and up and down movements of the real Glenn Miller Orchestra's trombones and saxophones while belting out the notes of the song, just like in the movie *Sun Valley Serenade*. He leaned toward another member of his platoon standing to his left. "Hey, those guys are really good!"

A young woman just in front of Gene turned and gave him a friendly smile. "That's Johnny Burkhart and his orchestra," she gushed enthusiastically. "Aren't they just the Killer Diller?!"

Gene smiled back at her and nodded in agreement as the private next to him took the girl's hand and pulled her a few feet into the press of dancers.

Looking once again at the band, Gene noticed their leader, tall and lean, with slick black hair and tanned skin, had a genuine command of his musicians and the music. Gene had heard about the somewhat famous local band and he could see that the accolades were not exaggerated. He watched until the band brought the song to its rousing conclusion, and the entire room erupted in appreciative applause.

"Whew, it's hot in here," Gene murmured to no one in particular, deciding at that moment to make his way to the far end of the large room where refreshments were offered. Before he moved away, he leaned to tap Pvt. Ackerman on the arm and order, "Keep an eye on our pot 'a gold."

Ackerman whipped off a smart salute, with a side wink, and turned his head back to the dancers. Mack had already grabbed another girl, this one in a bright green polka dot dress, as the opening strains of the next song began in earnest. Gene watched them for a few bars before the other dancers obscured his view.

Gene began making his way through the edges of the crowd – a.k.a. soldiers without dance partners good-naturedly waiting their turns – toward the refreshment area. He smiled as he recognized the song, Woody Herman's hip ditty, *Woodchopper's Ball*. The dancers on the floor made time with good footwork as the clarinet really let loose. *Man, that guy's good. That band's going places, that's for sure. I wonder if they've written any songs of their own...*

Turning his head and peering through the crowd, he caught a glimpse of Rooster being tapped on the shoulder as he jitterbugged with a tall blonde in a yellow outfit.

"Pardon me," Gene mumbled as he broke through to the far side of the room where the press of bodies was much less concentrated. He took a deep breath and reached up to adjust his hat, which had accidentally been bumped in the crush. Not for the first time, he wished he had opted for wearing just his khaki uniform shirt and trousers, with his folding cap, like the rest of the guys, rather than the more formal, and very hot, jacket and billed hat. *Maybe in a little bit, I'll mosey on upstairs and play a few games of pool. From the looks of that dance floor, it doesn't look like I'll be getting a chance to knock it out with anybody anytime soon.* "Ah well," he mumbled as he made his way up to the refreshment counter. *Guess I'll leave the hoofing to Mack and Rooster.* Several others were ahead of him and he had to wait his turn.

He smiled at the older woman behind the counter, figuring her for one of the chaperones.

She paused a second to assess the stripes on his jacket and quickly calculated his rank. "What'll it be, Sergeant?"

"Something tall, wet, and cold," he answered. She laughed and nodded as she fixed him up a tall glass of Coke and handed it over.

He took it and inclined his head in thanks as he stepped to the side and raised it to his lips, but paused as his eyes alighted on a vision in green heading his way…

CHAPTER 3

"Thanks, Miss," the good-looking soldier mumbled as he released Vivian's hand and raised his in a quick salute.

Vivian smiled sweetly at him and inclined her head with a murmured, "You're welcome," as the young man, whom she was amazed looked remarkably like a young Tyrone Power, turned away to find another willing partner just as the next song started up.

The air in the large room was heavy and smelled strongly of various perfumes, colognes, after-shave, hair tonic, and sweat. Her fingers reached for the handkerchief she had tucked into the belt of her dress, and tugged it loose, raising it to her face to dab at the perspiration. *Whew, I'm glad Mary June advised me to keep a hanky with me – she was right, I feel like a wilted carnation already and I've only danced three songs!*

She stepped back, gazing around for her friend as she tried to look inconspicuous, hoping another soldier wouldn't ask her to dance for a few minutes so that she could catch her breath. *My goodness…that last guy would win a dance contest on mere speed and stamina, not to mention technique. And his looks! I've got to find Mary June and see if she's ever seen him before…*

After a few moments watching the dancing and being unable to locate her friend, Vivian decided an ice-cold soda would hit the spot. Turning, she managed to wrangle her way back toward the wall through the press of bodies. "Excuse me please…pardon me…I'm sorry…"

She shook her head and smiled at a dozen soldiers and sailors on her way through, apologizing for being unavailable to dance for the moment, until she finally arrived at the refreshment counter.

"Hey sweetie, how're you holding up on your first night?" Mabel Franks, one of the women behind the counter, asked as she handed a sailor a glass of iced-tea.

"Whew, I thought I was prepared, but good gracious, I'm bushed already," Vivian grinned as she made her request.

Accepting the glass of bubbly grape soda, she took a long swallow, closed her eyes, let her head drop back, and sighed in pleasure as the cool effervescence permeated her core. After a moment, she moved to the side and looked around for an out-of-the-way spot to rest, trying to make room as more people crowded up to the counter.

All of a sudden, her whole body jerked to a stop as her eyes met those of a soldier standing at the wall several feet away. She stood stock-still and just stared. Never had she seen eyes that shade of blue before, almost turquoise, like the sky on a bright summer day. They were beautiful, yes, but…it was more than just his eyes that arrested her. It was as if she had experienced an electric shock when their gazes met, and her heart sped up triple time. For an endless moment, the world fell away and all sound ceased. She couldn't move or even breathe. He was watching her and with his glass two inches from his mouth, he nodded and his lips moved smoothly into a smile.

Then a sailor bumped into her and mumbled, "Sorry", jostling her into awareness again. The music from the bandstand and the voices and laughter all around rushed back into her consciousness with a roar.

Within seconds, a space next to the soldier at the wall opened up and she found herself moving toward it, as if her feet had made the decision. Hazily, her brain was wondering what the heck was happening as she looked up at him.

Appearing to be in his mid to late twenties, he wasn't overly tall, she judged maybe 5'10", and what she could see of his hair, under his billed cap, was dark and military short. Those blue eyes held determination and intelligence, validating the sergeant stripes on his jacket. His eyelashes and brows were dark, his face and neck clean-shaven and tan, his chin firm, and his lips smooth and perfect. He was handsome, yes, but not overly so…not like the Tyrone Power look-a-like that she had just finished dancing with – but with that young man she had felt nothing but amazement that he looked so much like a Hollywood star. What, then, was this sensation she was experiencing with this soldier? Something akin to the electricity one feels in the air when a lightning storm is about to begin. The hair on her arms bristled.

He asked her a question, but she couldn't hear his words. She blinked.

He tried again, and for a split second, she had the thought that he was experiencing the odd "lightning storm" feeling, too. This time, she heard his words. He had asked if she were feeling all right.

She blinked again and shook her head, suddenly frightfully embarrassed that she was acting like a complete dingbat, staring at him in rapt fascination as if she'd never seen a man before.

"Oh! Oh, yes. I'm fine…" she paused, racking her brain for words to string together that actually made sense. "I just got a little hot dancing a minute ago."

He nodded and smiled, a trifle *knowingly*. "You were dancing with *Mack*, no wonder."

Her brows puckered for a moment, wondering if she had missed something. "Mack?"

The sergeant's eyes widened as if he had just blabbed troop movements, and he cleared his throat – at least she thought he did, the music and voices around them were so loud, she wasn't sure – and then he mumbled, "Never mind," as he looked away and quickly gulped half of his drink.

GENE SWALLOWED THE large gulp and raised a hand to absently rub the back of his neck, which was experiencing a strange tingling sensation. Glancing around for a moment as he tried to understand what was happening, his eyes were soon inexplicably drawn back to the girl at his side as he watched her sip her drink and allow her gaze to dart around the soldiers nearby. Then, she turned her head and met his eyes again. When she did, he was irresistibly drawn toward her, like a helpless piece of lint toward the static electricity of his wool jacket.

Her eyes – for a moment they were the hue of a pair of buckskins he'd had as a boy and the next they were golden brown, like warm, clover honey, the kind his family's hives had produced.

He allowed his eyes to roam her face, damp with exertion, and immediately adored everything about it – her peaches and cream skin, her perfect lips and straight white teeth, her twinkling brown eyes, and her perky little chin. Her honey-blonde hair was alive with soft curls, and he wondered if they were natural or if she had used curlers like his younger sisters sometimes did. Somewhere in the recesses of his mind, he registered that she reminded him a bit of one of his favorite actresses, June Allyson – except that her voice was delightfully soft and smooth, and seemed to float across the space between them and slip effortlessly into his ears. Distractedly, he found it amazing that he seemed to have blocked out the noise and craziness around them and was able to focus solely on her, and he wondered if she was feeling the strange magnetism, too…

The stoic sergeant racked his brain to think of something to say to this young woman, and was aggravated that all of a sudden he seemed to have gone mute. Heck, he hadn't been this tongue-tied that time he met and talked to General Patton out at the base! He'd noticed her dress and realized she had been the girl dancing with Pfc. Makowski a few moments earlier, and had almost blurted out about the bet! *That would be a sure way to get us tossed out on our ears.* Simultaneously, he felt relief that he had stopped himself before he said anything, followed by a quick, unexpected surge of jealousy that flooded his chest as he wondered, although she hadn't known Mack's name, if she had been taken in by those Hollywood matinee idol good looks.

He took another drink of his cola as he allowed his gaze to sweep quickly down her body, admiring her pretty green polka-dot dress. Normally, bright green wasn't exactly his favorite color, but on *her* it looked wonderful. The soft short-sleeved tea dress with its button up, shirt style bodice and flared A-line skirt, perfect for twirling as she danced, accented her curves without being vulgar. It was that dress that had drawn his attention first, until the force of her gaze and her mere presence, had arrested his whole body.

Jumping Jehoshaphat, he hadn't expected anything like this tonight! Or had he…he'd been feeling like "something" was in the air all day – could meeting her be it? But even as that thought flowed through his brain, he mentally shook his head. Surely a girl like her already had a boyfriend – maybe even a fiancé. *If not, then Louisville is full of stupid, blind fools, that's for sure.*

"So…I've come to dances here a few times in the past…have you been coming long?" he asked, hoping she didn't think the question lame. At least he hadn't said the tired line, "Haven't I seen you here before?"

She smiled softly and shook her head. "No…matter of fact, tonight's my first night. I wasn't sure what to…" she paused as several men in sailor whites crowded past on their way to the counter. "What to expect. My friend has been a junior hostess since the club opened, and she warned me it gets crazy. I just wasn't ready for *how* crazy," she added with a tinkling laugh that seemed to fill his chest and reverberate down to his toes.

"Your friend?" he asked, only vaguely keeping his thoughts straight enough to talk and actually make sense.

She took another long swallow of her drink and gave a nod, her eyes scanning the crowd as she searched for said friend. "Mmm, there she is, right in the middle, in the purple dress, dancing with the tall soldier," she pointed and he inclined his head in acknowledgment. "Her name is Mary June…she's a very good dancer," she added, as if she were scrambling for something to say, much like he was.

"All the girls dance well…from what I've seen…" he murmured, trying to ignore the nearly overwhelming urge to lift a hand and touch her face or her hair.

Just then, one of the soldiers in his unit, Private Henry Gurke, shouldered by, while a swabbie came from the other direction, causing a jam. Pvt. Gurke lost his footing and stumbled toward them, causing Gene's protective instinct to instantly flare, and he turned and placed his body as a shield between Gurke and the girl. The bumbling soldier's weight fell against Gene's back and caused his body to push hers against the wall as she let out a startled squeal.

Suddenly, the girl was looking up into his face, her open mouth rounded in surprise as he stared down into her eyes. They were so close, their bodies were touching from chests to knees; he could feel the heat of her, as well as her soft curves. He got a whiff of her pleasing perfume, and her breath sweetened by the effervescent cola. Her hands had immediately braced themselves against his chest, and the condensation from the soda glass she still gripped in her right hand began wetting his shirt where his unbuttoned jacket had parted, but he barely registered the cold. His hands, with his now empty soda glass, had automatically braced on the wall on either side of her head, and he could see in her eyes that she was acutely aware of the feel of his body pressing against hers. Their stance felt quite intimate. *I wanted to get to know her better, but I sure wasn't expecting this!*

"Oh!" she gasped in surprise as he blinked his astonishment.

Do something, you idiot! Don't just stand here crushing her against the wall – she'll think you're a masher of the worst kind!

"Pardon me, I'm sor…" he began, but was interrupted by a loud clearing of the throat from their left.

"None of that, now! Soldier…you're a sergeant, you should know better than this," Miss Warren barked as Gene hastily took a step back. The woman gave him a fierce look that would have wilted the toughest drill sergeant, and then she took the girl by the arm and began ushering her back toward the dance floor. As they moved away, he could hear the older woman saying, "Really, Miss Powell, I would have expected better…" the rest of her words were drowned out by the music and the band. Gene watched helplessly as the girl allowed herself to be propelled forward, but she did glance back at him for a split second, as if to let him know she wasn't upset, that she knew he had only been protecting her from harm.

Quickly disposing of his empty glass, Gene followed along as the matron lead the girl back toward the dance floor. *Miss Powell…her last name is Powell…I wonder what her first name is…*

"REALLY, MISS POWELL, I would have expected better from you, especially on your first night," Miss Warren harangued. "To be caught in such a compromising position with a soldier you don't even know. I thought you understood the rules, young lady. There will be no fraternizing of that kind in the building. No kissing, no necking, no…"

"But I wasn't!" Vivian interrupted, embarrassed that Miss Warren thought she had done something improper. "It was an accident. The soldier and I were just talking and all of a sudden someone slammed into him from behind – all he did was place himself between me and harm's way. We weren't doing…what you said."

Miss Warren seemed to accept her explanation and backed

down a bit. "Well, all right. But don't allow yourself to be put in a compromising position like that again. Keep your distance. Some of these men, well…they haven't seen a girl in a while and…the flames of passion can be easily fanned…" the woman paused and visibly blushed – and Vivian did as well – as her meaning became clear.

"Yes Ma'am," Vivian murmured, acutely chagrined that she had managed to get into hot water with the director at her very first dance.

They had arrived back at the edge of the dancers and Miss Warren let go of Vivian's arm and took hold of her half empty soda glass. "Remember, you're here to help the soldiers and sailors have a good time on their leave…not just *one* soldier," she admonished as she gently pushed Vivian through the onlookers. One young private immediately asked Vivian to dance and she acquiesced, allowing him to sweep her out onto the floor as the band jammed away at Tex Beneke's version of, *I've Got a Gal in Kalamazoo*.

Vivian was acutely aware of Miss Warren's eagle eye as the soldier sashayed her around the floor, albeit a bit sloppily. They bumped into other dancers several times. Finally, they maneuvered around until Vivian couldn't see Miss Warren anymore and she heaved a sigh of relief. She smiled at her partner, who was a trifle on the short side, not much taller than her, and then took a quick look around to see if she could spot the blue-eyed soldier again. Her partner swished and swirled her around, only once stepping on her foot.

Suddenly, a cheer went up from across the room and couples began to part as a dancing pair really hoofed it up. The song was at the part where the singers were singing, "A-B-C-D-E-F-G…" and the couple on the floor broke into side-by-side tap dancing to the snappy beat. One would think they were a professional dance team. The other dancers backed up and gave them room to perform, clapping and laughing, and shouting encouragements to continue. Vivian and her partner joined the throng, with everyone caught up in the exhilarating spectacle.

All at once, Vivian recognized the good-looking soldier, the one who looked like Tyrone Power, was also dancing in the open ring, but the one who was tap dancing was a tall slim fellow with bright red hair – and a crazy cowlick. Soldiers all around were clapping and calling out to the two. Vivian heard the names, "Mack" and "Rooster" among the shouts. The girls dancing with them were keeping up, in perfect synchronization. Vivian applauded as she excitedly cheered, having the time of her life, and for a moment had forgotten her mysterious encounter with the blue-eyed soldier until she spotted him across the way, his attention now riveted on the two soldiers in the middle. His hands were around his mouth and he was shouting with the rest, and she knew he knew them personally. *He's a sergeant...I wonder if they are under his command...*

The band noticed what was happening and really launched into the swing of things, playing and singing for all they were worth. For a moment, Vivian thought the roof might just blow off.

The song seemed to go on and on, building and building, until finally came the rousing finish, ending with the two soldiers tapping, spinning, sliding, and showing off their respective dance talent. The red haired one even went down in the splits and then "slid" right back up, causing the crowd to squeal approval. By then, their partners were standing back and allowing them full reign, joining in the joyous atmosphere at the soldiers' showboating tricks as each one jumped high in the air and landed in the splits on the dance floor, the cymbals crashing in a rousing finish.

The crowd roared appreciation, rushing forward to pound the soldiers on the back in congratulations of their wonderful performances. The guys were all chuckles, side by side, bending over with their hands on their knees as if a bit winded. Vivian noticed her blue-eyed sergeant right there among the congratulators.

After a few moments, as if the band knew everyone needed a break, they struck up a slower, romantic tune – *I've Got a Feeling I'm Falling*.

Vivian watched as the sergeant she had already begun to think of as "hers" turned, his eyes zeroing in on her, and began to make his way over. As two other soldiers asked her to dance, she didn't even answer, just waited for Mr. Blue Eyes to reach her and extend a hand.

As if they were characters in a big screen movie, she placed her hand in his, and they started to dance...

CHAPTER 4

T HE GIRL FELT so good, so right, so responsive in his arms. They instantly gelled, as if they had been dancing together all their lives. No girl had ever danced so smoothly with him, or followed him so well. Like they were made for each other…

Was he dreaming? Things like this just didn't happen to him – to plain old Sergeant Eugene Banks, from Elizabethtown, Kentucky. If he could have put in an order for a girl with all of his personal likes and tastes, she would fit the bill to a T. What was even more, *she* seemed to be feeling the same thing that *he* was.

"My name is Vivian Powell. What's yours?" she asked softly, her cheek against his as they glided slowly to the smooth music.

Vivian…such a beautiful name…and it fits her…

"Sergeant Eugene Banks. But, um…my friends call me Gene."

"Gene Banks. I like it. Everyone calls me Viv."

"Viv Powell. I like it," he echoed, not caring two beans that he was smiling like a chowder head.

Her hand fit so perfectly in his, like a precisely machined part inside one of his tanks. Her cheek against his felt just right, and her dress swished against the legs of his uniform pants as they moved together to the music in perfect synchronization.

Wow.

All his befuddled brain could register was just…WOW.

As the mellow male voice crooning the mesmerizing melody

continued, some of the words registered in Gene's mystified mind and he chuckled softly against her cheek. She pulled back just enough to look up into his eyes, and once again, the power of her honeyed gaze made him catch his breath. He nearly stumbled.

"What's funny?" she queried softly, her eyes roaming slowly over his face, up to his cap, down to his lips and his chin, then back up to his eyes.

Should I tell her what I'm feeling? Or will she think I'm a sap headed dope? Well, she'd be right. With one look, she's clobbered me, turned me into a slack happy slob, but I've never felt happier in my life. Like the song says…I've got a feeling I'm falling for nobody else but you…

He grinned down at her as he smoothly guided her around the floor. "I was just listening to the words of the song…the guy says he's flying high…she caught his eye…he's tingling all over." He hesitated, gauging by the sparkle in her eyes how she was taking his admission. Gene decided to lay it on the line. "Baby, I've never felt this way before…but…I bet all the guys tell you that," he added, a bit of the old self-doubt raising its ugly head. Surely he only imagined that she was feeling the same thing…

Her eyes continued to twinkle as she took in everything he was saying. It was as if the wheels were turning in her mind and she was trying to decide what to say. He swallowed, suddenly nervous. Had he fouled everything up one minute into their first dance? Would she laugh and make fun of him with her friends later?

Then, she smiled and leaned in to press her cheek to his again. "Good. I was a bit afraid it was just me. Glad to know I'm not the only one off the cob."

Gene chuckled at her phrase, which meant she was feeling as goofy about him as he was about her.

He snuggled a bit closer, being careful not to press her *too* close, after that dressing down they had when he had unintentionally mashed her to the wall with his body. "I thought this kinda thing only happened in the movies," he whispered next to her ear as he expertly turned them away from a couple dancing too close.

"Me, too," she sighed, almost purring like a contented cat. "I told my friend I didn't think I'd have a good time. I nearly didn't come tonight," she admitted, amazement in her voice.

"Mmm, I'm so glad you did," he breathed as he twirled her around again.

"Me, too," she said again, and he felt her hand edge up to the nape of his neck, the touch of her fingers causing goose bumps to erupt and race down his back.

Just then, he felt an extremely unwelcome tap on his shoulder.

He opened his eyes, but didn't stop dancing, as protocol would insist. One of the privates in his unit hovered there with a comical look on his face. His eyebrows were raised, fully expecting his sergeant to relinquish the girl for the remainder of the song. Gene glowered at the younger man. Quickly deciding to use his sergeant status to his advantage, he ignored the fact that it was frowned upon to pull rank in situations such as this. *Oh well. There's a war on. Rules be hanged.*

Gene practically growled, "Go take a powder, Private."

"Yes, sir!" The private squawked as he snapped to attention and saluted. Without thought or question, he turned on his heel and retreated to the other side of the dance floor, only turning back once at his scowling commander.

Vivian leaned back at his words and looked around; having been unaware someone had even interrupted them. "Who was that?"

Gene took his eyes off the retreating would-be interloper and grinned at her, feeling a bit hazy-headed like he had one summer when, on a dare from a school chum in grade school, he had sucked nearly all of the helium out of a balloon so he could make his voice sound like a chipmunk.

"Just some knucklehead that thought he was gonna take you

away from me before the song was over."

She grinned back at him and then snuggled against his cheek again.

He felt like he'd died and gone to Heaven.

WAS THIS REAL? How could something like this happen so fast? Was it just six months ago that she had thought she would never get over Walter? Vivian clamped her lips together, stifling a sigh that at that moment, she couldn't even remember Walter's last *name…*

Eugene Banks. Sergeant Eugene Banks. If we married, I'd be Vivian Banks… She almost giggled as she silently sing-songed, *Vivian Banks works in a bank while her husband drives a tank.*

She tried to control herself and quit being so silly. How could she be thinking of marrying this soldier after only one short conversation and one nearly completed dance? At that thought, a bit of her happiness deflated. When the song ended, the rules dictated that she had to dance with another soldier. She wasn't supposed to dance with the same soldier two dances in a row. But…how could she let him go? How could she watch him take another girl in his arms?

Oh goodness, I'm losing my mind. But he feels the same way…he just told that private to take a hike. The rule sheet she had signed flashed before her eyes… You must not spend all your time with just one soldier. You must not allow a soldier to get fresh with you while on the property. You are not to allow a soldier to escort you home. When she had signed the sheet, she'd had no clue how those rules would chafe in such a short time.

But oh…how good she felt being held in his arms…and they danced together so well! This was so wonderful, like something in a movie up on the big screen. So, life really does imitate art at times…

Her eyes closed. She and Gene seemed to be floating on a cloud to the lovely strains of the music. She smiled at the words of the song as his arm around her back tightened a little more…the guy was singing about traveling single, chancing to mingle, and being all a-tingle…

Tingle…man, he said it.

ALAS, AS THE old saying goes, all good things come to an end. A few more times through the chorus and the song drifted to a stop.

The soldier and the junior hostess leaned back and looked into one another's eyes.

"Thanks for the best dance I've ever had in my life," Gene avowed, his fixed stare holding Vivian's.

"You're welcome, Sergeant," Vivian mumbled, somehow unable to release his hand. She watched as he raised that hand, bringing hers up to his lips and her eyes fluttered shut. When he pressed those lips to the backs of her fingers, she sighed. His lips were warm and soft, just like she knew they'd be…

When she opened her eyes again, another song was starting up – a fast one this time. Before she knew it, a sailor in whites came along and scooped her into his arms, calling over his shoulder, "Thanks for warming her up, Sarge."

Before the sailor swept her around, she saw Gene's face, and the look in his eyes; a look that told her he wasn't going to seek out other girls to dance with.

At that moment, Vivian made up her mind that at her first opportunity, regardless of the reason she was there, she would take a "break" from dancing and seek out her blue-eyed sergeant.

UNFORTUNATELY, THAT BREAK didn't come for another hour. By then, Vivian was out of breath and her feet were screaming from the half-size-too-small pumps she had foolishly worn. She had danced with at least two soldiers per song, and all but one were fast numbers. However, the band was tired as well, and mercifully, they stopped to take ten.

Vivian had wound up in the arms of the red headed private, the one they had called Rooster, who had been in the impromptu dance-off earlier with the Tyrone Power twin. He was a great dancer, but was a might too energetic for her at that point. She wondered how he'd been dancing all this time and seemed to be nowhere near the end of his stamina.

When the number ended and the music stopped, he grinned happily and said, "Thanks, Miss. You're number forty-five."

Vivian frowned, not understanding. "I beg your pardon?"

He chuckled. "Never mind." Then, his gaze focused over her shoulder and he grinned again. "Hey Sarge."

Vivian turned her head and smiled a welcome – Gene was standing just behind her, his eyes boring into hers. *Those eyes...* once again, she felt that lightning sensation zinging all over her body.

"I'm ahead by three," the private jabbed his sergeant in a foolhardy manner.

Gene gave the private a nod, but his eyes didn't leave Vivian's. "As they say, Pvt. Deal, it ain't over till the fat lady sings."

The private chortled and gave his commanding officer a lazy salute, which Gene automatically returned.

Gene waited for the private to move on. Once he did, he and Vivian stood just contemplating one another's dreamy expressions for a moment.

"Hi," he greeted softly.

"Hi," Vivian answered. "Is he one of your men?" Vivian asked, feeling a bit silly with them just standing there in the middle of the emptying dance floor, staring at one another as if in a trance.

"He is," Gene answered, clearly disinterested in discussing the other soldier.

Finally, he seemed to rouse himself and looked over his shoulder. "Is it all right if you...get something to eat with me?"

Vivian glanced around, looking for Miss Warren, or Mary June, but her friend had been scarce the entire time. "I'm not sure..."

Making a decision, Gene gently grasped Vivian's arm and gave it a gentle tug. "How about we go find someplace quiet to rest a spell."

She decided to throw caution to the wind. "That sounds like Heaven."

The couple walked together out of the large room and down the hall, where quite a few of the others seemed to be headed as well. They joined the throng in a room at the end of the hallway where food was being prepared. Waiting in line, not saying anything, but extremely aware of one another, they ordered a sandwich and coffee, and then wandered out into the hall and up the stairs.

Vivian had not had an opportunity to tour the facility when she had signed on, as she hadn't wanted to be late getting back to work, and she had been barely on time for the dance that evening.

"What's up here?" she asked as they climbed the staircase.

"Different rooms, one with pool tables, one with ping pong tables, one with card tables...ones with a few chairs for just relaxing and maybe reading a book..."

Vivian knew without him saying it that he was heading for one of the latter rooms.

At the end of the second floor hallway, they found such a room. It had a few comfortable chairs and a couch. Several low tables held magazines strewn haphazardly, and shelves with books lined the walls. At the moment, no one else was there, and they sat down in chairs to take a few bites of their sandwiches and sip their coffee. Each one marveled at how comfortable they were in one another's presence.

When they finished their snack, Gene wiped his mouth, stood, and held out his hand, pulling Vivian up on her feet and over to the couch, where they settled side by side.

"Oh, that hit the spot. I hadn't realized how hungry I was. I didn't eat much supper," Vivian shared, briefly watching him as he turned slightly so he could drape one arm on the back of the couch behind her shoulders.

"Me either."

Alone with him, seemingly far away from others, Vivian was suddenly a bit nervous. What did she know about him, anyway? He wouldn't…try to take advantage of her, would he? Maybe this wasn't such a good idea…

"So…" she began, moistening her lips and observing him again. "Tell me about Sgt. Eugene Banks."

He smiled and reached for one of her hands that was resting in her lap, focusing on it as if it were the most interesting object in the world. Her heart kicked up a notch.

"Oh…Sgt. Banks is just an average Joe." Looking up and catching her raised eyebrow, he chuckled. "I was raised not far from here – in E-town…my parents had a farm. Got two younger brothers and two younger sisters…"

"You're the oldest," Vivian stated the obvious, trying to concentrate on his words when her whole body was acutely aware of his every move, the warmth of his chest, his thigh pressed against hers, the sound of his voice, the touch of his skin as his hand caressed hers…

"Yep. I'm the odd one. The rest of my family has medium brown hair and either brown or hazel eyes, but I've got dark hair and blue eyes." He paused for a moment as a look of something like pain flitted across his features before he masked it and went on. "Pop used to tease Mom that she'd had a fling with a traveling salesman and I was the result."

"Goodness!" Vivian gasped, but when he flashed those blue eyes at her, his lips pulled up in a half grin.

"He was kidding. They used to tease each other all the time."

"Used to? Do you mean they are…" she faltered, not wishing to ask if his parents were dead.

"Oh, I guess they still do. I don't see them much anymore." He shrugged, let go of her hand, and for the first time that evening, he took off his peaked cap and leaned forward a bit to place it on one of the tables. Then, he reached up to run his hand over his hair and tug at his collar and tie.

Stealing a look at her, he smiled as if he were a bit embarrassed. "Mind if I take off my jacket?"

She shrugged. "Not at all. I imagine you're a trifle warm in it…"

"Yeah, but, I didn't want you to think I was, well…planning on trying something," he explained. He grinned as he watched the meaning of his words dawn on her and she blushed a bit and looked down at her hands once again in her lap. Gene leaned forward and removed his jacket, tossing it on the couch next to him, and then sat back, his arm once again behind her shoulders.

"That's better. Now…where was I?"

"Your parents used to tease one another," she prompted.

"Oh yeah. So…when I was nineteen, I hopped a bus and came to Louisville to visit my aunt and uncle, and got caught up in the big Flood."

"Oh my! We heard all about it, but it didn't reach where we lived. Was it as bad as they said? My father wouldn't let mother or I go anywhere near what he termed 'that filthy downtown floodwater'…"

"You bet it was bad. But I got put on a rescue boat team with some pretty good fellas. We saved more people out of our rescue station than any other," he boasted, smiling at her appropriately impressed expression. "Plus we stuck around, helping to bring food to those who stayed for the duration out of fear of looters. After that, I bounced around a bit, joined the CCC's, and stayed in after my hitch to become a foreman at several camps in Illinois.

Then, the war started. I got called up and they sent me to Knox. I'm twenty-five, and I'm a staff sergeant, or more specifically, a motor sergeant, over one of the motor pools for the 1st Armored Division."

She smiled at him as he stopped and just gazed into her eyes, so deeply that she looked away and drew in a breath, smoothing her hair a bit. *Oh my goodness…I've got to get hold of myself or he'll think I'm an Able Grable on the prowl for a man!*

He cleared his throat. "So, that's who Sgt. Eugene Banks is. Now, who is Vivian Powell?"

She stared back into those eyes that seemed to look straight into her soul and drew her lip between her teeth with a soft laugh. "Oh, I'm afraid Vivian hasn't led such a colorful life as Sgt. Banks. Let's see…I'm an only child, I grew up in the house on Cooper Chapel Road where I still live with my parents…"

"That's in Okolona, right?"

"Yes, it is." She gave a nod. "Um…I went to school in Okolona and graduated, I got a job right out of high school at a bank downtown on Fifth, where I'm a teller, and I turned twenty-one last December." Thinking her life sounded boring compared to his, she added with a small, self-conscious shrug, "That's it."

His eyes seemed to pierce into hers, as if he suspected there was something she wasn't telling him. "That's it? No…boyfriend…fiancé?"

She gasped. "No, of course not! Would I be sitting here alone with you if there were?"

He grinned, obviously relieved and pleased. "No, I guess you wouldn't."

She hesitated for a moment, debating whether or not to mention it, then added quietly, "There *was* a boyfriend…his name was Walter. He…well, let's just say, that didn't work out."

"Mmm," Gene hummed deeply, leaning a bit to touch his forehead to her temple. "I'd say that guy must have been an idiot to let you get away."

"I agree," she quipped, and they both chuckled. "So...what exactly does a motor sergeant do?"

"Well, let's see...the book says that a motor sergeant is a Maintenance Platoon Sergeant of an Engineer Support Company assigned to an Engineer Battalion. He is responsible for the overall management of scheduled and unscheduled maintenance of wheeled, ground support, and construction related equipment. Also, he is responsible for the tools, equipment, and facilities, and for the management, supervision, training, professional develop-ment, health and welfare of five NCO's and ten soldiers in his unit."

"My goodness, that sounds like a lot!" Vivian exuberated breathlessly, more than a little impressed. Gene just shrugged, characteristically humble.

"It has its ups and downs."

She sat huddled with him, contented, fingering the emblems and decorations on his uniform as he quietly explained what each one was...arm-of-service, branch-of-service, unit insignia, marksmanship, his hash marks or rank stripes, his staff sergeant chevrons...

After a while, she debated over voicing her next question, but then finally decided to as it was important to her. Clearing her throat, she ventured, "Are you a believer, Sgt. Banks?"

"Yes. Yes, I am, Miss Powell," he responded with firm, steady conviction, and with no hesitation.

She smiled in relief of the one aspect that could have driven a wedge between them. "Good. So am I, Sergeant."

"I figured as much," he smiled back.

They sat together for a few more minutes, just enjoying one another's company, listening to the faint strains of the music starting up again directly below, and softly sharing words of praise for Johnny Burkhart and his band. She felt a twinge of guilt that she wasn't downstairs attending to her duties.

Finally, Vivian turned her head. Her eyes met his only inches away as she leaned back against his arm. She let her gaze drop to his lips, so smooth and utterly *kissable*, and then back to his eyes again.

Gene smiled and whispered, "Whatcha thinkin', Miss Vivian Powell?"

A memory of Walter's voice from the past, sneering that she was a prude, decided at that moment to rear its ugly head. Suddenly, a rebellious boldness came over Vivian, and she turned toward Gene a little more, touched the material of his shirt above his heart, and admitted gently, "I was just wondering, Sgt. Banks...what it would be like to kiss you."

His eyes flared in surprised reaction, and then those lips of his curved into a very sexy smile. "Mmm, is that right, Miss Powell?"

"That's right." Her eyes twinkled mischievously.

He let out a soft snicker as his eyes sparkled in response. "Well, I think I can provide the answer to that mystery."

Their connection held for a few moments as their awareness of one another skyrocketed, and then Gene reached up to touch her chin with the tips of his fingers and she turned her body a bit more into the curve of his. He gently leaned in and joined their lips.

The effect was immediate and powerful – more so than either had expected. Breaths hitched as sparks flashed, fireworks exploded, and hearts galloped like racehorses on Derby Day.

Her pulse thudded in her ears and she melted into his embrace as his lips skillfully moved over hers, warmly, and oh so thoroughly.

It was a kiss of a lifetime.

It was a kiss neither of them would ever forget.

CHAPTER 5

G ENE LAY ON his bed, hands under his head, fingers linked, and staring up at the ceiling only faintly illuminated by a bit of moonlight shining in the window. He turned his head and picked up his watch from the bedside table. 2:43 am.

He couldn't go to sleep. A certain honey-eyed girl wouldn't leave his brain, or his body for that matter, alone.

Eugene Banks was no innocent. He'd been on lots of dates, with lots of different...*types*...of girls. He dated in high school. He had gone with the other enlistees when they all wanted to blow off a little steam, into the small towns near the CCC camps and hung out with the local girls. He'd even had a couple of dates since he'd been stationed at Knox. But *never* had anything happened to him like meeting Miss Vivian Powell. One look – *one look* – from her practically knocked him off his feet! *And to think...she's been right here, in Louisville, practically my whole life and I never met her before.*

Drawing in a deep breath, he blew it out slowly and shook his head in amazement.

But he had a problem. She was a junior hostess at the service club and one of the club's strictest rules was the hostesses were not allowed to date the soldiers. He understood the reason – if all of their girls started dating the soldiers they met there and the soldiers became steady beaus, said beaus would not want to come to the club and watch their girls dancing with other servicemen for three hours. Said girls would then no longer be junior hostesses, the beaus would insist. No-sir-ee. Gene knew first hand how miserable it was to be relegated to the sidelines, and Vivian wasn't even officially *his girl!*

But the memory of their kiss…as his best friend from his CCC days used to say, *shut my mouth and beat me daddy eight to the bar*…the warmth of her lips, the little sighs and the softness of her body against his, the whole rightness of the two of them together. It had been like the best dream a guy could ever have, totally unreal…and totally real.

He cringed now as he remembered what had interrupted their kiss. Warden Warren. *She must be part bloodhound, because she had sure sniffed out where one of her new girls was "resting", and boy howdy, did it hit the fan.* Poor Viv, she had been so embarrassed to be caught red-handed, or more to the point, red-lipped, with a soldier on her first night as a hostess. *Miss Warren sure lit into her.*

She had practically dragged Vivian out of the room and down to the dance hall, and never took her eyes off of her the rest of the evening – well, at least the last forty minutes until the dance was over. Then, the old broad had made sure Viv was in the group as the new girls were ushered out the door and across the hall for an evaluation of their first evening as hostesses. Viv had cast a quick glance at him, and that was the last he had seen of her.

After waiting around and not catching a glimpse of her again, he had belatedly realized he needed to put in for a bunk in the sleeping quarters on the third floor of the USO club – but no such luck. He'd waited too long and every bunk was spoken for. There was nothing left to do but take a jog outside and hope he wasn't too late to catch the bus heading back to the base. He'd made it with seconds to spare – it was pulling away from the curb and he'd had to flag it down!

Now, here he was, stewing in his own juices and racking his brain to figure out what he was going to do about this situation with Vivian Powell.

What he didn't know was if she had been kicked out – or would continue her duties as one of Louisville Service Club's Junior Hostesses.

If she didn't…how would he see her again?

Monday at noon…

"WHAT'LL IT BE, ladies?" the big-boned waitress asked as Vivian and Mary June climbed up onto the last two open stools at Tafel Drug Store's lunch counter.

"Hey Gerti. I'll have a hot roast beef sandwich and a large iced tea, please," Vivian responded as Mary June scanned the menu on the wall past the woman's head. Gertrude nodded as she wrote down Vivian's order on the pad in her hands, and then raised her eyes to other girl. The woman waited, a tiny bit of aggravation showing on her face. "Be right there!" she called out to a man on the other end that waved a hand trying to get her attention.

"Give me a…hamburger with everything but onions…and a chocolate malt," Mary June finally told the harried server.

The woman scratched out the order and then turned to pin it to the revolving rack as she bent a bit to call to the cook back in the kitchen, "Gimme one bossy on a board, and then burn one, drag it through the garden and hold the rose!"

"Comin' right up!" came the response.

As the woman moved back down the counter to take care of other customers, Mary June watched her go, and then turned back to her companion. "She always cracks me up."

"Yeah," Vivian replied, but was obviously pre-occupied.

"Hey – you've been walking around all morning with your head in a cloud. What's up? What was Miss Warren giving you the business about Saturday night? I was so aggravated that we couldn't get on the same bus going home because I was dying to ask...and who was that soldier I saw you going upstairs with...and *why* the heck did you go up there with him?" the girl paused for a breath after her rapid-fire delivery.

Vivian picked up the tall glass of ice tea that the waitress placed in front of her and took a sip from the straw. She glanced around, trying hard not to simply blurt out the answers to the questions and confide in her friend – which was what she had been dying to do all weekend. They had both hurried in to work that morning with not a minute to spare for conversation. Usually able to chat during the bus ride to the bank, wouldn't you know, they had been stuck at either ends of the bus for the entire route and a traffic jam had caused it to get to their stop ten minutes later than scheduled.

Finally, she couldn't hold back anymore. She had to tell her best friend about her blue-eyed sergeant. "Oh Mary June! What a night!" she exclaimed. "Miss Warren saw me talking to him...once next to the refreshment counter...and once in a reading room upstairs. We went up there to find a quiet place to just talk. His name is Gene Banks. He's a sergeant, and he's stationed out at Knox."

Mary June reached for her milkshake and took a long draw from it, never taking her eyes from her friend. "Aaaaand," she prompted.

Vivian peered her way, and couldn't hold back the smile that overtook her face. "Oh Mary! I can't believe something like this has happened – to *me!*"

"Like *what?*" Mary June practically screeched, before covering her mouth with her fingers to stifle a giggle. "Viv – spill it!"

"I...I think I'm in love," Vivian squeaked, a blush coloring her face as her best friend's eyes rounded and her mouth dropped open. "I've never felt anything like that with a guy before – and certainly not with *Walter*," she added, suppressing a shudder. "It's like something out of a movie – when our eyes met…I felt tingles all over!" she stopped for a moment and shrugged self-consciously. "Listen to me, I sound wacky, I know, but…"

"Viv!" Mary June squealed. "Tell me everything!"

The waitress brought their lunches at that moment, giving both girls the "eye" as she laid down the plates. The friends waited until she moved on, and then for the next few minutes, between bites, and mindful of the clock on the wall, Vivian told her friend the dreamy details of her encounters with the handsome sergeant – although she played down the particulars of the kiss. Still, the other girl could barely keep her voice down in her reactions.

"Oh honey, I'm *so* jealous. I've been going to the dances for over a year hoping to meet my Mr. Right, and only managed to get my feet black and blue from dead hoofers who can't dance. You – on your first night there – meet the soldier of every girl's dreams!"

Vivian wiped her mouth on her napkin and then smiled dreamily. "I know…it doesn't seem real – and yet somehow…it's the realest thing that's ever happened to me." She paused and looked her friend in the eye. "If that makes any sense," she laughed.

"It does to me, honey," Mary June agreed.

"And to think…I almost didn't go to the dance. He said he usually doesn't have a good time at them, and on several he had just stayed upstairs playing pool with the fellows."

"So…is he coming back for the next dance?"

"I don't know…once Miss Warren found us upstairs and dragged me away from him," at that, she paused again and felt another blush suffuse her face, "we didn't have time for any parting words – and she wouldn't let me get anywhere near him for the rest of the dance. Then when she was herding all of us new girls into the room for our 'evaluations', I only caught a glimpse of him…"

"What did she say? I mean she didn't kick you out, did she?" Mary June asked worriedly.

"She gave me a stern warning – which was a bit embarrassing in front of the other girls – and lectured all of us about the rule sheet we had signed and why the rules are important." Vivian met her friend's eyes for a moment before adding, "I understand why the rules are there...but, oh Mary...meeting Gene was the absolute last thing I had expected! Truly, I only joined to help out a worthy cause..."

"Of course you did, sweetie! I know that. But, if you see him again while you're there, you'd better watch out. A couple of girls got kicked out a few weeks ago for 'conduct unbecoming a junior hostess'," she mimicked Miss Warren with a roll of her eyes.

Vivian's eyes widened for a moment, imagining the shame of that happening to her.

Mary June caught her friend's worried look and rushed on, "I'm so happy for you! You deserve to meet a swell guy, after all the lies and junk Walter put you through." With their lunch break nearly over, the girls laid the proper amount of coins on the counter and gathered their things to go back to the bank.

As she turned to head toward the door, Mary June tossed back over her shoulder off-handedly, "I just hope he doesn't wind up being too good to be true."

Vivian jerked to a halt, her friend having said the one thing that could sling mud onto her pristine memory. *Yes...what if he realized what I was feeling and just played me for a fool? What if everything he said truly were just "lines"? What if he thought I'm a loose woman – gracious, I practically begged him to kiss me! What if he says those things to every girl he dances with?* Swiftly going over every look, every nuance, every scrap of body language between them, Vivian shook her head, silently arguing, *No, he couldn't have been faking or lying. Those eyes...I could see the truth of his words in his eyes as he spoke them...but then again, I didn't suspect Walter was lying to me either, before I stumbled upon the truth...* She closed her eyes, remembering the day she had happened upon her ex-boyfriend in the arms of another girl – another girl who had sneered at her to "Get away from my boyfriend!" *Oh Father in Heaven, please, please, please, let Gene be everything he seems to be!*

When she started walking again, catching up to her friend, Vivian murmured, "Me, too, honey…me, too."

THIRTY-FIVE MILES SOUTH, in a mess hall at the base, Gene reached for a piece of chocolate cake and added it to his tray. Pushing it along until he had chosen all of the items he wanted, he picked it up and carried it to a nearby table with only a few corporals at one end. They greeted him and he returned the welcome before sitting down to eat his meal.

His mind was swirling with various things, not the least of which was a certain sweet-voiced young woman who danced like an angel and kissed like a…

Whoa there! Shaking his head, he made himself focus on his job – mainly some trouble with the engine of one of the big Diamond T cargo trucks. Two of his best mechanics couldn't seem to figure out the problem. Could it be sabotage? Bad fuel? He sure didn't need this today, when his mind couldn't seem to stay on task.

He sat chewing his food as well as the problem until a few minutes later when Corporal Dan Brown approached the table.

"Hey Sarge, mind if I join you?"

"Help yourself," Gene responded with a smile and gestured with one hand toward the seat directly across the table. He liked Cpl. Brown. The two of them had been friends a long time, since they had served in the C's together. Brown was a few years younger, and had worked with Gene in two of the forest camps. Matter of fact, Gene had even saved his life during a dangerous, but quickly contained fire, and the younger man had vowed he owed him one. When war had been declared, both of them were called up and joined at the same time – and both had been sent to Knox.

"How goes it?" Gene asked as the other man settled in to eat.

"Can't complain. Captain Moore's all right. Strict, but a good egg, you know?"

Gene levered a large bite of mashed potatoes into his mouth and nodded. He knew the corporal had recently been assigned to their unit captain's office, handling typing, filing, and other duties.

"Speaking of that…" Cpl. Brown continued. "Thought you'd like to hear something I found out today…"

Gene eyed him as he reached for his cup of coffee and took a sip. "Oh yeah? What's that?"

The corporal grinned at him and took a bite of his meatloaf, teasingly making him wait while he chewed and swallowed. Gene didn't take the bait to get antsy, but merely took another leisurely bite of his meal. Finally, Cpl. Brown, surreptitiously looked around to make sure he wasn't being overheard, then took a drink of his ice tea and leaned a bit closer over the table. "You've been nominated for promotion. Overheard a bit of a conversation. Capt. Moore is needing to fill a first sergeant slot. I heard him say there were things he was checking out before the panel convenes."

Gene's eyes widened a bit. This was excellent news. More pay. More recognition. More responsibility. On the heels of that thought was…would the higher rank impress Vivian? He refocused on the conversation when he realized the corporal was waiting for him to respond.

"Thanks for the heads up, Brown," he grinned.

In spite of the fact that Gene outranked him, the corporal knew he wouldn't make him adhere to protocol. He winked at his friend and said in a low voice, "No sweat, Banks. Us old C buddies gotta stick together." Then he shoved a large bite of mashed potatoes in his mouth and wiggled his eyebrows.

Gene chuckled and shook his head.

The corporal swallowed and took another drink of his tea, obviously with more on his mind. "Hey Sarge, it true what the fella's are saying?"

Gene met his eyes and shrugged. "What?"

"Scuttlebutt has it that you were caught alone with a girl in one of the reading rooms at the USO in town Saturday night, *makin' whoopee*, no less."

Gene felt his face and neck heat up and cursed the malady he'd suffered all his life – that of a man actually blushing.

The corporal saw the heightened color right away. "It's *true?* Boy howdy!" He tipped back his head and laughed. "The fellow that told me said she was *some* dish, a real looker. You latched onto a real Able Grable, huh Sarge?"

Immediately, Gene's temper flared. He leaned forward, his sky blue eyes darkening to the hue of sapphires as they pierced the other man with the intensity of an arc welder, and pointed an index finger into the corporal's face.

"*Don't. Call. Her. That.* She's *not* that kind of girl. It was a *kiss*, that's all. We weren't *making whoopee*."

The corporal's eyes shot open and he leaned back a bit. "Whoa, ease up." He looked around quickly to see if anyone noticed their conversation. "Don't snap your cap, Sarge. I didn't mean nothin', just flappin' my gums."

Gene clamped his lips, breathed in deeply through his nose and ground his teeth together as he forced himself to relax a bit back onto his seat. Surprised at his own reaction, he averted his eyes from the startled look in Cpl. Brown's.

A strong wave of guilt swept over Gene as he thought about what he had done from the perspective of what others would think. How could he have taken such a chance like that? Squire her to a room at the end of the hall – *alone* with him? To risk ruining Viv's reputation – and on her first night as a hostess! His father had raised him better than that. *Her* father would probably want to take a baseball bat to him if he finds out…

The corporal slowly resumed eating, watching his higher-ranked friend as if he were a round of live ammo.

After a minute, Gene looked up and met the other man's eyes. "Sorry, Dan. That was out of line. I had no call to bust your chops like that."

Cpl. Brown responded with a nod. Resorting to their pre-military friendship, he couldn't resist venturing, "I've never seen you carry a torch this bad before, Gene…even the times we double-dated while we were in the C's. She must really be something…"

The smitten sergeant allowed a small smile as he looked away again, seeing Vivian in his mind as she gazed into his eyes and boldly declared she was wondering what it would be like to kiss him. And man, oh man, the result had about knocked his socks off.

"She's something, all right. As special as they come."

"She got a name?" the corporal grinned.

The prettiest name in the world…

"Matter of fact, she does, Corporal," Gene grinned back. "Vivian."

CHAPTER 6

T HE WEEK HAD dragged by for Sgt. Banks. One crisis after
another had cropped up, almost like something or someone
was pulling out all the stops to cause him no shortage of
aggravation.

First, the problem with the engine in the Diamond T turned
out to be the diesel fuel injectors, and the fact that someone,
somehow, had substituted used (albeit cleaned up and looking
new) injectors for new ones. Used injectors that were clogged and
unable to allow the diesel fuel to flow correctly. Out of desperation, and after his mechanics had put in two new sets from off the
shelf, Gene had examined one and found it to be faulty. Now, the
questions were – how, why, and who?

On the heels of that, two privates in his unit got into a fistfight over a girl and he had to physically break them up – and got
punched in the mouth for his efforts – *and* he then had to figure
out a solution, since both men seemed to be constantly at each
other's throats. If that wasn't enough, on Wednesday he had
awakened with a massive toothache, as a result of the punch,
which had necessitated an hour in the dentist's chair; not his
favorite place to be. Thursday brought a torrential rainstorm that
washed out carefully constructed earthen mounds on the tank
practice range and several of his tanks had suffered damage that
his crew had to scramble to repair.

Friday, Pvt. Deal, a.k.a. Rooster, who had won the previous

Saturday night's bet by three dances, was accidentally pushed off a loading dock and broke his leg. It was a severe break – a compound fracture. Gene and another private in the unit had a hard time getting the injured man into a jeep and over to the post hospital. The poor guy had done his best not to scream out in pain.

On Saturday morning, Gene trotted up the steps of the hospital to check on him.

Peeking around the doorjamb of the ward, Gene saw the private laying in bed, his leg trussed up in some kind of contraption with wheels and pulleys, and a cast from foot to thigh. Gene could tell from one glance at his face that he was in quite a bit of pain.

Mustering his sympathy into morale-boosting encouragement, Gene stepped into the large room and walked to the bed, then stood waiting for Deal to acknowledge his visitor. After a moment, the private turned his head and saw him, and it was obvious that he was trying to hide the true degree of discomfort he was experiencing.

"Hey Sergeant Banks!" he greeted, making as if to push himself higher in the bed.

Gene came forward quickly, one hand lifted toward the stricken man. "Hang on there, Roo! You just lay still and rest. I just came by to see how you were doing."

"Oh, I'm all right. The doc says it could have been worse," he paused and waited for Gene to raise his brows in question. "I coulda' broke both legs!" he joked with his trademark silly snicker.

Gene laughed along with him, shaking his head at the happy-go-lucky private.

"Hey, listen, Sarge, I want to thank you for helping me out, taking me to the hospital and all…"

With a shrug, Gene played down the thanks. "I didn't do much, Deal. Mainly just drove the jeep."

The private's expression changed and he looked his commanding officer in the eye. "No…I appreciate that…that you cared, you know? The way you kept making sure…" he wavered, and both of them looked away in embarrassment. "Aw heck, you know what I mean," he finally mumbled.

"Yeah…" Gene murmured, then shook his head at himself as he remembered the gift he had brought the private and had kept hidden behind his back – a copy of Silver Screen Magazine with Deal's favorite actress, Rita Hayworth on the cover in a sexy pose, wearing a flowered bathing suit and sporting a large red flower in her hair. He handed it to the private.

"Wow, thanks!" the young man exclaimed, fixing his eyes on the delightful picture. "Don't she just knock your socks off?" he sighed. Momentarily forgetting, he moved his leg and then let out a yelp.

Gene moved forward, instinctively reaching toward the leg as if to try and help, but stopped himself just before touching it. "Hey man, watch out now," he cautioned as Deal settled back down in the bed.

"Yeah…how could I forget this big paperweight attached to me, huh? Looks like I won't be winnin' any more bets with my hoofin'."

The sergeant met the other man's eyes again, determined to connect and encourage. "Hey – stow that. That leg is gonna heal just fine…and you'll be out on that dance floor again, hoofing it with the best of them, *and* winning other bets. You hear?" He paused, waiting for the younger man to acknowledge. "You just do everything the docs and the nurses tell you. You'll see."

"Yes, sir," Pvt. Deal mumbled, although he visibly seemed to perk up a bit as Gene's words sank in and gave him hope that he might just recover.

After a moment, Deal changed the subject.

"So…what do you think is going on with the truck parts?"

Gene balked for a second. He had thought that no one but his mechanics knew about it, but then realized that a thing like that can't stay hidden under a bushel for long. He raised his shoulders in a shrug.

"I don't know…but mark my words – I aim to find out."

VIVIAN FUSSED WITH her hair, wrestling with a stubborn curl that wanted to do its own thing. "Agghh!" she growled, lowering her arms and staring at her reflection in the mirror over Mary June's dresser as the girls finished getting ready for the dance.

"Aw, come here. Lemme see what I can do," Mary June mumbled, turning her friend so that she could get at the offending curl. With a few squirts from a bottle, she brushed out the lock and then fixed it back with a hair comb. "There. Now, leave that in until we get to the dance, and then take it out. If you leave it in all evening, it'll probably fly out when your soldier twirls you around," she added with a giggle.

"*If* he's there…" Vivian sighed. Her emotions had been to the moon and back, and all around the maypole all week. Of course he couldn't call her on the telephone, as he didn't have her, or rather her family's number, and he didn't know her father's name, so he couldn't ask the operator to find it. But…seven days is a long time to stew, dream, and wonder. Now, she was just a bundle of nerves.

"Of course he'll be there…unless he couldn't get leave…" Mary June commented, grinning at her friend when Vivian's eyes rounded. "Oh! I didn't even *think* of that!"

Mary June laughed and hugged her friend. "Don't *worry* about it. Just go, dance, try to have a good time, and if he's there, he's there. Okay?"

"Easy for you to say," Vivian mumbled, but flashed her friend a grateful smile and leaned in for a quick hug.

Spying the clock on the nightstand, she squealed, "Eeek! We'd better hurry!"

Now cheerful, the girls gathered their purses and sweaters for the chilly trip home on the bus later, and left the room. Mary June's older brother sat lounging in a chair listening to a prize fight on the radio and glanced up when the girls came into the living room. He'd agreed to take them in his car.

"'Bout time. I got things to do and places to be. Let's go," he playfully griped as he stood and opened the door for them to precede him. Mary June gently elbowed him in the ribs as she passed. This was a game they played all the time – he griped about driving her somewhere, but in truth he was a very protective big brother and took his responsibility seriously. The three chuckled as they trooped out to the car.

THE BAND BEGAN their third song, Glenn Miller's *String of Pearls*, and Vivian brushed her hair back from her face with one hand, unconsciously fiddling with the tormenting rogue curl. Her partner from the last dance flashed her a grin of thanks and handed her off to a fellow in sailor whites with the flap collar uniform.

They started moving to the mellow music, the sailor a homely fellow, but a passable dancer. Vivian tried her best to concentrate on him, but at every opportunity, when facing in the direction of the doorway, she searched the newly arriving soldiers for one particular face and hat. She fought the disappointment each time she didn't see him.

"You lookin' for somebody special?" the sailor asked when the song was nearly over. The sad, almost rejected look in his eyes made Vivian cringe with guilt.

"Oh, no…I was just looking to see how many soldiers would show up tonight," she crossed her fingers at his shoulder and silently asked for forgiveness for the lie, then she managed a smile at his reassured look.

"It sure gets packed in here. I was here last Saturday night, but I didn't manage one dance."

"Oh?" she asked distractedly.

"Yeah…you're a good dancer, Miss. I know I don't do so good…and I ain't much to look at. I thank you for sayin' yes."

Vivian forced herself to meet his eyes and saw the sweet vulnerability in his face. Her heart went out to him and she smiled encouragingly. "You're welcome, sailor. That's what I'm here for. And your dancing is fine. There are just so many of you all, compared with how many girls there are…I'm afraid not everyone gets the chance to dance. You shouldn't take that personally," she added sweetly. He perked up and sent her a big grin.

"Thanks, Miss."

They made polite conversation for the rest of the dance. He told her a bit about where he was from and what his job was in the Navy. She mentioned she worked in a bank.

The song ended with Vivian facing away from the door to the hall. As the sailor gushed another thank you and the next song began, a familiar voice just behind her ear softly inquired, "May I have this dance?"

Electricity zipped down her arms and legs and her breath caught in her throat as she turned and looked up into what was already her favorite pair of blue eyes in the whole world – those in the dear face of her blue-eyed sergeant.

"You most certainly may," she returned.

Gene's grin flashed in the bright lights of the ballroom as he took her in his arms, undoubtedly pleased that the song – Artie Shaw's version of Cole Porter's *Begin the Beguine* – wasn't a particularly fast dance, and he could hold her instead of swinging her around.

After a moment of basking in the pure joy of being with Gene again, and with her temple nestled against his smooth jaw, Vivian ventured, "I wasn't sure you would come tonight."

He leaned back enough to look into her eyes; the familiar tingles fizzing through each of their bodies.

"Wild horses weren't going to keep me away...although a flat tire on the bus tried its best," he smirked.

"Flat tire!"

"Yep. You never saw a flat get changed faster let me tell you. We were all falling over each other trying to help the driver," he laughed. "Probably looked like a bunch of Keystone Cops."

Vivian laughed as they came close again, the nervousness, dread, and doubts melting away as they moved in total synch to the music. It was effortless, like they were made for each other...

"This band is so good," Gene spoke softly near her ear after a few bars of outstandingly smooth clarinet. "You can bet they're going places."

"Yes. They can play anything," Vivian mumbled, her eyes closed. For the first time all evening, she was thoroughly enjoying a dance.

"Did you get in much trouble last week?" Gene finally broached the subject he'd been agonizing over since the last glimpse he'd had of her the previous Saturday night.

She shook her head against his cheek. "Not too much. Miss Warren balled me out and gave me a warning...but my friend also warned that we should be on our best behavior..."

Gene nodded. "I get it. Hands off after this dance, right? Grrr," he playfully growled.

Vivian giggled. "I'll be feeling the same way when I see you cutting a rug with another girl."

"Nah. I'll probably just hang around...but hey, think we could sneak one more in a little later?"

"I think that can be arranged," she smiled dreamily against his smooth, freshly shaved face and breathed in the wonderful scent of his already familiar aftershave. They spent the rest of the song dancing quietly, each one thoroughly engrossed in the feeling of being in the other's arms.

Too soon, the song ended and they had to part ways.

In his peripheral vision, Gene spied Warden Warren glaring their way, so he leaned in and whispered in Vivian's ear, "Until later, baby."

"Count on it," she quipped back as he released her. She turned and smiled up into Pvt. Makowski's handsome face.

"I'll take over from here, Sarge," Mack teased as the trumpets began blaring out the notes of Artie Shaw's *St. Louis Blues*.

Vivian gazed longingly at Gene as Mack swung her away.

Later seemed like a lifetime away.

A FEW SONGS later, Gene settled against the wall with an ice-cold Dr. Pepper and just watched the action. He figured he could have gotten another girl to dance, but in truth, he just didn't want to. Now that he'd met Vivian, he didn't want to hold another girl in his arms. No other girl even held a candle to her. She drew him like a bear to a bowl of honey.

As he sipped his drink, he watched her with some unknown marine. She looked breathtaking in her pretty pink and white flowered dress. The white collar around the squared neck, and the two white-trimmed pockets on the front of the skirt set off the design perfectly, and somehow fit her personality – sweet and innocent with a touch of spice. When he had first walked up to her, he had noticed the dress and he wondered if it were new. Something told him it was. She'd looked adorable in the green one, but this one was even prettier in his opinion. The color looked gorgeous on her. *But then, I bet she's one of those girls that would look good in a flour sack.*

Now, she was smiling politely, and dancing marvelously as the "Gyrene" twirled and swished her around, making the A-line skirt of her dress flare becomingly.

After a while, her dance partner maneuvered her out of

Gene's view, and he turned his attention to perusing the crowd. Spotting Corporal Alvin Fisher, his supply clerk, among the watchers, Gene raised his glass to him and the man wound his way through the sideline to Gene's side.

"Hey Sarge."

"What's doin', Fisher. You enjoying yourself?"

"Yeah, I danced the last one, but got beat out for this one, so I'm waiting," he laughed. "How about you? You dance with *her* yet?"

Gene cast a sharp glance at the corporal, but didn't see anything nefarious in his manner, so he relaxed a bit and grinned at him. "Matter of fact, I did."

"That her there in the pink dress, dancing with that Gyrene?"

"Yep."

The corporal took the hint that his sergeant wasn't going to engage in idle talk about the girl the whole unit had heard he had gone instantly bonkers over, so the younger man wisely shrugged and changed the subject.

"Been thinking about those injectors."

"Me, too," Gene mumbled, looking at his companion, who was in charge of supplies, parts, and tools for his unit.

The other man met his eye and gave a nod. "I'd like to get my hands on the jerk that switched 'em out. Whatdya think? Is it like, somebody doing sabotage, or…think it could be somebody with some kind of racket going on? Could he…could he be sellin' army stuff on the black market or something?"

"That's what I'm thinking. That whole box was the same way – used, clogged injectors that had been wiped off and packaged as new. Somebody went to a lot of trouble."

"Yeah…but *who?*"

Gene drew in a deep breath and let it out in a frustrated huff. "Your guess is as good as mine, Fisher. But I know one thing."

"What's that, Sarge?"

"When I find out who's doing this, he's gonna wish to high heaven that he had decided to stay on the right side of the law."

CHAPTER 7

GENE WAS RIGHT there at Vivian's elbow when the band put down their instruments for a break.

She thanked her partner before turning and smiling up at Gene, her face beautifully flushed from dancing five fast numbers in a row with a variety of talented partners. The last one, a short, stocky member of the local coast guard, wearing the traditional dark blue uniform with white stripes on the collar and a dark blue cap, had just about danced her feet off; in addition, he had swung her out and back so many times she was nearly dizzy.

"Whew! I was never so glad to hear anyone say, 'Let's take ten' as I was just now," she gushed, panting as she tried to catch her breath.

Gene chuckled as he took her arm and began to escort her off the floor. "You know, I never realized being a junior hostess to a bunch of lonely, attention-starved GIs was such a hard job."

She glanced up at him and saw the teasing twinkle in his gorgeous eyes. Managing to keep her wits about her, she quipped back, "You just try it, Sergeant, while wearing high heels, struggling with stockings whose seams insist on going crooked, and striving to keep your makeup from smearing and your hair from wilting." Realizing she had just told him some quite personal details, she looked away and felt her face heating up even more than it already was.

Gene laughed out loud at her candor and dipped his head in

surrender. "I give. I certainly would not wish to go through all of that…with all of that," he chuckled.

"Oh, you," she chided, aiming a half-hearted soft slap at his head, which he skillfully ducked.

"How about we just grab some quenchers and find a corner somewhere…somewhere decidedly *not* private," he specified.

"Sounds wonderful."

After getting her an ice-cold cherry soda, and another Dr. Pepper for himself, Gene steered them to the far corner of the refreshment room where they found one lone bench not even big enough for two. Gene, of course, urged her to sit, while he braced a foot against one end and leaned over her with his back to the room so they could have a modicum of privacy.

Vivian took a long drink with her eyes shut, allowing the bubbles to navigate their way down through her core and revitalize a bit of her weariness. Then, she leaned back against the wall and gazed up at him, her eyes doing a bit of navigating themselves as they traveled over him from his cap down to his shiny black service shoes.

"You wear a uniform well, Sergeant Banks," she complimented. "Spit-shined and perfectly creased."

He inclined his head with a jovial smile. "Thank you, ma'am."

Then with a wolfish grin, he wiggled his eyebrows. "And may I say, that pink dress is quite becoming on you. I like it even better than the green polka dot one from last week. Makes you…kind of glow."

Vivian smiled and dipped her head in gratitude; quite pleased he had noticed the new dress that she had purchased at Lerner's that week, in direct hopes that he would like her in it. It also pleased her that he distinctly remembered what she had worn the week before. That knowledge made another round of tingles fissure through.

For a few minutes, they talked about the weather and the upcoming Derby, which neither planned to attend. Then, gathering her courage, Vivian said, "Sergeant. May I ask...do you go to church?"

Gene dropped his foot to the floor and stood up straight, a bit taken off guard by her question, since he hadn't been thinking in that direction. He cleared his throat and reached up to fiddle with a tie that wasn't in need of adjustment. "Well, I used to. I'm afraid I got out of the habit. Actually...I haven't been to church since I arrived at Knox. Well, that's not quite true – I've visited the chapel out there a time or two after Pearl, but..." he shrugged to a stop.

Vivian watched him, trying to discern his thoughts on the subject. Finally, she said, "Well, I only asked because I wondered if...if you would like to join me and my family tomorrow. But, if you'd rather not..."

"Oh no, I mean...yes, I think I'd like that. Where do you go to church?"

"Little Flock Community Church," she answered, and provided the address. He promised he would make it a point to come, as he had planned to stay over at the club anyway and had already reserved a bunk.

"Your parents will be there...right?" he asked, suddenly a bit nervous to actually meet her father. He wondered what, if anything, she had told her parents about her first night as a USO hostess.

"Yes...is that a problem?"

He looked into those honey brown eyes that already had the power to render him as helpless as a paratrooper without a chute, and he shook his head. He suddenly realized he would willingly submit to anything for the chance to spend time with Miss Vivian Powell.

"No ma'am. I look forward to meeting them."

Her smile warmed him right down to his toes, and he was already wishing he could remove his jacket again as he'd done the week before. *From now on, I'm leaving this dad-blamed jacket at the base.*

As Vivian opened her mouth to say something else, they both heard the band striking up a fresh song.

Vivian laughed and resolutely stood up on her aching feet, which were blessedly feeling better after their brief respite.

"No rest for the weary!" she joked as she took his arm and allowed him to escort her back into the ballroom. They strolled past Miss Warren, and the woman gave them a nod of approval.

Gene took Vivian's empty soda glass from her hand and placed it on a table as they passed by, and then when they hit the floor, he swept her into his arms.

"I believe you stated earlier that I could have seconds."

She couldn't help but laugh with joy at his silly grin. "I believe I did."

This time, they shimmied and spun to a rousing version of the crazy tune *Slap That Bass*. Both of them began to laugh and chortle so much at the silly words and the snappy tune that they were missing connections and looking the fool. Couples dancing nearby chuckled at their antics.

By the time it ended, they were both winded and fell into one another's arms, both having the time of their lives.

If each one hadn't thought they were smitten before – they certainly would now.

GENE CLEARED HIS throat and unconsciously reached up to tug at his tie as he sat next to Vivian in church the next morning. She looked warmly over at him and sent him a tiny smile.

He returned it, and then put forth a valiant effort to pay attention to the pastor's sermon. It wasn't that the man was a boring speaker, or that the topic wasn't relative or interesting. On the contrary, Pastor Rodgers was the kind of preacher that proved points in Scripture by using stories from his personal life that were quite entertaining, and had just the right amounts of humor or suspense. It was just that sitting that close to Vivian was wreaking havoc with his concentration. *Get hold of yourself soldier! You're acting like a love-struck teenager. Straighten up!*

His fingers toyed with the edges of his cap as it rested on one leg. Inevitably, his gaze strayed back her way again as he became acutely aware of her hand moving down to tug at the hem of her slightly tight skirt as it rode just above her knees. He swallowed and looked away, feeling positively wicked that he should be picturing her legs as he sat in *church* of all places!

Another twenty minutes went by, during which Gene was able to follow the pastor's points and gain some fodder for contemplation. Then, the invitation was given, the last song – *Just as I Am* – was sung, and the congregation was dismissed with a prayer.

Gene stood and placed his cap under his arm, extending a hand to help Vivian stand.

"Well, young man. Did you enjoy the service?" asked Vivian's mother, Barbara, with a smile as she fiddled with her purse.

"Yes, ma'am, I did," Gene truthfully answered as he smiled at the woman, whom he guessed to be in her late forties. Still attractive, her hair was the color of Vivian's, with just a touch of gray at the temples, but she had hazel eyes – he had noticed right away that Vivian had inherited her father's honey brown eyes. Mrs. Powell was a sweet woman, quiet and demure. She was dressed in a fashionable, but several years old, dress of peach colored crochet over a cream lining. The outfit was trimmed in black and on her head she wore a smallish black felt hat trimmed with a peach ribbon.

"I appreciated the invitation," Gene glanced at Vivian with a smile. "I'm afraid I've been a bit remiss in my church-going for much too long. This was a good refresher."

Barbara looked delightedly up at him, obviously pleased with his response. Vivian's father, George, a large man with dark hair and black-rimmed glasses and wearing a gray suit, had stood also, but remained silent. He hadn't said much since he had been introduced to Gene on the porch outside when they had first arrived, and Gene wondered once again if he knew about the *kiss*.

Barbara glanced at her husband and received his slight nod, and then extended a hand to Gene. "My husband and I…and I'm sure our daughter…would be pleased if you would join us for Sunday dinner, Sergeant Banks. Would you do us the honor? We're having chicken and dumplings," she added with a twinkle in her eye.

"Thank you, ma'am. I'd be delighted. Chicken and dumplings are a favorite of mine," he replied with absolute veracity.

They moved out into the aisle and began to stroll toward the door, pausing to shake hands with Pastor Rodgers and share a bit of small talk before continuing on down the outer steps.

Gene placed his cap on his head as Mrs. Powell looked around and remarked, "Did you drive, Sergeant Banks?"

"No ma'am, I hitched a ride."

"Ah well, then, you can ride to the house with us. Come along," Barbara ordered sweetly as she took her husband's arm and allowed him to escort her to the car.

Gene peeked at Vivian from under the bill of his cap and grinned. *I know she signed an agreement not to date the soldiers she meets at the club, and I hope she doesn't get in trouble, but…*

Extending his elbow, she took it with a sparkling smile. His heart flip-flopped in his chest. Together the four strolled across the parking lot.

"MA'AM, THAT WAS the best meal I've had in years," Gene declared several hours later as the four of them sat around the dining table. He leaned back in his chair, both hands rubbing his overly full belly.

"Oh, it was nothing, Sergeant. Just something I threw together at the last minute," Vivian's mother demurred, one hand touching the back of her hair, which wasn't in need of smoothing. "But, thank you."

Vivian lowered her head to wipe her mouth with a napkin, hiding her smile. She had barely stopped a bark of laughter at her mother's remark, since she had been a witness to the woman scurrying around the kitchen as she prepared the meal, mumbling phrases like, "Oh, I do hope the sergeant likes my spices," and, "Oh, I wonder if the sergeant prefers rolled dumplings better than drop…"

Vivian had floated between helping her mother in the kitchen and hovering in the living room with her father and Gene. From what she could tell, the two men were enjoying a friendly conversation. Each time she had stuck her head in, they had been chatting about various things like her father's job as a machinist for the Louisville & Nashville Railroad, the aggravation of dealing with so many items being rationed for the war, the merits of different car models, or Gene's job at the base. On her last eavesdrop, they were somberly talking together about the losses our military had suffered at Pearl Harbor.

Now, wishing to have some time alone with "her" sergeant, Vivian pushed back her chair and laid her napkin beside her plate.

"Mother, is it all right with you if Gene and I go for a walk? I could use some exercise after that meal. But…if you need me to help clean up…"

"No, no, you two go on," her mother immediately encouraged, punctuating the statement with a few flicks of her napkin in the general direction of the dining room doorway.

Gene rose and thanked his hosts again, before moving to follow Vivian as she made her exit. Soon, they were outside in the bright sunshine, strolling along side by side down the paved road with houses on one side and acres of empty land on the other. The weather was perfect. Gene had removed his jacket and hat well before they ate their meal, leaving them both on a chair in the living room.

The sergeant cleared his throat and shoved his hands in his pants' pockets. "I appreciate your mother inviting me for dinner. She's a great cook." He shot a look her way as if realizing what he'd just said. "I mean…that is…unless you helped. I mean…I'm sure you're a good cook, too," he stumbled to a halt and clamped his lips.

Vivian sent him a side glance and then erupted in laughter. "I did help, what she would *let* me, that is. Despite her words to the contrary, she worked very hard to impress you with her cooking prowess."

He tipped his head back and laughed. "I see."

She grinned at his laughter and stopped to lean over and pick a spring wild flower from the side of the road. Twirling it in her fingers, she resumed walking as she assured, "I'm a pretty good cook, too, although she usually doesn't let me have the run of her kitchen. So, I can't say I'm as proficient as Mom yet, but…"

"It just takes experience and practice, like anything else. I'm sure someday you'll set a fine table for your husband and family." After that statement, Gene's eyes widened and he sent her a quick look, which she caught from the corner of her eye, but she merely nodded acquiescence and kept strolling. She wondered if his words had conjured images in his mind of them with their children sitting down to dinner in their own home, as they had in hers.

After a few moments, Vivian slipped her hand in the crook of his elbow and ventured, "So…how was your week?"

He smiled down at her. "Would it make sense to say…it went by like a snail and yet a racehorse at the same time?"

She softly giggled and gave a quick nod as she thought of her own week, alternately wishing it would hurry by so that Saturday night would arrive, but also dreading it in case it didn't turn out the way she hoped. "I know exactly what you mean."

Pursing his lips, he said, "Do you remember Rooster? I mean

Private Deal, the one with the bright red hair and the cowlick?"

She did, indeed. "The one who did that side-by-side dance with the private who resembles Tyrone Power? What's that one's name...Mack?"

He nodded, not surprised that she would refer to Mack's resemblance to the celebrity. Almost everyone did. "Yep. Well, Rooster broke his leg Friday. It's pretty bad."

Vivian gasped and turned her head to meet his eyes.

"The docs operated on him and he's in traction at the post hospital. I think he's a bit worried..." he paused, sympathy clear in his eyes.

"Well, modern medicine has come a long way. I'm sure, with time and exercise, he'll be all right. Look at *me*," she smiled and patted her left leg. He sent her a confused look and she explained, "I broke my leg in three places when I was fifteen, but it healed just fine." Waiting a moment, she added with a mischievous grin, "Why, I can even keep up with the likes of Sergeant Eugene Banks on the dance floor."

Gene chuckled and laid a hand over her own on his arm, caressing it fondly. "Yes, ma'am, you surely can."

The day and their camaraderie felt so wonderful. Vivian realized she hadn't been so completely at ease with a man in...well, *ever*. She sighed contentedly and laid her head against his shoulder as they continued to stroll, thinking Sgt. Gene Banks was about as perfect as a man could get.

"What else happened this week?" she asked, just to keep the conversation going. Already, she loved to hear Gene's voice, no matter what he was saying. The timbre of it always drifted into her ears and filtered down inside her body like honey on a piece of warm toast. *Such a nice, masculine voice,* she sighed silently as she listened to him talk about a torrential rain dissolving some earthen mounds, and then about a fistfight between two of his men – and how one of them knocked one of his teeth loose!

"Oh my! Let me see!" she gushed, stopping and turning to

him as he obligingly grinned widely at her, pointing to the offended incisor.

"It's fine now. The post dentist did a great job," he assured, choosing not to tell her what a painful ordeal it had been.

"I did get some bad news, though," he admitted softly.

She tilted her head up at him and watched as he clamped his lips together for a moment. "I found out my best friend from high school was killed..."

Viv gasped in sympathy and touched his arm. "Oh Gene!"

He nodded solemnly. "His name was Russ...Russ Calhoun. He'd gone into the Navy early in '41, and was sent to Pearl." He stopped a moment with a sad sort of smirk and shook his head in self-disdain. "I remember teasing him that I was jealous that he got to go to Hawaii...all play and no work – nothing but Hula girls and fun times... So, he sent me a package with a dancing Hula doll and a picture of him on the beach with his arms around two beautiful girls in grass skirts with long lovely black hair. At the bottom, he'd written – *to Gene – eat your heart out Army boy*." He took a deep breath and blew it out slowly. "He'd been injured during the attack on Pearl Harbor. The docs had patched him up, but...he got an infection, and..." he swallowed hard, giving a little shrug.

"I'm so sorry, Gene," Viv murmured, peering up at him as they stood in the bright sunshine together. "Matter of fact, we received some bad news this week, too," she admitted softly. "My cousin, Bill...my Dad's brother's son...they used to live next door and we'd been inseparable until they moved to Illinois when we were both twelve. He was the brother I wished I'd had... He joined the Marines in January, immediately after hearing about the attack on Pearl, and had been sent to Camp Pendleton. He was killed in an accident this week. He was in a jeep...he wasn't driving...it flipped over..." she stopped, her eyes misty.

"Aw honey," Gene whispered. Sometimes, the war seemed far away and almost unreal – but it had a way of making itself very real when news of casualties reached the ears of loved ones and friends. He drew her into his arms for a moment and they stood together, each remembering good times with their fallen loved ones and lending heartfelt support to each other.

Finally, they pulled back and stared into one another's eyes, as their shared grief added another layer to their burgeoning feelings for each other.

By mutual silent agreement, they resumed their walk; he with his hands in his pockets, and she with her hands gently gripping his arm. At her prompting, he told her a few more incidents about his week, but stopped short in his explanation of the injector problem.

Vivian looked up at him, wondering why he stopped. "Did you find out what the problem was?" she asked, a bit concerned that his expression had hardened – just a bit, but enough for her to notice.

"Yes and no," he replied, and she pondered why he was suddenly being so vague.

"Yes and no?" she encouraged.

Gene shook his head slightly, as if reminding himself of something, and then cast a glance around at their surroundings.

"So, how long have you and your parents lived here? I mean, did you grow up in that house?" he asked, inclining his head back toward her home and effectively changing the subject.

Something about that set off alarm bells inside her head. What was he keeping from her?

Politely, she explained that she and her parents had moved into the house when she was ten, and then talked a bit about where they had lived before and things about the neighborhood.

After a while, the odd feeling of him withholding something from her went away and gradually they moved back into their normal give and take.

Vivian had no idea, however, that it wouldn't be too long until the suspicion of Gene keeping secrets would come roaring back with a vengeance.

CHAPTER 8

A NOTHER WEEK CREPT by for the smitten couple. Gene spent it performing his duties and avoiding run-ins with his decidedly unpleasant roommate. On Wednesday when yet another truck developed injector trouble, and the base supply warehouse was still out of replacements, the captain issued the command that an emergency run be made into Louisville to pick some up.

It had been some time since Gene had run an errand, matter of fact he hadn't since he had received his sergeant stripes, but he didn't really mind. All of the privates and corporals under him in the unit were busy with repairs and other duties that were of a timely nature. Rooster had been his gopher, so to speak, but with him still laid up in the hospital, the errand had fallen to Gene.

Now taking his hat off as he entered the captain's office later in the day, Gene acknowledged Cpl. Dan in the outer room with a nod and then turned to see the captain motion him inside.

"Did you get them, Sergeant?" Captain Moore asked as Gene moved through the doorway and saluted.

"Yes, sir. No problems. They said they would send the bill to the procurement office."

"That's fine," the captain replied. Observing his sergeant, he gestured for Gene to shut the door. Gene complied and took a seat in the chair the captain indicated.

"What do you make of this, Sergeant? Any ideas? Any leads?"

"No, sir. It was done on purpose, that's for sure. The problem is, we can't know for sure when, since it's been weeks since we've had to replace any injectors. There are any number of people who would have access to the supply room."

"Have you noticed any keys missing?"

Gene thought a moment. "No sir."

"For now, keep an eye out for anything suspicious. I've alerted the MP's and they are adding extra patrols in the area after lights out. I have a suspicion that you have stumbled onto something that could be the tip of the iceberg. If you see or hear anything, inform me immediately. That's all, Sergeant."

Gene rose to his feet and saluted, "Yes, sir." The captain returned the salute and went back to his paperwork as Gene went to the door.

"Oh, and Sergeant?"

Gene pivoted on his heel and faced his superior again. "Yes, sir?"

"Keep this under wraps for now. Tell no one who doesn't absolutely need to know – 'Loose lips', 'The Walls Have Ears', etc. That's an order."

"Yes, sir."

The captain returned Gene's second salute and resumed his work as Gene turned to leave the office.

The more Gene thought about this mystery, the more it rankled him. With a scowl, he changed direction and headed off to chat with a few of the other motor sergeants and see if anything else was afoot – without letting any of them know what he was up to.

THE FOLLOWING FRIDAY afternoon, Vivian counted out her cash drawer and finished her day, anxious to get on with her evening. When she and Gene had parted on Sunday night after the final dance – which she had danced with Mack – they had arranged to go to dinner and catch a movie. She could hardly wait to see him.

"I hope you have a good time with your sergeant tonight, honey," Mary June offered as she gave her own makeup a final going over in the employee's restroom at the bank in preparation for the bus ride home.

Vivian grinned at her over her shoulder as she wiggled into the dress Mary June had leant her for the evening. "I plan on it. Do me up?"

Obliging, she stepped close. Finding she was unable to resist needling her friend a bit, she asked, "What're you going to do if Miss Warren finds out you and Gene are going out – and he came to church with you?"

Viv glanced at her over her shoulder as her teeth caught her bottom lip. "I know…it's not like me to break rules like this, but…oh Mary, I can't help it!" With a tiny sigh, she added, "I'm going to keep my agreement to attend the dances and dance with any soldier who asks. Gene understands. But, if we get caught and Miss Warren dismisses me from being a hostess, well…" she shrugged one shoulder, "he's worth it."

With a thoughtful expression on her face, the other girl fastened the buttons at the back of the dress. Then, the girls worked together to arrange Vivian's hair, pulling back one side with a lovely comb in the shape of a butterfly embellished with crystals. The rest of her hair cascaded around her shoulders in perfect honey-blonde waves.

When they finished and stared at the mirror, both girls were smiling from ear to ear at the result.

Mary June let out a slow whistle. "Whew! Honey, you're gonna knock that man's stripes right off his uniform!"

Vivian giggled as she fiddled with the skirt, murmuring self-consciously, "My goodness, I've never worn anything so…*provocative* before." The short-sleeved dress hugged her figure perfectly and was quite becoming. The smooth material had a pattern of large flowers in various shades of pink, it sported a square open neck and cinched waist. The effect finished off with a sash of the same fabric that hung fetchingly at Vivian's hip and ended halfway down the length of the pencil skirt. She had paired it with white open-toed pumps.

Her friend chuckled and hovered around her, tugging and smoothing. "Aw, it's not that bad. It fits you better than it fit me," she added with a snicker.

"Thanks, honey. I appreciate you lending it to me. Okay, well...I guess I'm as ready as I'm going to get!" Once more Vivian leaned close to the mirror to blot her lipstick and then picked up her purse and sweater, along with a bag containing her work dress and shoes. "I just need to stash this in my desk."

Mary June consulted her wristwatch and gave a soft shriek. "Jiminy Cricket, the bus!"

Vivian laughed as her friend gave her a quick hug, flashed two thumbs up, and disappeared out the restroom door with a hollered, "See you tomorrow night – don't take any wooden nickels – and don't kiss any wooden sergeants!"

GENE CHECKED HIS watch for the third time and eyed a bus passing the '39 Buick Century convertible in which he sat. He had borrowed the car for their date from another sergeant who owed him a favor. It was a sharp looking car, wine colored with a tan top and matching interior.

Reaching out a hand to run it appreciatively over the smooth upholstery, he mused that he was thankful his friend had been so accommodating, as he hadn't relished trying to take Viv out to dinner and a movie if they were going to have to walk everywhere, catch a bus – if they could even time that right – or pay for a taxi.

I'd like to buy a car this nice some day. He had never owned his own car, having not needed one at the CCC camps, nor since he had joined the army. If he needed to get around, he'd usually use a jeep. But now… *Maybe I can start putting some lettuce away for one every payday, once I make First Sarge…that is IF I make it,* he reminded himself. *If I don't find out who the creep is that tampered with my supplies…*

For a moment, his euphoria at being able to take Viv out on a real date, in a swell car, and have her all to himself for the evening, dimmed a bit as he thought about the still-nagging question of the switched diesel parts. He'd been investigating and surreptitiously interviewing some of the other sergeants through-out the base, and had found out that each one had faced the same or a similar issue over the past two months. But – no one had seen or heard anything out of the ordinary.

Gene shook his head in frustration. *It beats the heck outta me. But if I get my hands on that lousy no good son of a—*

Just then, the door of the bank opened and a familiar woman sprinted to the bus stop, barely making it in time before the driver closed the door. If he wasn't mistaken, the woman was Vivian's friend, Mary June…

He watched as the bus started up again and moved into traf-fic. Horns blared and people sidestepped one another as they traversed the sidewalks of Fifth and Market, hurrying home on a Friday evening.

A minute later, the bank's glass door opened again and Gene's breath caught in his throat as Vivian stepped out, wearing a gorgeous pink flowered dress. It hugged her curves in all the right places. *WOW! Would you look at that!* Momentarily struck dumb, his mouth went dry and his heart kicked into overdrive.

Vivian moved to one side of the door to allow a man to exit, nodding to him as he apparently wished her a good evening. She looked around then, scanning the area with a white clutch-type purse shielding her eyes against the afternoon sun.

Gene physically shook himself out of his stupor and moved to open his door to get out. A loud horn blasted as the large front end of a late model Dodge zoomed past. His heart nearly stopped as his head whipped to the left. He yanked the door shut and let the car go by, and then slid out quickly and made his way around the front, waving to Vivian.

His heart was still hammering from the near collision, and now her smile of welcome nearly bowled him over. *Holy mackerel, she's gorgeous.* He hurried over and took her hand as he reached her side.

"Hey beautiful," he greeted, his voice husky as his heart still pounded in his chest.

Her face pinkened with a lovely blush. "Hello handsome."

He allowed his eyes to caress the vision that was Vivian, from the top of her hair, to her beautiful face, arresting eyes, and those gorgeous lips, all the way down that amazing dress and to her cute little feet in a pair of white shoes.

"Mmm, don't you look *gorgeous*," he murmured, his eyes sparkling approval.

"You like?" she grinned.

He nodded and pulled her a bit closer, trying valiantly not to grab her and kiss her senseless. "I *like*."

She pursed her lips for a second and then raised one eyebrow fetchingly. "Mission accomplished, then."

He chuckled at her candor, and lifted his hand to caress her cheek with the backs of his fingers. Just above a whisper, he admitted, "I thought tonight would never get here. 'Bout lost my mind waiting."

Those delightful honeyed eyes of hers twinkled in the sunlight. "Same here." They stood like that, motionless, until someone cleared their throat and mumbled, "Pardon me" as they made their way around the couple.

Gene forced himself back to the business at hand. Sweeping an arm toward the car, he announced, "Madam, your *chariot* awaits." Her laughter tinkled merrily as they started over.

"My goodness, this is some chariot. I *approve*," she purred as they reached the passenger door.

Belatedly, he thought about his decision to put the top down and he hesitated. She met his eyes. "I can put the top up if you'd prefer…"

"Oh no, don't. I love convertibles. Don't put it up on my account." She viewed the automobile with admiration, caressing the shiny paint on the fender. "It sure is…what's that term they say now? …*On the beam.*"

Gene totally agreed with her assessment that the car was A-one. "It belongs to a pal who owed me a favor."

"*That's* the kind of pals to *have*," she teased with a cute grin.

He opened the passenger door and Vivian sat down and gracefully swung her legs inside.

Gene swallowed hard and closed the door, blocking the lovely view of a set of swell gams.

"And now I owe him one," he said quietly to himself as he made his way around to the driver's side door and quickly slid inside, eager to get their date underway.

"All right, my dear. First stop – The Seelbach Hotel's Derby Room."

GENE HELD THE door for Vivian as they exited the restaurant and then fixed his garrison cap back on his head. He took his place on the street side of the sidewalk and tucked Vivian's hand in the crook of his elbow.

It was beginning to get a bit breezy on the downtown street and the warmth of his arm through the fabric of his shirt felt wonderful. She squeezed his forearm, noticing the firm muscle under the material, and sighed softly. Then closing her eyes, she breathed in his delicious masculine scent, which she was sure was uniquely part Gene and part Old Spice after-shave. Her father wore the same brand, but it never smelled that good on him!

Thinking back to when Gene had hurried around the front of the car to her side, she hadn't been able to help but admire the picture he made in his khaki uniform, with his cap at just the right angle, tie knotted just right, trousers creased to perfection, and black shoes gleaming.

"That was great," he interrupted her musings as he rubbed his belly appreciatively. "Haven't had a meal that good since...last Sunday and your mom's chicken and dumplings." He sent her a cheeky grin.

She shot him a "Yeah, right" look. "Oh, come now, Sergeant. Surely my mother's chicken and dumplings can't compare to the connoisseur's delights of the chef at The Derby Room. He would be highly insulted." She held up a one-sheet flier about the restaurant, which she had picked up on the way out the door as memorabilia for her scrapbook. "Why, it says here," she read from it, her tone playfully pretentious. *"Every item on our menu begins with the finest meats, fruits and vegetables on the market, selected and prepared with utmost care – cooked and seasoned to delectable taste by our new chef, who comes to us direct from Chicago. Economical and oh, so good – get dinner for just sixty-five cents!* Now I ask you, how could Mom's chicken and dumplings trump that?"

Gene just beamed and turned his head a bit to look into her eyes as she smiled up at him. She wondered what he was thinking as she teasingly batted her eyes for good measure, but found she was unable to stifle her giggle.

"That's all well and good," he conceded. Then he sent her a wolfish grin. "But honey, never underestimate the power of a home-cooked meal. No disrespect to Chef What-Ever-His-Name-Is from Chicago, but it's true what they say about the path to a man's heart."

"Mmm, I'll have to remember that, soldier," she murmured contentedly and he chuckled as they strolled down South Fourth toward the movie theater.

The couple had eyes for only each other until several yards

further on, when they both heard a man's voice holler, "Well, I'll be a son of a gun! Gene Banks, in uniform?"

Gene looked up and broke into a grin from ear to ear at a couple walking toward them. "Chief? Is that you?"

The two men laughed and sped the last few steps toward one another, reaching out with right hands to connect in firm shakes, while their lefts gave friendly slaps on their backs.

"I ain't seen you in…what's it been? Four years? Five?" Vic Matthews, Gene's friend from the days of the '37 flood, exclaimed.

"Yeah, about that," Gene agreed, still pumping Vic's hand. "Good to see you, Vic. Good to see you."

Both men cheerfully stepped back; Vic to once again draw near the woman he was with, and Gene to put his hand at Vivian's back.

Vic proclaimed proudly, "You remember my wife, Louise."

Gene inclined his head toward her with a friendly smile. "I sure do. So you two did get married. I'm glad. Nice to see you, Louise."

"Hello Gene," she nodded.

Drawing Vivian a bit closer, Gene said with his voice just as filled with pride, "Viv, remember me telling you about Vic Matthews, my old rescue boat skipper?" She nodded that she remembered as he went on, "Vic, Louise, this is Vivian Powell."

Vivian had been gazing at the other woman, noticing her quiet beauty and dazzling smile, and she could not mistake the way she kept looking up at her dark-haired, dark-eyed, dashingly handsome husband in complete adoration. Another thing Vivian noticed was – the woman had on an identical dress to the one she was wearing! The only difference being that the colors in Louise's were shades of blue while hers were pinks, but the style was exactly the same.

With a twinkle in her eye, Vivian quipped, "Nice to meet you both. And Louise – I must say, I love your taste in clothes."

All four erupted in laughter.

Louise smiled in a friendly manner, smoothing one hand down the skirt of her dress. "I was about to say the same to you. But I think I like yours better. Those pinks look wonderful on you."

The men talked for a few minutes, catching up on missed years. Vic seemed suitably impressed at what Gene had achieved in the C's and in the Army, but Vivian thought he was a bit vague when it came to what he was doing now. She glanced at Gene, but he didn't seem to think anything of it.

Eventually, the girls stepped closer to speak a few words woman to woman while the men reminisced. They each found it funny that both dresses were borrowed from their best friends to go out to the movies with their men. The girls hit it off right away and Louise mentioned that perhaps they could get together as a foursome sometime in the future.

"I'd love that, and I'm sure Gene would, too," Vivian assured.

Suddenly, Gene brought up his arm and checked his watch. "Hot dog! Viv, if we don't hurry, we'll miss the start of the movie," he said as he turned, reaching for her with his other hand.

"What movie are you going to see?" Louise inquired.

"A new one is playing at the Rialto called *Saboteur*, with Priscilla Lane and Robert Cummings," Gene answered. "It's by that Hitchcock fella, so it should be pretty good. The next showing is 7:15."

"Oh Vic, what do you think?" Louise turned to her husband as she addressed them all. "We've been trying to decide all evening between *Flying Tigers* with John Wayne and *Woman of the Year* with Spencer Tracy and Katherine Hepburn. This one might be even better..."

"I don't know...I was looking forward to watching the Duke whip 'em into shape..." he paused, looking down into his wife's sparkling hazel eyes. Vivian knew before he said the next words that they would be joining them. It was obvious the man was smitten with his wife. "But, I guess. If that's what you want," he added softly.

Gene laughed out loud as he remembered all of the evenings the old gang had spent running around together – in that crazy ancient black hearse. She'd had him tied up in knots even then. Evidently things were no different now. "She's still got you wrapped around her pinky finger, I see. Huh, boss?"

Vic turned his head and flashed his old friend a mischievous grin. "Oh shut up, *Green Gene.*"

"Hey!" the sergeant shot back, albeit laughingly. Vivian shot him a querying look and he mumbled, "Uh…I'll explain that later."

VIVIAN LINGERED FOR one more moment in the doorway of the elegant and amazing Rialto Theater, which was considered the finest and most costly movie house in Louisville. She'd heard its construction had cost over one million dollars when it opened in 1921. Viv had never had the pleasure of seeing a movie there before, and she wanted to savor the experience. This was a night for memories, and she knew she would never forget the venue's breathtaking chandeliers of Bohemian crystal, the great marble staircase, and the walls overlaid with gorgeous tiles and fantastic mosaics. Finally, with a soft contented sigh, she allowed Gene to tug her out the doors with the others.

"Wow, that was some ending," Louise Matthews declared as the four made their way out of the building. "I don't think I'll ever forget it." She took her husband's arm and looked questioningly up at him as the two couples began to stroll back to their cars. "Did you enjoy the movie?"

"Yeah, it was pretty good," he answered. "I liked the news-reels, too. That bit about that defense plant in Akron, Ohio that's turning out anti-aircraft guns was interesting – and the stuff about how they get mail to the G.I.'s overseas, and how most of the guys were saved when the Yorktown was sunk."

"And those poor people on Malta, being bombed so much – I felt so sorry for them," Vivian added.

"Yeah," Vic agreed. "The movie was good, too, though. That poor schmuck, Barry Kane, blamed for something he didn't do, but nobody would cut him any slack. It sure was full of twists and turns. That Hitchcock fella can sure spin a good yarn." Turning to look at Gene, he asked, "What'd *you* think about it, Sarge?"

"It got me fired up, I'll tell you that," Gene answered. "Guys like that Fry, they get me. How could anybody do something like that – betray America, set bombs and start fires, and hand a man a fire extinguisher filled with gasoline and watch him burn! And then, that old Charles Tobin – he sure was a piece of work. Lousy traitors," Gene grumbled, as if he were distracted about something.

Vivian squeezed Gene's arm and shuddered as she remembered the all-too-real final scene. "I hope I don't have a nightmare about that awful Fry falling from the top of the Statue of Liberty. It was so *real…*" she shuddered again. "I almost felt sorry for him by then."

"Yes, me too," Louise agreed. "If only Barry had grabbed his arm and not just his sleeve…" The couples navigated around other people who were hurrying to catch the next showing.

"Something I didn't quite get, though," Louise continued, "was why Pat had such a hard time believing Barry was innocent. She should have been able to sense he was an honest man and telling the truth. The poor guy; I felt so sorry for him."

"Oh I know," Vivian agreed. "By then, she was in love with Barry. Her heart should have told her the truth, no matter how bad things looked. Remember how the circus people's immediate belief in him convinced her of his veracity, but then later she overhears him in that Soda City place, bluffing his way out of the tight spot they were in – and right away, she doubts him again. I found that a little far-fetched."

Gene grinned at her and couldn't resist querying, "So, if it had been *you*, you'd stand by your man no matter what, huh?"

She met his eyes dead on and nodded, not a shred of doubt in her mind. "You bet I would."

"Mmm, I'll have to remember that, Miss Powell," he teased, paraphrasing her earlier statement.

They both laughed.

Vivian, however, had no idea that before too long, her own words would, as they say, make a liar out of her.

CHAPTER 9

G ENE PULLED THE car up in front of Vivian's house and turned off the motor. They'd had such a wonderful evening that neither one wanted their date to come to an end.

Even as the hour grew late, they had dawdled along the way, attempting to postpone the inevitable. After stopping for a milkshake at a corner soda shop, Gene had driven slowly all the way to her house. There was nothing else to do – they had to say goodnight.

Each one sat for a moment, contemplating their end-of-date kiss...only their second one – they hadn't had the opportunity to indulge since their mammoth first kiss. Gene almost laughed that he was actually nervous.

He cleared his throat and ventured, "Well...I guess I'll walk you up."

Vivian gathered her purse and sweater, glancing at him as she did. "All right."

Gene climbed out of the driver's side and rounded the car, opened the passenger door, and extended a hand to help her out. She took it and he drew her forth, marveling at the tingles he felt from the mere touch of their hands.

Politely tucking her hand in the crook of his arm, he strolled with her slowly up the walk, silently cursing the fact that he'd suddenly become tongue-tied. It seemed that she was, too.

They reached the porch and mounted the steps side by side.

Vivian cringed a bit that her parents had left the porch light on, which was drawing moths. She batted one aside and moved a bit away. Then, with Gene's help, she draped her sweater around her shoulders.

"I had a wonderful time tonight, Gene."

"Me, too. The best date I've ever been on. That's a fact, ma'am," he added, exaggerating his Kentucky twang. Vivian giggled at his silliness.

"And your friends, they were very nice. I liked them both."

"Yeah, they're great."

She seemed to be casting about for something to say, and then suddenly looked up at him with a mischievous grin. "Now, what was that about *Green Gene?*"

Gene tipped his head back and laughed, albeit not too loud, since it was so late.

"The guys called me that on the boat one day when I ate something bad and got sick. Even puked over the side…" Vivian wrinkled her nose at him. "Sorry," he grimaced. "They said I turned green right before." He shuddered at the memory. "Anyway, on and off all day it would hit me. So by the end of the day, I was Green Gene – and they never let me forget it," he ended with an embarrassed chuckle.

"Oh, that's awful, you poor baby," Vivian cooed, lifting a hand and cupping his cheek.

"You *know* it." He raised a hand and laid it warmly over hers as they stared at one another. A moth chose that moment to flutter at Vivian's cheek and she swatted at it. He turned them so that he was closer to the light.

"Um…I guess I'll see you tomorrow night, then?" she asked softly as she looked up into his face, but his features were now in shadow with his back to the glow.

He cleared his throat again, wishing the captain hadn't given him an absolute order to go undercover on Saturday night to follow a lead. It was a logical thing to do, the captain just didn't realize it was cramping Gene's style something awful.

However, the worst part was, Gene couldn't tell Vivian the truth. He'd been given direct orders – and if there was one thing about Gene Banks, he was a man who followed orders. It was a matter of personal pride for him. He chose his words carefully…

"Well, no. I won't be able to be with you. The captain ordered me to do…something," he hoped he didn't sound as shady to her as he sounded to himself.

From the look on her face in the harsh porch light, he had.

"You're not…oh…" she murmured softly, and he could see she was hurt. Of course she felt slighted – it was like he was saying he had something more important to do than spend time with her, but in his heart that was the farthest thing from the truth.

"I'm sorry. But…this can't be avoided."

"Well…what *is* it? Can't you explain?" Vivian asked, apparently trying to control her feelings.

Gene sighed regretfully and slowly shook his head, keeping his voice gentle. "I'm sorry, but I can't. I'm a sergeant, remember…sometimes, duty calls. It's…official army business."

At that, her expression softened a bit and her lips turned up in a slight smile. "Oh, I see. 'Loose lips sink ships' and all that?"

Gene chuckled. "Yeah. Something like that."

"All right, Sergeant. I'll let you off the hook this time," she acquiesced. Then with a teasing twinkle, she brought up a hand and pressed a finger to his chest, adding, "Just don't make a habit of it."

Gene laughed out loud at that and gave her a perfect salute. "Yes, sir! Whoops, I mean…Yes, Ma'am."

Vivian giggled at his play, and then her eyes grew serious when he lowered his hand and let it fall softly down to caress her shoulder and neck.

"Oh honey…you don't know how I wish I could get out of it," he murmured, his voice husky. Slowly, he brought his hand up and let his fingers cup her chin. "But...I'll try to make it to church on Sunday."

"That would be nice," Vivian whispered, her senses totally zeroed in on the feeling of his fingers on her skin.

He leaned slowly forward, gently drawing her face toward his until his lips met hers. The feeling was electric, just like their first kiss. Each one took a surprised breath, and then melted into one another. Gene's lips moved over Vivian's, caressing and warm as he breathed in the subtle scent of her perfume. He lost track of time as the rest of the world faded away and the universe became filled with only the two of them. Behind his eyelids, sparks seemed to dance. It was magical.

Finally, Gene forced himself to pull back, leaving each of them to shiver in reaction to cold reality. Did the night just get cooler? What was it about their kisses that seemed to wipe them both out?

With a dreamy smile, his voice low and thick, he said warmly, "Good night, sweet Vivian Powell."

"Goodnight, wonderful Staff Sergeant Banks," she answered just as dreamy.

"I hope Sunday gets here double-time."

"Triple."

She turned with a soft smile and opened the door, before slipping quietly inside. Just before she allowed the gap to close, she gave him one last wiggle of her fingers and a whispered, "Goodnight."

He watched the door close and heard the lock turn, then walked to the car and stood for a moment just looking up at the porch. Then he got in the car, started it up, and drove away, feeling as if the night had lost its enchantment because Viv was no longer at his side – and it would be thirty-six hours before he would be able to hold her again. Part of his brain was amazed that she had become so important to his life in such a short time.

And for the first time since he had joined the C's so many

years before, he wished he didn't have to follow orders.

EARLY SATURDAY EVENING, Staff Sergeant Blake Hendricks, Gene's very own self-appointed vexer, walked into their shared room with a towel wrapped around his middle, while he vigorously dried his hair with another. He stole a quick look over at Gene lounging on his bunk flipping through the latest copy of *Stars and Stripes*. It didn't appear to Hendricks that his roommate was preparing for a night out.

With a smirk, he taunted, "What, aren't you going into town tonight? Your new girl drop you already?"

Gene clamped his teeth together and shot a look at the other man. "What girl?" he asked innocently.

Hendricks scoffed as he tossed the towel on his bunk and began getting dressed. "It's all over the barracks – *Sgt. Banks has a girl down at the USO and she's a real dish,*" he mocked.

Gene refused to let the man get his goat. He merely turned the page in the newspaper and lifted one shoulder in a careless shrug. After a minute, he asked casually, "What's it to you?"

The other man threw him a look as he buttoned up his shirt. "Absolutely nothing, Banks. Less than nothing."

Gene just drew in a breath and let it out in a controlled sigh. "That's good."

For some reason, that made Hendricks angry. Probably because he found it so difficult to ruffle Gene's feathers, no matter how hard he tried. The man always seemed to be one degree short of the boiling point. Evidently he could tell that Gene was trying not to smile, so he stopped his movements and sneered, "You really tick me off, Banks, you know that?"

At that, Gene lowered the paper and swung his legs to the floor to sit up on his bunk, glaring straight back at the obstinate fellow staff sergeant. "What's your *beef*, Hendricks? You've been on my case since day one and I ain't done jack to you. What's up?" He waited while the other man finished dressing and grasped his cap from off the chair on his side of the room. "You got a beef with me, out with it. 'Cause I tell you what; I've had just about enough of this unprovoked animosity." He could practically see the steam coming out of the other man's ears. "Well?" Gene pushed.

Hendricks crammed the hat on his head, obviously still angry. "Like you don't *know*," he spit out.

With that, he stomped out and slammed the door to the room.

Gene stared after him open mouthed. *What in the Sam Hill did that mean? That guy's nuts!*

After a few moments, Gene shook off the unpleasant altercation and began to get ready to obey orders for the night. Drawing an older uniform out of the bottom of his footlocker, he began to hurriedly change into it. *I wish they'd give that jerk his own quarters. I've about reached my limit of sharing "temporary" quarters with him...*

Once dressed, Gene waited until the barracks had fallen silent and he could no longer hear noise outside, figuring most of the post had left for their weekend liberty. It was dusk as he crept out of his room and shut the door behind him. Reaching the outer door, he looked around before slipping out and heading off to his destination – hopefully to get to the bottom of the supply mystery.

VIVIAN SMILED AT the young sailor who awkwardly thanked her for his dance, practically stumbling over his feet that seemed too big for his body. It was her sixth dance of the night and the ballroom at the USO seemed hotter and more crowded than usual. *Whew, I need something cold to drink,* she mused as she tried to make her way through the over packed room.

Politely pushing her way through the crowd of soldiers and sailors, she grinned as she came upon her friend Mary June, who seemed to be heading in the same direction.

"Hey girl," Mary June greeted as she hooked arms with Viv.

"Hey. Boy, is it busier tonight or is it my imagination?" Vivian huffed as she finally made it through the back of the crowd and over to the refreshment corner.

"Yes, it does seem so. I've lost track of the number of dance partners I've had already – but I can count the bruises," Mary June laughed. "Seems like I'm getting the ones with two left feet tonight."

"I wish the band would play more slow songs," Vivian giggled.

Her friend nodded in full agreement. "*Boogie Woogie Bugle Boy* about did me in. The sailor I danced that with kept tossing me over his shoulder – once I thought I was going to land on my head!" she giggled, only half teasing.

They collected their refreshments and navigated to a far corner to try and get a few minutes' respite, talking idly about one thing and then another.

A little time went by and then Mary June rose up on tiptoes, peering at something near the doors to the main hall. "Hey," she reached over to tap Vivian on the arm, speaking loudly to be heard over the music and the noise of the crowd. "I thought you said Gene wasn't coming tonight."

Vivian's heart ramped up as she focused on her taller friend. "He wasn't...why?"

"Well...unless my eyesight's gone kaflooey, he just came in and he's standing to the left of the doors talking with some other soldiers."

Vivian stretched up and even hopped up and down a few times, trying unsuccessfully to see over the heads of the dozens of people between them. "I can't see...are you sure?"

"Far as I can tell from here. He's not in his usual uniform, though, so maybe it's not him," Mary June answered. The crowd seemed to push against the girls as more enlisted men crowded into the large room.

After a minute, Vivian gave up and gazed around her at the mass of bodies. "Well, he knows I'm here. He'll find me."

A full song went by and then Mary June was coaxed back into the mix of dancers. She called over her shoulder, "I'll see if we can dance our way over there. I'll point him your way."

Vivian nodded and a few moments later, she was cajoled to dance as well. She barely heard anything her partner was saying, as she was so intent on spotting Gene. *Perhaps he finished his assignment early. Yes, that must be it...*

Finally half way through the song, the dancers nearest the door parted just enough for her to catch a glimpse of him. As Mary June had said, he was just to the left of the doors. Relaxing against the wall, he had one foot braced and both hands in his pockets. He appeared to be just watching the action. The crowd thickened again and she lost sight of him. Frustration mounted and she wondered why he hadn't sought her out yet.

Another song started, with yet another partner. Without actively taking the "lead", she couldn't really influence where they headed as they navigated through the mix of gyrating bodies, dodging elbows and arms, but they did manage to get closer to her intended direction. Perhaps her partner could tell she was interested in something on that side of the room and he was trying to be accommodating.

Suddenly, the dancers parted and about ten feet away, there was Gene wearing an olive green uniform that didn't seem as tidy as was his norm. The pants weren't creased and his tie was crooked. He wasn't wearing his billed hat, but had a garrison cap tucked in his belt. Vivian strained to see him clearly, but the crowd tightened again and her partner swung her away. She nearly stumbled; the incident having left her shaken.

What in the world is going on? Perhaps it's not him... Wait...he said he had an assignment…could he be on some kind of… No, that's crazy – what kind of assignment would he have here at the USO? It's not him, that's all there is to it.

The night got no better as it dragged on. Several songs went by as Vivian performed her duty and danced with whoever asked, until finally she caught sight of Gene again – this time dancing! Gene was *dancing* with another girl! Vivian only managed a few seconds' glimpse, but she was sure it was him and he seemed to be thoroughly enjoying himself.

Vivian felt sick. *Why is he doing this?*

An hour later, Vivian was finally able to make it over to where she had seen him as the crowd had begun to thin out, but he was nowhere to be found. He could have gone upstairs or even left the building, she had no way of knowing.

And he hadn't sought her out even once.

CHAPTER 10

S UNDAY WENT BY slowly for Vivian. Gene didn't make it to church – but then, he'd said he would "try" to make it. Vivian had tossed and turned all night wondering why Gene had come to the dance when he had said he couldn't, and then he hadn't even tried to seek her out! The whole thing gave her a familiar and unwanted feeling.

Walter had lied to her and tried to keep the truth from her that he had another girlfriend. Now, was Gene lying to her as well? How well did she really know Gene? Actually, she had only met him a matter of weeks ago. She had known Walter for four years, but hadn't *really* known him at all before he had broken her heart. She knew she had trust issues, but she had thought that with Gene it wouldn't be a problem. He had seemed so perfect… Now, she just didn't know.

Vivian waited all day, but Gene never showed. Once, she had picked up the telephone to try and call out to the base to get in touch with him, but found that their home's line was dead. *Great. Someone probably hit the pole again. I hope it's fixed soon…* But it wasn't, and Sunday ended in silence from Vivian's blue-eyed sergeant.

On Tuesday, Vivian finished up a quick note to Gene. Signing her name, she hastily read it over before sealing it to put in the post.

Dear Gene,

Not sure what happened Saturday at the dance, but I wanted to let you know that I signed up to ride on the bus with some of the other girls out to the base Friday night for a dance at the NCO club. I hope you will be there. Perhaps we can talk? I'll be sure to save a few spots for you on my "Dance Card", ha ha. See you then...unless you're busy...

Regards,
Vivian

Satisfied with the wording and that she hadn't come right out and accused him without letting him explain, Vivian folded the single sheet and put it in an envelope she had already addressed to Staff Sergeant Eugene Banks with the base address. She sealed the flap and placed a stamp on it just as Mary June finished with her last customer before their break for lunch.

"Did you tell him you're coming out to the base on Friday?" Mary June asked as they gathered their purses.

"Yes," Vivian answered, then paused as she looked at the envelope in her hand. "I hope I'm not being presumptuous..."

The girls began making their way to the door as Mary June turned her head to glance at her friend. "Nah. The way the sergeant has been acting toward you, it seems to me like he's thinking about staking a claim. You've got a right to know why he did what he did Saturday night. Surely he can tell you without giving away 'troop locations' so to speak."

Vivian sighed, hating the cloud that had settled on her budding relationship with Gene. Things had been going along so smoothly until this...

"You're right. Let's get lunch before that clock beats us back."

They laughed as they exited the building, only stopping long enough, on their way to their favorite soda fountain, for Vivian to slip her envelope inside the nearest mailbox.

FRIDAY NIGHT SLUGGISHLY rolled around, and Vivian finished freshening up her lipstick in the employee ladies room at the bank. She and Mary June had already changed their dresses and were ready for the dance. They would walk the short distance to the club and board the buses to make the thirty-five mile trip out to the army base. The same buses would bring all of the girls back to Louisville and deliver each young woman safely to her own home as a thank you for their service.

Viv's stomach was filled with angry butterflies.

She met her friend's eyes in the mirror. "Oh Mary June, I'm so nervous. What if I get out there and…and he doesn't want me there…or…"

"Now, hold on. Just relax," she responded without interrupting the smooth application of her lipstick. "If Sergeant Banks does not show for the dance, just hold your head up and your arms out – they'll soon be filled with willing male bodies in khaki and olive drab, honey, believe me. And Mr. Banks will be the one out of luck." She gave Vivian a saucy wink. "Okay?"

Vivian laughed as she blotted her own lipstick, much of her nervousness receding. "Okay."

Finished with their preparations, Vivian smiled and picked up her things. "Let's get this show on the road."

Twenty minutes later, they were boarding the bus to go out to the base.

The busload of chattering girls set out from the club for the seventy-mile round trip to Fort Knox. What an adventure. Once past the city limits, US 31W, aka Dixie Highway, was merely a narrow two-lane road full of potholes and Vivian didn't think they would ever get to the top of that hill at Muldraugh. It seemed to go on forever. She could hear the bus' engine straining.

Mary June and Viv made the trip on a shared seat about midway towards the back, and had fun listening to the others relate their funniest USO GI stories. Mary June threw in a few of her own, but Vivian merely soaked everything in.

"I had a country boy a few weeks ago who said he wanted to teach me the 'chicken reel' – and then he proceeded to show me how it's done!" one buxom redhead cackled. "Believe you me, this gal is not gonna be caught dead flapping my arms and crowing like a chicken, not for all the tea in China. Or should I say...all of the *Sergeants* out at *Knox!*" The squealing laughter rose to such a crescendo, the bus driver nearly put his hands on his ears.

A cute brunette chimed in, "After the last dance on Saturday, the sailor I was with leaned over and whispered, 'Tell me where ya live and I'll come by tomorra' and gitcha. We'll have us a good ol' time on the town.' When I politely told him no, but thank you, he snapped his fingers and mumbled, 'Dag Nabbit, another filly turnin' me down'."

The girls laughed and giggled over one another's stories. So many were leaving their seats and stretching to give each other curlers or stockings, that the driver finally threatened to pull over to the side of the road and make them walk the rest of the way if they didn't stay seated. That got their attention in a hurry.

Finally, the lights and buildings of the installation came into view in the distance.

Off to the left, the girls could see the famous United States Bullion Depository, or "Gold Vault" as everyone called it, set far back off the road and obviously well guarded. Viv had heard about it, of course, as had everyone who lived in the surrounding area as well as the nation, but she'd never had the opportunity to see it. She knew it had been built in 1937, and it was rumored to store, in addition to gold, important documents like the Declaration of Independence, the US Constitution, and more. It was an impressive structure, and in the waning light of evening, it resembled a glowing island. A circular drive encompassed all four sides of the building and the bright lights illuminated its beautifully manicured lawns.

Just past the depository, the driver turned right, onto the base and Entrance Drive, which was a long street with buildings on both sides and a huge flagpole at the end. It was the heart of the main garrison. The girls quieted once the bus rolled into Fort Knox proper; several of them, including Vivian, stared wide-eyed out the windows for their first view of one of the US Army's premier, permanent posts.

They rolled past a gorgeous brick, two-story administration building, and then a long white structure with a sign that indicated it was the *Post Exchange*. She knew that meant it was kind of like a general store. Further down they passed a large multi-storied, two-winged hospital, a good-sized theater with a white-columned portico, and a lovely chapel with a round, stained-glass window above the double front doors.

Vivian could see two tall, checkered water towers off in the distance. For the first time, she realized Fort Knox was like its own little city. There were lovely houses for the married officers with children. There was a school, playgrounds, a swimming pool; the streets boasted quaint lampposts. Right there on base, they had everything one needed to live and function. For a moment, she sighed thoughtfully as she imagined living there with her military husband, and raising children alongside other military wives.

Finally the driver turned down a street and pulled up in front of a large rustic stone and timber building with a long creek-rock-edged sidewalk leading from the curb to the curved staircase and the front door.

"Here you are, ladies. The Noncommissioned Officers' Club."

Vivian looked over at her friend and drew in a breath, blowing it out through pursed lips. "Okay, it's now or never, I guess."

Mary June laughed and gave Viv a playful push. "Aww, you

worry too much. Get yourself up and let's get in there – a whole bunch of handsome NCO's are waiting to dance with us!"

The other girls laughed as they made their way down the aisle of the bus.

"WANT A BREW, Banks?" Sergeant Philip Lowe asked as he offered to hand Gene one of the brown bottles of beer he had smuggled into the party. The dance tonight was in honor of Sergeant Major Brice Holland's fortieth birthday – his wife had requested. However, all alcohol was supposed to have been locked away in deference to the majority of the USO girls being under twenty-one.

"No, man," Gene shook his head and glanced around. "Mrs. Holland sees you with that, you'll be spending the night in the clink."

Lowe shrugged and took a swig of beer before stashing it.

Gene took a quick look at his watch, wondering where on Dixie Highway the buses were right then. He was anxious to see Viv.

Less than a minute later, he and the others heard the distinctive motors of the buses pulling up outside, and his face transformed into a wide grin. He then took a place in line with the other officers to watch the girls streaming into the club, resembling a contingent of colorful butterflies.

Pretty soon – there she was! Walking right behind her friend, she looked this way and that as she and the others made their way inside. Then, their eyes met and he thought hers looked a bit uncertain for a moment. But, then she smiled and gave him a nod. *Is she still upset about Saturday? If so, I'm gonna have to take her mind off of it. There's a war on, and if she's gonna be a sergeant's girlfriend, she'll have to get used to plans being interrupted.*

He'd been looking forward to this night ever since he received the invitation and then found out Viv was coming. His arms ached to hold her again, and he couldn't wait for the dance to start so he could claim her for the first song—and as many as he could, since it was a private party and the normal USO rules didn't apply.

When all of the girls were inside, Mrs. Holland stepped up to a microphone at the end of the large rectangular open room where a small contingency of military musicians had been assembled. She was a lovely woman, tall, dark haired, and wearing a gold, long-sleeved satin evening dress.

"I want to welcome all of you and I thank you for coming and helping my husband celebrate his milestone birthday. There are plenty of snacks and soft drinks in the room to my right," she pointed toward a doorway. "Everyone have a good time, and a bit later, we'll let birthday boy cut his cake," she added as everyone laughed. Her husband grinned and grabbed her for a kiss, prompting whistles and cheers. Enjoying herself, she kissed him back with gusto, and then turned to signal the band to begin playing. Their first song was the smooth ballad *You're Getting to Be a Habit With Me*.

As one, the men in uniform charged over to the girls, like Derby horses when the gates are flung open; and Gene went right along with them. It only took seconds for him to reach Viv's side, take her hand, and pull her into his arms to begin swaying to the music.

"Hi," he murmured, loving how she fit so perfectly in his arms. "Wow, has this been a long week. I was so glad to get your note that you were coming to the party." He waited for a few seconds. "I'm sorry I couldn't make it to church. Did you have a good week?"

He pulled back and looked down into her face, which seemed a bit guarded. She peered up into his eyes and then averted her gaze. "Viv? Honey, what's wrong? Are you mad at me about church?"

Viv drew her lip between her teeth for a moment and then met his eyes again. "I was just wondering about Saturday…"

Gene's brows furrowed. "Saturday? What do you mean? I told you I had an assignment."

She nodded, hesitant to delve into the subject. It had been bothering her all week, however, so she forged on. "I just was surprised, that's all. I mean…the least you could have done was give me a smile."

A shadow crossed over Gene's features as he tried to make sense of what she was saying. Didn't she understand he'd been on assignment? What did she mean give her a smile?

"I wanted to, honey. Heck, I wanted to do more than that," he teased, trying to coax a smile from her. "Believe me, I wasn't enjoying myself."

They had settled into a comfortable dance position, cheek to cheek, but at that sentence Vivian leaned her head back again, her expression perplexed.

"You weren't? Well, you certainly fooled me!"

Gene locked his gaze with hers for a moment, shock radiating through his body. He was starting to get a bit unnerved. Had she seen him? He shook his head, emitting an uncertain chuckle.

"Baby, I don't know what you're talking about, but couldn't we just forget Saturday and concentrate on here and now?"

Sadness seemed to seep into Vivian's beautiful eyes and she let out a resigned sigh, lifting one shoulder in a tiny shrug. "I suppose so. If you want me to believe you weren't having fun with that girl, then you must be a very good actor."

Gene's heart skipped a beat and his eyes widened. "You saw me?"

"Yes of course, did you think I wouldn't?" she answered, her eyes incredulous that he should even ask such a question.

He studied her face for a minute, the wheels whirring behind his eyes.

"Where?"

"At the dance, of course."

Relief flooded his limbs and he laughed as he drew her close again, murmuring in her ear, "You must have just been imagining things and conjured me up. Can't say I'm insulted. But…what *I* want to do is concentrate on tonight. I have it on good authority that there is no 'one dance' rule for this shindig."

The ballad ended and the band immediately launched into *Boogie Woogie Bugle Boy of Company B.* Gene had always been proud of the music the Army band could produce, but tonight they were outdoing themselves. Plus, several of the USO girls could sing quite well and had volunteered to join the band on the temporary dais, delivering more than a fair job on the lyrics. Everyone on the floor kicked it into high gear, whooping and hollering, and jitterbugging to beat the band. Gene and Viv were no exception.

By the second verse, Viv was laughing, spinning, and twirling, and transformed back into the girl he had fallen in love with, much to Gene's relief.

NOW VIVIAN WASN'T sure of *anything.* On Saturday night, she would have *sworn* that soldier at the club was Gene. He had looked just like him…or *had* he? His uniform was a bit unkempt compared to Gene's usual penchant for neatness and…something about how he danced, talked, and comported himself wasn't, well…*Gene.* Was his hair a bit lighter? Maybe he was a bit heavier, even an inch shorter perhaps? *Okay, it wasn't him. Just some other soldier that kind of resembled him. I've heard it said that everyone has a double somewhere in the world. Gene's just happens to be in the same town. I wonder if he's a soldier at Knox…Or…* Vivian almost laughed out loud at herself. *Maybe unconsciously I'm expecting Gene to cheat on me, to lie to me, and he's right, somehow I conjured him up.*

Her relief was palpable. As her limbs relaxed, she almost lost rhythm with the silly song.

Her spirits buoyed, she allowed herself to have fun with Gene, dancing tune after tune with him and reinforcing her belief that he was one great hoofer, and one very sweet guy. Her favorite moments, however, were the slow melodies, when Gene would draw her into his arms and they would glide effortlessly around the floor, their awareness of one another blocking out the reality of anyone else being in the room. She knew she would never tire of feeling his warm arms surrounding her, his hand holding hers, his wonderful Old Spice aftershave lending to an invisible cloud of bliss.

I'm so glad I decided to come to this party. The club is so nice, she mused as she opened her eyes, her cheek pressed against Gene's as she gazed at their surroundings. The big, open area boasted beamed ceilings, polished hardwood floors, a creek stone fireplace, and large windows that looked out over acres of smooth, green lawn dotted with tall majestic trees. It smelled wonderfully of cedar, aftershave, and a trace of cigarette smoke, which Viv figured was probably from the dozens of officers who frequented the club and sat around smoking, drinking brown bottles of beer, and playing cards and games of pool – or so the girls had said in the bus on the way there.

That song ended and another fast kicker started up – *The Beer Barrel Polka.* Everyone let out a whoop and began trying to perform the circular shuffling, twirling steps. Neither Viv nor Gene knew the dance, but they looked at one another and shrugged with matching grins, determined to give it a go.

Soon everyone was chortling and calling out insults as turns and kicks got all discombobulated. Several couples were doing a fine job and Viv and Gene did their best to emulate their moves. Finally as the song came to an end, the band decided to take five and everyone drifted over to the refreshment tables.

Vivian drew the back of her hand over her forehead and then fanned her face. "Whew, I worked up quite a thirst," she giggled, accepting Gene's proffered clean white handkerchief with a smile.

She dabbed her face with it.

"What do you want to drink?" Gene asked, naming the choices.

"Oh, I'd love a Grapette," she answered and he reached to get a bottle, removing the lid before handing it to her.

She took a deep drink and sighed at the pure effervescent pleasure it afforded.

"You having a good time?" Gene asked, taking her elbow and guiding her over to some chairs against one wall.

"Oh yes, this is so much fun," she gushed, truly meaning the words. Looking around, she added, "This is a nice clubhouse…do you…come here often?"

He took a long pull of his Dr. Pepper and looked around with a shrug. "Some. I have a few buddies I play cards or shoot pool with. But…" he reflected and turned her way; almost as if he were embarrassed at what he was about to confess. "I don't smoke, and I don't much care for beer or liquor. The fellows rib me about it…you know, calling me a teetotaler or a Puritan, or strait-laced…or my favorite – Mr. Buzzkill," he laughed and she giggled with him, leaning close.

Gene shrugged again. "I'm not a Puritan. Heck, I used to smoke when I was a teen, just like everybody I knew. My dad and my brothers smoke. We even raise tobacco on our farm. I just quit because I got tired of smelling like an old ashtray – and tasting even worse – and like my uncle used to say, 'spending good money just to light it up and let it burn'." He stopped and looked around before he continued. "I get a beer once in a while, if I'm in the mood – and if it's ice cold and I'm as parched as a desert. But…well, you know how it is."

Vivian had been watching him, secretly so glad to know for sure that he didn't regularly drink or smoke, as they weren't habits of which she herself was very fond. She reached over and laid her hand over one of his. He looked into her eyes and she smiled.

"I'm glad. Personally, I wouldn't like you as much if you

smelled like an old ashtray all the time," she teased, her eyes twinkling merrily.

He grinned, those blue eyes sparkling as he allowed them to caress her hair, her face, her dress. "You're wearing your green polka-dot again. I sure like it...on *you*, I mean...it looks good on you," he stumbled, as if he had suddenly gotten tongue-tied and – was he blushing? Do men really blush?

"Thank you, Sergeant."

He chuckled and leaned near, whispering in her ear, "None 'a that. I'd say you and I are way past the 'Sergeant' and 'Miss Powell' stage...wouldn't you?" His warm, deliciously Dr. Pepper-scented breath fanned her cheek and sent tingles all the way down her spine, almost as if she'd taken a slug of the bubbly drink itself. She gave a hazy nod of agreement and her eyelids drifted shut. For a moment, every thought went right out of her head.

She was vaguely aware that the music had begun again – this one a ballad, Bing Crosby's, *Only Forever*. It was amazing how they kept playing songs that said what was in her heart...yes, she wanted to be with Gene forever, to have him grant all her wishes, to come near when he beckoned...how she would always remember the first time she'd seen him smile...

She opened her eyes when Gene leaned back, expecting him to extend his hand and ask her to dance...but he was staring past her head – and his expression was anything but dreamy and happy.

CHAPTER 11

V IVIAN WATCHED AS Gene's eyes, which had narrowed and hardened to an icy blue, seemed to be tracking movement. Concerned at his immediate change in mood, she turned to see what had captured his attention just in time to see another man with sergeant stripes on his sleeves come to a stop right behind her. The man was stocky in build, a few inches shorter than Gene, with dishwater blond hair and hard green eyes.

Suddenly, she realized Gene had tensed up, like a tiger ready to pounce. Through gritted teeth, he growled, "Thought you weren't coming to Sergeant Holland's party, Hendricks." His tone suggested he very much wished that had been the case.

The other man ignored the comment, choosing to mutter instead as his eyes raked Vivian from head to foot, "So, this is the dish, huh Banks?" Gene didn't move or respond, but just as she felt him begin to lean protectively closer, the other man offered her a hand. "Wanna dance, doll face?"

Out of habit she acquiesced. Taking Hendricks' hand, she shot Gene an apologetic glance, and allowed the other man to help her up and over to the dance floor where he pulled her straight into his arms – way too close. She was immediately uncomfortable.

She tried to push back and create some space between their bodies. "Please, Sergeant…not so close…" she requested softly.

His rigid arms refused to yield as he led her in a slow swooping turn, his hard chest pressed to the softness of hers. "Isn't that what you girls are here for? To dance with us *lonely GI's* and give us a little pleasure?" The way he said the last word seemed as if he meant something entirely different, and Vivian's heart started to pound. Something about this man made her fight-or-flight response flare to life. The disagreeable odor of beer on his breath made her nearly gag. He'd been drinking...was he drunk? Is that why he was acting this way?

"Y—yes," she stammered, her mouth suddenly dry as she searched for a way out that wouldn't offend the sergeant. She wished fervently that Gene would cut in. Viv tried to turn her head and see where Gene was, to perhaps send him a message of help with her eyes, but Hendricks kept her body molded to his and her back to where they had left Gene as he swayed with her to the music. He wasn't nearly as good a dancer as Gene and she had trouble following him. Everything seemed out of synch.

"I bet you've been giving *Banks* pleasure, haven't you, doll," his voice slithered into her ear. His hot breath caused shivers to race down her body that were anything but pleasurable.

"S—Sergeant Banks and I enjoy one another's company, if...if that's what you mean," she gasped, forcing herself to keep dancing when all she wanted to do was push him away and run back to Gene. Her displeasure and near panic must have been evident on her face, as several of the girls dancing with other soldiers nearby kept giving her sympathetic glances.

The man then had the audacity to allow the hand that was pressing against her back to begin a slow slide toward a part of her that he shouldn't be touching. "C'mon baby, relax. I'm your lover boy's roommate. The name's Blake. I can show you a good time – way better than Banks. Don't limit your favors to just one guy." His hand reached its target and he whispered his next request in her ear. Vivian felt her face flame red at his vulgar words.

Without thinking, she wrenched out of his grasp as his eyes

and mouth opened in surprise, drew back her arm, and slapped him straight across his face. "How *dare* you," she hissed, her eyes filling with tears of embarrassment and hurt.

Before she could blink, Gene was there. Charging up like a ferocious lion, he moved her out of the way, and put his whole body behind the force of one hard punch, straight to the other man's mouth. It sent him to the floor and even skidding down a few feet as the women nearby squealed and the music stopped.

Several dancing couples nearest the action rushed to intervene. Two of Gene's friends grasped his arms as if they figured he would go after Hendricks again, while two more hauled the other sergeant to his feet. The dancers had scooted back, making an open area around the disturbance.

Sgt. Maj. Holland elbowed his way through. "Gentlemen, what is the meaning of this?" he demanded.

Gene's face was red with anger and he was panting as if he'd run up a hill in full combat gear. He was glaring at Hendricks, his fists tightly clenched.

Vivian had covered her mouth with her fingertips, mortified to have caused the ruckus.

Suddenly, Mary June appeared at her side with Mrs. Holland on the other, while several of the other girls came around them to unconsciously give Vivian support. Everyone was staring at Sgt. Hendricks as he glared back at Gene, both his lips split and bleeding from connection with Gene's hard fist. Hendricks yanked his arms out from the grasps of the other men and dug a handkerchief out of his pocket to dab at his mouth.

"Well?" Sgt. Maj. Holland demanded again.

Neither man seemed willing to speak up.

The thought that this could get Gene into trouble crossed Vivian's mind. He had shared with her that he was up for promotion to a higher rank, and if this caused him to lose that opportunity, or worse yet, lose his sergeant stripes, she would never forgive herself. Oh, why had she agreed to dance with that horrible man?

Mary June, never a gal one could call shy, spoke up in heated defense of her friend. "I saw the whole thing. That sergeant there," she pointed at the sulking Hendricks, "was holding my friend extra close while they danced and...well...putting his hands on her. Then, he whispered something in her ear and she slapped him for it."

Sgt. Maj. Holland shifted his eyes to Vivian and then over to Gene. "And I suppose you came rushing to her defense, Sergeant?"

Vivian cast a glance at Gene and was relieved that the other men had let him go. "That's right, sir," he answered. He was just standing quietly now, although his breathing was still rapid and he was unconsciously rubbing the knuckles of his right hand as he waited for his commanding officer to continue.

The commander turned and affixed his gaze onto Hendricks like a spotlight. Viv wondered if he'd had trouble with the man before. From his expression, it seemed so.

Finally, the sergeant major barked, "I should throw you both in the stockade..." but he paused as his wife moved to his side and curved her hand around his elbow. She looked up at him, sending him a silent message. Smiling into her eyes, he seemed to relax a bit as he patted her hand. "But since it's my birthday party, and my *wife* doesn't want it spoiled..." he stopped and shifted his focus between the two men.

"Hendricks, I want you to apologize to this young woman, and then confine yourself to quarters. You're to report to my office first thing in the morning." The tone of the order left no room to argue.

Sgt. Hendricks flicked a final glare toward Gene, and then turned his gaze to Vivian. Straightening to his full height as if coming to attention, he inclined his head in her direction. "I apologize for my unsavory behavior, Miss." Then with a snap, he saluted his superior and stiffly stalked off toward the door. Once it closed behind him, everyone in the room seemed to breathe a bit easier.

Sgt. Maj. Holland turned to Gene. "Sergeant Banks, you know I allow no fighting amongst my men. However…" he paused, seemingly appraising Gene's thoughts, and then his eyes twinkled. "Since you have apparently appointed yourself the young woman's Sir Galahad…my *wife* requests that you be allowed to stay at my party." Everyone chuckled, including Mrs. Holland, as she looked up at him adoringly.

Then, the commander turned his attention to Vivian. "Miss…" he paused, eyebrows raised.

"Powell, Sir. Vivian Powell."

He smiled kindly, and something about him reminded her a bit of her father. "Miss Powell, please accept my apology as well, for how you were treated. No young woman should volunteer for the USO and be subjected to manhandling such as that. Might I suggest that you and your rescuer spend a few minutes outside in the cool evening air to collect yourselves, and then return to the dance when you are ready?"

Vivian's eyes widened, utterly surprised at his suggestion. But when Gene drew near and extended his elbow, she took it and smiled shyly at the commander. "Thank you, Sergeant Holland."

She and Gene headed toward the door to the rear, opposite the one through which Hendricks had departed, as the music began to play again.

GENE CLOSED THE door behind them and sucked in a deep breath, striving to release the last bit of spent fury from his body.

Furious was the word – he'd been watching Vivian dancing with his nemesis, and when he had seen Hendricks crushing Viv in his arms like that – and then had the audacity to put his hand on her bottom – he had charged like a raging bull.

But then, once the offender landed on the floor with blood seeping from his busted lips and two of Gene's friends had grabbed hold of his arms, he knew he'd just blown his promotion right out the window. If so, it was worth it to avenge Viv's honor and get her away from the filthy hands of a man like Hendricks.

He turned his head and looked down at her as they strolled toward the club's newly finished swimming pool with its surrounding concrete benches. She seemed to have calmed down. Good. When he had seen that she was upset almost to the point of tears, he had wanted nothing more than to break free from his restraints and slam Hendricks' teeth down his throat. He shook his head. Normally, he wasn't a violent man, but his *roommate* knew just how to push his buttons.

"You okay?" he asked softly.

She looked up at him, her hand holding onto his bicep tightening a bit as she smiled.

"Yes, I am now." Then with her grin flashing in the moonlight, she added, "Thank you, *Sir Galahad,* for coming to my defense."

They both snickered softly as he led her to a bench and made sure she was seated comfortably. He lowered himself next to her and took her hand in his.

"Is that man really your *roommate?*" she asked, wondering how in the world these two men could share a room, when they were so vastly different.

Gene blew out a frustrated breath. "He told you?"

She nodded.

"Unfortunately, yes. He was transferred here about two months ago and they put him in with me while new barracks are being built. In the morning, I'm requesting a new Bunkie, or permission to move. I've had a belly full of Staff Sergeant Blake Hendricks."

"What an awful man…he'd been drinking. Is that what made him act that way? Is he a mean drunk?" she asked, thinking about a man two doors down from her parents' house on Cooper Chapel Road who always created havoc when he'd had a few too many.

Gene cringed, hating to even talk about Hendricks. "I apologize for that. He was doing it to needle me."

"Needle you?" Viv asked, staring at him in the soft light of the moon.

"Yeah…" he wavered, running a hand back through his hair. "He's always on my case, but more so lately. He acts like there's some kind of score to settle between us. Anyway, tonight he came in while I was getting dressed and started right in. Your letter was on my bunk and the scumbag picked it up and read it. Then, he tells me that if he didn't have other plans, he would come to the party and sweep you off your feet and away from me. Then, he shows up. I'm sorry he took his dislike of me out on you, Viv."

Vivian shivered in the cool night air and Gene automatically raised an arm to wrap around her and pull her against his side so that he could lend her some of his warmth. "He's a despicable man. Let's talk about something else," she declared, giving him a small smile.

"Good idea," Gene answered softly, leaning to touch his cheek to her forehead.

"So…I've never been out here before…I had no idea Fort Knox is so…*much*," Vivian ventured, chuckling a bit at her lack of words to describe the immenseness that was *Fort Knox*.

Gene laughed. "You wanna hear the history of Fort Knox?"

Viv grinned at him and snuggled a bit closer. "Sure."

"Well, now you see, I'm an authority on everything Fort Knox," he flashed a boasting smile at her. "Since I was a kid, growing up on a farm in Elizabethtown, I was fascinated by this place. Anyway…it dates back to the Civil War when both Union and Confederate armies – but not at the same time, of course," he joked, "bivouacked nearby at Fort Duffield."

"Fort Duffield? I've never heard of that."

"Well...it wasn't actually a fort. It's really just a high vantage point near the river with maybe a small building or two, and some tents. That area of the river was like a gateway between the North and the South."

"Okay," she murmured, gazing up at him as if he were the smartest man on earth. It made him sit a bit taller with pride as he continued.

"So...the US Army decided they needed a permanent post for training the military and chose this area. The government bought about 40,000 acres and most of the buildings of a tiny town named Stithton, a small farming community that was here in Hardin County. Then, they renamed the area Camp Knox, after Major General Henry Knox, who was Chief of Artillery in the Revolutionary War and the first Secretary of War."

"Why did they choose here?"

"Several reasons – one being rail lines and the Louisville, Henderson, and St. Louis Depot already here and established, that could play a large part in transporting soldiers to the camp. By 1925, Camp Knox had added 33,000 more acres and had become the largest military reservation in the United States."

Vivian gasped, unable to imagine something so vast. "But, why do they need so much land?"

Gene pursed his lips. "That's a good question – the answer is that this is a training facility. New recruits need to learn how to survive out 'in the wild'. This area has lots of thick red clay Kentucky mud, and acres upon acres of rugged terrain and hills – so rugged, by the way, that foot soldiers who've marched up and down those legendary hills even dubbed one 'Misery' and another one 'Agony'." He made a funny face like he was miserable and she laughed at his silliness. "Plus, the recruits are trained on the guns and tanks, so the gun tubes spit out smoke, fire, and boom after boom year-round on the vast empty ranges, and that needs to be far enough away from civilization that we aren't too much of a disturbance. Now where was I...oh yeah. The Army decided

Camp Knox would be the new headquarters for the *mechanized* cavalry. So, in 1932, the name was changed to *Fort* Knox and the Army's oldest mounted unit, the 1st Cavalry Regiment, arrived and exchanged its horses for armored combat cars." He grinned at her awed expression.

"Then, they really stepped up construction on some of the buildings you may have noticed on your way in – everything from a new hospital, administration buildings, quarters, barracks, and housing for soldiers and officers with families, a movie theater, a chapel...recreation clubs like this one," he indicated with a nod over his shoulder. "Oh, and I almost forgot – the Gold Vault. I could tell you details about that place that you'd probably think I was making up, like the bombproof roof, poison-gas booby traps, alarms, minefields, razor wire electric fence – and it's rumored that the lower level where the actual vault itself is can be totally flooded in sixty seconds to defend against intruders. It's an amazing feat of construction and engineering," he added, staring out into the dark in admiration.

"Yes, I saw it. It's quite impressive. It's a beautiful building, too," she agreed.

He nodded, "Beautiful, yes, but don't ever try to approach the gates, they might shoot you on sight and ask questions later." He was only half kidding.

She gave him a playful push and he chuckled before continuing, "We've got new recruits and draftees arriving all the time, so building never really ceases. Part of my job is keeping the construction equipment in fine working order. They're still raising barracks; many they're calling temporary, are two-story clapboard shelters. But some are permanent brick buildings. One over to the south of here that's nearly finished is three and a half stories tall and 455 feet long. Even with all that, we can't seem to keep up with the demand. Some guys even have to sleep in tents for a while when they first arrive. At last count, the installation has grown to over 3,000 buildings and owns over 100,000 acres."

Viv laughed and shook her head. "You know your stuff, don't you, Sergeant? And to think, all of this has been here most of my life and I didn't have a clue."

He gave her a playful salute. "Just the facts, ma'am."

Her eyes sought out his face in the moonlight as she asked softly, "Gene…you've never said, but…will you be sent overseas with the rest of the soldiers?" She seemed to be holding her breath waiting for his answer.

He raised his hand and let his fingers gently play with a strand of her hair. "Well, not all ground soldiers go off to fight. There's a 'war' to fight right here at home, too, that needs men – the support and supply side. If *we* don't do our jobs properly, *they* can't do theirs. My job is very important, helping stateside where the training takes place, keeping equipment and vehicles – training and non-training – in working order. That will never stop until the war is over. So, the answer is, it's unlikely, but I guess it's always a slim possibility, depending on how the war goes. But, if I'm needed over there, I'll go. Any soldier worth his salt in the United States Army would," he added with a shrug.

They gazed at one another for a moment and he could tell she was thinking, or maybe even praying, that he wouldn't be called to do that particular duty. Suddenly, he was overwhelmed with the desire to kiss her, as the thought of their last kiss – on the front porch of her parents' house – came rushing back in full detail. He leaned in and she raised her chin, her eyes fluttering shut…

Just as their lips met, the door to the club opened and Sgt. Lowe stuck his head out to holler, "Hey Banks! Miss Powell! Mrs. Holland said to get in here so her husband can cut his cake. She says she's tired of cutting rugs!" He added with a laugh.

Viv and Gene looked at one another and burst out laughing as he took her hands and hauled her gently to her feet.

Then holding hands, they ran together to the door.

CHAPTER 12

M ID-MORNING THE NEXT day, Gene knocked on the door of Capt. Moore's office and entered at his command.

When he did, he paused for a moment as his eyes met those of Sgt. Maj. Holland sitting in a chair in front of the desk. He saluted both men and stood awaiting further orders.

"At ease, Sergeant," the captain said, returning the salute and motioning with one hand, "Have a seat."

Gene swallowed uncomfortably and cast a glance at the sergeant to his left. The sergeant major smiled, encouraging him with a wave to be seated. "Relax, Sergeant Banks. This is just a 'put our heads together' meeting." The man's smile told Gene that the sergeant major hadn't changed his mind from the evening before; that he didn't intend to have him reprimanded for punching Hendricks in the mouth.

"I wanted to get Sergeant Holland in the loop on this investigation and get his ideas," the captain explained.

Gene gave a nod and relaxed in his chair.

"I've been doing a bit of investigating myself, Banks," Sgt. Maj. Holland began. "I think the culprit may suspect we're closing in, because none of my supply rooms, nor the warehouse, has reported any more discrepancies since the initial ones were found. The Captain said that you saw something while on stakeout last Saturday?"

Gene sat a bit straighter in his chair. "Yes, sir. I was hiding out across from the entrance when a jeep pulled up. A man and woman got out, went over to the doors, and talked a bit. I could tell the woman was wearing a nurse's uniform and I could see the man pointing and gesturing. I admit, however, that I was too far away; I couldn't see them clearly enough to identify them, just hair color, height, etc., and I couldn't hear anything they said. But I knew that neither one had any business being at the doors of the warehouse at 2:00 AM. Other than that, however, they didn't do anything suspicious enough."

The captain nodded and shuffled through some papers, picking one up and remarking, "This is a list of everyone the MP's stopped or saw with a jeep that night, and I'm having them check into alibis now. I think we should have things narrowed down in a matter of days." He handed Gene the list and as he scanned it, his eyes widened just a bit when he came to one name. However, he quickly squelched the reaction.

Before Gene could ask if the captain was going to assign him to stakeout duty again that evening, the man said, "Sergeant Holland has ordered one of his men to watch the warehouse tonight, Banks, in case you were about to ask. You have the weekend free." Gene grinned in spite of himself and then the captain added, "Oh, and I understand from Sergeant Holland that you and the sergeant who bunks with you had a bit of an altercation at his party last night...over a certain young junior hostess from the USO in town. Miss Powell, I believe is her name?"

Gene's heart instantly began hammering in his chest. *Oh no, here we go...* The captain could, of course, override Sergeant Holland's decision to forgo his reprimand, and that could very well bring a grinding halt to his promotion. *Well...whatever happens, he'll just have to accept it and go on.*

He moistened his lips. "Yes, sir."

The captain moved his papers to the side and picked up a file, which he opened and read several items while Gene began to sweat. He had dreaded going back to his room the night before, knowing another confrontation was a given, but his "roommate" hadn't been there. The idiot had disobeyed a direct order and had not confined himself to quarters! Idly, Gene wondered if the fool had gone AWOL.

Finally, Capt. Moore glanced up and met Gene's eyes. "Sergeant Hendricks will be moving his belongings to his new quarters…after his forty-eight hours in the stockade are up, that is. The MP's stopped him for blowing right through a stop sign in a jeep last night, nearly made them run off the road. They escorted him to the lockup. Just to let you know, so you wouldn't report him as being AWOL."

Gene barely stopped himself from gasping in relief. "Yes, sir."

"That's all, Banks. You're dismissed." The captain smiled with a bit of a glimmer in his eyes and added, "Enjoy your liberty."

"Thank you, sir!" Relief shot through his body as Gene climbed quickly to his feet and gave each man a salute, his wide grin impossible to contain.

As he walked out the door and placed his garrison cap back on his head, he didn't see the two older officers in the room grinning and shaking their heads in total understanding.

"WELCOME AGAIN, SERGEANT. You're becoming a regular," the girl at the door said with a friendly smile. Her eyes seemed to be brimming with some kind of secret knowledge and he wondered if she was one of Viv's friends.

Gene winked at the girl, paid his quarter, and moved on into the club. The atmosphere was alive with the music of Johnny Burkhart and his orchestra playing *You're a Sweet Little Headache*. Gene chuckled and shook his head as he made his way inside. *Wonder what Viv would do if I called her that? Nah, I wouldn't do that, 'cause she's not a headache. She's an angel.* He quickly scanned the large, already packed room, and finally spotted her right in the middle – and she saw him at the same time. She smiled and lifted her head in a nod as he waved.

He moved to the side and just let his eyes feast on her. She was wearing a new dress – at least, new to *him*. And man, did she look great in it. It was periwinkle blue with a big square white lace collar and a wide, twirl-able skirt – which at the moment was twirling to beat the band. Gene's face moved into a grin from ear to ear. *That little minx, she's showing off for me. Look at her go.* She and her partner for the time being, a tall skinny sailor in dark blue bell-bottoms and a white "gob hat" were swinging up a storm. Viv was shimmying, whirling, spinning, and moving her feet, keeping up with every move the sailor made. Every time the sailor swung her out, she would face Gene and fling her hand up in the air in a cute little wave. He chuckled and tipped his head back in acknowledgment.

Soon, the dance was over, and Gene pushed off the wall, heading toward his girl. However, it was the Andrew Sisters' rousing version of *Bounce Me Brother with a Solid Four*, and when he reached Viv, she put her hand up to his chest and teasingly shook her head. "Sorry, Sergeant. I have you penciled in for the next slow song."

At first, he was a bit taken back, but then quickly realized she was right – it was so much better if they could dance cheek to cheek.

He bowed gallantly to another soldier who had come up to ask her, and stepped back joining those on the sidelines. The man grinned his thanks and took Viv's hand as they started Jitterbugging to the fast, crazy song. When that one ended, the band followed it immediately with *Don't Sit Under the Apple Tree*. Viv gave him a sweet smile and a shrug, wiggling her fingers at him when another sailor snatched her hand and swung her into the dance with him. For Gene, it was getting a bit old to be watching and not *participating*. She was just too darn fetching.

Ahh, then finally, the song came to a close, and the opening strains of *I Know Why, And So Do You* began. Gene wasted no time in getting to Viv's side as she politely turned down a private with, "Sorry soldier, this one belongs to *him*."

Gene took her in his arms, matching his cheek to hers, and let out an exaggerated sigh of relief. "Man oh man, I thought I'd never get to do this!"

Viv giggled and let him glide them along to the lovely tune. "I was beginning to wonder myself."

They were silent for a few lines, but Gene hummed a few bars, whisper-singing the line about her smiling at him and him hearing gypsy violins.

"Did you get in any trouble from last night?" Viv asked softly as they swayed to the music.

Gene smiled and shook his head gently. "Nah." Then he remembered his soon-to-be-ex-roommate and added, "Hendricks did, though – the stockade for forty-eight hours. Then he's moving to other quarters."

"Good riddance," Viv immediately growled and Gene had to chuckle in agreement. He hoped that he would have the room to himself, at least for a while. *If not, please God, at least make 'em give me a good egg.*

The song was over too soon for Gene's liking, but Viv said she was thirsty, so she held tight to his hand and together they moved off the dance floor and toward the refreshment corner. He smiled as he followed along, glad to know that she just wanted a few more minutes to talk to him and he would *almost* have her all to himself.

They got their beverages and made their way over to several tables that had been placed along the wall on one side. Sitting down at one, they leaned toward one another and sipped their soft drinks, trying to hear each other over the music.

"Can you make it to church tomorrow?" Viv asked before taking a long drink.

Gene nodded as he sipped his Dr. Pepper. "Yep. I've got my buddy's car again. He had to take an emergency leave because his dad died. He left the car on base and said I could use it. He's from New York and he said they go everywhere in taxis there."

"Oh, I'm sorry about his dad…"

"Yeah, me too…" Gene paused, averting his eyes a bit and thinking about his own father that he hadn't seen for far too long. Viv stared at him.

"How long has it been since you've seen *your* parents?"

The corner of his mouth lifted at her question. "What are you, a mind reader?"

She laughed and reached out a hand to cup his cheek, suddenly serious. "No…but I can read your eyes…why don't you go see them tomorrow?"

His heart sped up a bit. *Hold on, why should I get the jitters about seeing my folks and my family. Just because… well, that shouldn't make any difference…*

Gene's eyes met hers and he reached up to cover her hand. "Only if you go with me."

Viv's eyes flared a bit and then she looked thoughtful. "Are you sure? I mean…what would they think?"

At that, Gene broke into a slow smile and brought her hand around to his mouth to plant a kiss on her fingers. "They'd think their son and brother is bringing home the prettiest girl in Louisville, just to meet them. Deal?"

Viv laughed at his playful compliment, and Gene's heart thrilled to think that maybe, just maybe, she found him irresistible. "Deal, Sergeant." She took another swallow of her drink and looked around, her eyes widening a bit. "Uh oh. Enemy sub at three o'clock. I'd better get."

He got the message and gave her a quick acknowledge with a tilt of his head. "I'll see ya on your next break, honey."

She hopped up from her seat and beat a hasty retreat back toward the dancers, passing Miss Warren with a smile and a salute.

The woman accepted the gesture, and then turned to give Gene *the eye*. Walking over to the table, she greeted him, "Good evening, Sergeant. You've been a regular at the club for some time now." She turned and looked to see Viv already in the arms of a sailor in white. "But you've been minding your p's and q's. I've been watching."

Then she did something totally unexpected. She *winked* at him! "Keep up the good work, young man."

"Yes, ma'am," Gene replied, flabbergasted. As she walked away, he shook his head, thinking, *Well, I'll be a monkey's uncle. Wonders never cease!*

AFTER CHURCH THE next day, Gene maneuvered the '39 Buick Century convertible onto Highway 31W, heading south, and turned his head to flash Vivian a grin. "You sure you're okay? Too much wind?"

She had insisted he could keep the top down, having come prepared with a silky scarf to tie over her hair. As they picked up speed, the wind whipped the ends of the scarf around and she reached up to keep them still as she looked over at him.

She grinned back and shook her head. "No, not at all – I love it."

"Okay," he said over the noise of the road and the wind. "But if you change your mind, just sing out."

"I will. Finish telling me about Bing…"

"Well, he sang every song request we could throw at him," he said as he finished telling her about the singer, Bing Crosby, making a personal appearance at the base the week before. "He sure had a busy day. I heard he went to Churchill Downs and entered his own horses in several races out there, and then he played in a golf match for the Army-Navy Relief Fund. After that, he was supposed to have a 15-minute interview at the Fort Knox field house, on our radio station WINN, but he was late and so to make up for that, he and Senator Chandler and Governor Myers, whom he'd played golf with, had a 90-minute ad lib song and gag session. It was a riot."

"I wish I could have seen him. I just love his voice, and his 'Road' pictures with Bob Hope. I've seen all three of them, *Road to Singapore, Road to Zanzibar, and Road to Morocco.* They're hilarious. I hope they do more of those."

Gene beamed cheerfully in agreement. "Yep, best comedy team in show business."

"They sure are."

They rode along for a minute, perusing the familiar landscape that was the route to Fort Knox and enjoying the perfect weather – not a cloud in the sky. Viv commented on what a glorious day it was.

"Oh look! There's more Burma-Shave signs!" she giggled and pointed as she spotted a small wooden sign up ahead, situated close to the edge of the roadway and painted red with white letters. Put up on the highways across the country by the Burma-Vita Company, which produced a brand of brushless shaving cream called Burma-Shave, the little signs, usually five or six in a set with a few words on each one, were spaced about 100 yards from each other, and intended to be viewed in a series. Taken all together, they made up a witty rhyming message. The last sign in the set always displayed the product logo. It was an extremely successful advertising gimmick.

Vivian read each portion of the rhyme aloud as they rolled past. "No lady likes...to dance or dine...accompanied by...a porcupine...Burma-Shave." They both laughed.

"So true!" she chuckled.

Gene shot her a mock expression of insult. "So, if I had come to the dance that first time and hadn't shaved – you wouldn't have danced with me?"

She pursed her lips together, obviously trying to look serious, but failing. She shook her head with a decisive NO. "Nope. Uh uh. Not a one."

"Well, Jiminy Crickett," he quipped, raising a hand and rubbing his smooth chin. "I'm sure glad I used that good ol' Burma-Shave, then!"

She grinned teasingly and adjusted her scarf in the breeze before looking over at him. "Church was good today, wasn't it," she stated.

He nodded with a smile, glad that she had convinced him to get back in church. He hadn't been going regularly since everyone had gone the Sunday after Pearl Harbor and he'd realized over the weeks since getting back "in the groove" that he'd been nursing some anger against God. Just another thing meeting Viv had done to improve his life…that, and shaming him into contacting his family.

Now, he thought about their morning. He had spent the night at the club again, and had made it out to her church in plenty of time. "Yeah. I really like how your pastor tells so many stories. That one today about taking his wife out for their first date and forgetting his wallet – and she had to pay for the meal – the way he told it sure was funny."

Viv laughed. "Yeah, sometimes I wonder that Margaret even married him. And he's got a blue million stories. I've probably heard every one of them, but they never seem to get old or worn out – and he always ties in good points with them."

"Like today…talking about forgiveness and unconditional love and trust." Gene shook his head, reaching back to unconsciously rub the back of his neck. "It was like the man was reading my mail."

She smiled in complete agreement. "He's quite good at that."

Another minute of silence went by and she gazed over at him again. He seemed to be deep in thought. "Did you get a call through to your parents?" she asked, suddenly realizing that if he hadn't, they would be dropping in on them unannounced.

She was relieved when he shook his head in the affirmative. "Pop had a telephone installed a few years ago, and I'm glad of that. Before, we could only get a call through the corner store up the road. That was a pain; let me tell you. It was long distance from downtown Louisville, but it was worth the money."

Viv smiled, remembering when her family had the same situation. She waited, hoping Gene would expound on the subject, but he didn't. Finally, she ventured, "What did they say?"

He shook his head as if he'd let his mind wander. "Huh? Oh, they said fine. They'd love to see me, they'd love to meet you, and Pop had just been hunting and brought back a deer, so we'll have venison steaks on the grill and Mom's making potato salad and some other things, and a chocolate cake...I just hope she's not using up all her ration stamps on us..."

Something in his voice made Viv look closely at him. "Gene...how long has it been since you've seen your family?"

He pressed his lips together and took in a big breath. Then, she saw him swallow as the muscle in his jaw moved and he clamped his teeth together. *Oh goodness...what is he not telling me?*

Finally, he admitted, practically under his breath, "Two years."

Viv's mouth dropped open. She couldn't *imagine* not seeing her mother and father for that long of a time span. "Oh Gene! W...why?"

He glanced at her and then reached over and took her hand, tugging her closer across the bench seat. She came willingly. Steering with his left hand, he stared straight ahead while the thumb of his right hand stroked the backs of her fingers. He was quiet for a few minutes and she let him gather his thoughts.

Finally, he began. "There's something I want to tell you...something I've never told another living soul. I...I found out a few years back that...I was *adopted.*" He shot a look at her face, like he expected her to react negatively. She didn't, she merely squeezed his hand and sent him a small encouraging smile. When he didn't elaborate, she prodded, "And...?"

He shrugged and she could tell the subject was very hard for him to talk about. But...somehow she knew he *needed* to talk about it.

"How did you find out? Did your parents tell you?"

He snorted and shook his head. "My brother."

"Your *brother* knew, but you didn't?"

Pulling in a deep breath, he nodded and unconsciously moved his arm up to press their entwined hands against his chest, as if to relieve pain buried there.

"One day, me and my brother Jack...his name is Jackson, well...we got into it. I can't even remember what the fight was about. Just scrapping, like all brothers do. I was nineteen, and he'd just turned eighteen... In the middle of the argument – we were in the barn milking the cows, of all things – he yelled, 'Well, at least I'm not *adopted*, like you!' and then he clamped his hand on his mouth and looked at me, his eyes round as saucers. I felt like the bottom dropped out of my whole existence. For some reason, I didn't go ask my parents. I believed him; I guess because of the expression on his face maybe, but deep down in my gut, I knew it was true. I kind of went berserk for a minute and...I punched him. Knocked him clean down on the dirt floor – first time I'd ever done anything like that to Jack, we'd always been close, you know? And then I just...ran."

"Ran?"

He nodded, driving by habit as the memories swam before his vision. "Mom was visiting a sick neighbor, and Pop was out hunting. I ran in the house, threw some things in a bag, and started walking down 31W – in the rain. Eventually, I hopped a bus, and rode to Louisville, to my uncle's house. My dad's brother."

"My goodness! I bet your parents were frantic when they came home."

"They were. They questioned Jack and he just said I went crazy and ran off. He told me later Mom walked the floor all night, praying for me..." he paused again, his eyes glistening. "Uncle Jerry called Pop the next day...or rather, he left a message down at Weaver's...that I was with them and I was all right. Then...he and Aunt Ida...they told me the truth."

Vivian squeezed his hand and waited, letting him unload at his own pace. She watched him shiver, and her heart compressed knowing that it hurt him so much, even after the time that had passed.

Finally, he began, "My parents were living in Baytown, Texas, when the big Goose Creek oil well came in. Hundreds of men went there from all over, some with their wives. Well...I was born...and my real mom died having me. I don't know anything about my real father. My parents had been married for three years and Mom was afraid she wasn't going to have any children...they took me and gave me the Banks' name. Three months later, my mom found out she was pregnant. After Jack and then Laura were born, Pop quit the oil field job and they moved here to E-town. He bought the farm with money he'd saved up... They never told anyone the truth, except Aunt Ida and Uncle Jerry."

"Well...then how did Jack know?"

Gene shook his head with another soft snort. "He said he got up one night to go use the outhouse, and Mom and Pop were in their room with their light on and the door shut. It was almost Christmas, and Jack thought if he listened at the door, he might hear them talking about Christmas presents...instead, he heard 'em talking about *me*."

"Oh no...how old was he?"

"About twelve," Gene shrugged. "He said he never intended to just blurt it out like that. But once the cat was outta the bag, he couldn't stuff it back in."

Vivian laid her head on Gene's shoulder, her heart aching for the hurt young man that he still was deep down. But...even though she, herself, couldn't really identify or understand what he was feeling – surely it wasn't as terrible as he made it seem. She bit her lip for a moment, striving for words that would comfort him as he continued.

"I'd always kind of wondered why I didn't look like anybody in the family…" he admitted softly. "I always felt like…like there was something I didn't know that I *should* know, just kind of lurking in the shadows, waiting for me to find out. But, I sure didn't dream it would be *that*. I told you Pop always teased Mom that I was the product of her messing around, and I'd kind of thought…" his voice slowed to a stop and he gave a small shrug.

"Gene…I'm sure your parents love you. I'll bet they love *you* just as much as they love their…*other* children…"

He slowly blinked, his eyes serious as he drove, and she knew he'd heard those words before. "I know. We've talked about it. I know they love me…my brothers and sisters love me…I guess it's just…" he wavered, trying to articulate very deep, confusing feelings. "My dad, he'd always been a straight up guy, you know? I never knew him to lie – to *anyone*. Over the years, I'd heard more than one person say, 'If Banks said it, you can take it to the bank.' I was always so proud of him…wanted to be just like him. Then…I find out he'd been *lying* to me all my life – and Mom too."

Vivian laid her hand on Gene's chest and pressed it against his heart, which she could feel was thumping hard. "Gene…I wouldn't call that a lie, the same as speaking falsehoods. They just didn't *tell* you something. I bet if you had asked them, they would have…"

He shook his head, but didn't disengage himself from her. "I asked him that, and he looked me straight in the eye and said, "Son, I'd have to say no. I'd probably not ever have told you…because your mom and I were afraid you'd react, well – just like you did."

"Oh honey…" Vivian murmured.

"That was two years ago. I haven't been back since. Not even when I was first sent to Knox."

Viv pressed a bit closer and laid her head back down on his shoulder to try and give him moral support. He turned his head a bit and gave her a tiny smile, nuzzling his cheek against the top of her head.

Then, he turned his eyes back to the road with a sigh.

CHAPTER 13

THEY HAD PASSED Fort Knox and motored through Radcliff, and now as the familiar landscape and rolling hills of his home came into view, Gene's hand started to sweat on the steering wheel. He swallowed and tried to smile at his companion.

"We're almost there."

Her hands flew up to her scarf and she scooted over a bit, reaching for her purse on the floorboard. "Oh goodness, I need to make sure I look…"

"You look *beautiful*," he interrupted, reaching over to grasp her hand again and bring it to his lips.

She smiled shyly, but still turned the rearview mirror to the right so that she could see herself and make a few hasty repairs. Vivian yanked the scarf off her head and smoothed her hair as he slowed the car to turn right onto a gravel road. There was a rural mailbox next to it, with the words "Banks Family" barely decipherable along the side. The letters had once been bright white. He knew, as he'd been the one to paint them, back in the carefree days of being John Banks' oldest, and proudest, son.

He slowed to a stop and gazed in both directions. The gravel road went straight for about four hundred yards until it passed some trees, then it veered to the right. Vivian stared at two wire fences with wooden posts made from straight, uniformly sized tree branches running down both sides of the drive, with acres of land stretching out on either side.

"How far does the property go?"

"We've got 150 acres. The house and barns sit right in the middle," he motioned toward a barn with a red painted metal roof that they could just make out. "The house is beyond those trees," he added softly.

After a few moments, he drew in a big breath and let it out slowly. Turning his head toward her, he mumbled nervously, "Here we go," and let the car move forward.

Once they rounded the stand of trees and the house came into view, Vivian relaxed back onto the upholstery, as an unexpected peace seemed to settle down onto her shoulders like a warm cape on a windy day. It was a typical farmhouse, with two stories, three dormers, and a deep front porch that ran the width. Somehow, it exuded warmth and family…and love.

As Gene brought the car to a stop and set the brake, the front door slammed open and a boy of about thirteen came running out, his light-brown hair fluffing in the breeze. "Gene! You're here! Mama, Gene's here! He's drivin' a swell car!" the boy stopped in mid-run and stared for a moment at Vivian, and then he added over his shoulder, "And he's got a pretty lady with him!"

Vivian laughed and put her hand on the door handle, but Gene said quickly, "Lemme get that," as he pushed his door open and climbed out. The boy met him as Gene rounded the front of the Buick and they collided into a brotherly embrace. They stood swaying together and Viv could hear the boy, his voice muffled against the front of Gene's shirt, "It's been so long since I've seen ya, Gene. I've missed ya. Why haven't you come to see us?"

Feeling a bit odd just sitting in the car, Vivian quietly let herself out and stood next to the passenger side as a woman with straight, light brown hair threw open the screen door of the house and came to the edge of the porch. She was wearing sturdy brown shoes, and her full apron covered a blue flowered, short-sleeved dress. She put one hand up to her mouth, and then descended the steps, heading straight for Gene. He let go of his brother just in time to catch her as she flung herself into his arms.

"Mom," Viv heard Gene utter, his voice husky with emotion. Viv wrapped her arms around her middle and turned her head away, beginning to get choked up.

Immediately, an older man came out the front door, followed by another man who appeared near Gene's age, and two young women. They were all smiling through tears and waiting for the woman to finish her greeting before they started down the porch steps.

Finally, Gene separated himself from the woman and made his way over to Viv. He took her hand and drew her forward.

"Mom…" he paused, looking past her to the others, and amended, "Everybody, I want you guys to meet Miss Vivian Powell." Turning to meet Viv's eyes, she could see his were damp. "Viv, this is my mother, Phyllis Banks. And my little brother, Jeff…and my Dad, John, my brother Jack, and my sisters, Laura and Julie," he completed the introductions. Vivian greeted each one as they were named and pointed out, and then Phyllis came toward her with a big smile and outstretched hands.

"Welcome Vivian."

"Thank you, Mrs. Banks…"

"Welcome to our home," she continued. "You two must be starved, it's nearly one o'clock. Come on in the house and we'll eat before everything gets cold," she encouraged, turning and hooking her arms around one of Gene's and one of Viv's as she ushered them forward. The others greeted Viv and shook her free hand as everyone made their way inside.

Once they crossed the threshold, Viv came to a halt to take in the large, comfortable living and dining room area and to breathe in the mouth-watering scent of hot food on the stove.

Mrs. Banks remained by Viv's side as the others advanced toward the table set with the family's best dishes. Impulsively, she gave the girl a quick hug, and whispered in her ear, "I have a feeling you had something to do with this visit…and if I'm right, I want to thank you."

When she pulled back, she smiled, teary-eyed, and Viv smiled back, her own eyes just as moist. Viv couldn't quite make her voice work to answer, so she just gave a nod.

Somehow, Vivian knew in the space of those few moments that she had just met people who would become very important in her life. She chanced a glance at Gene, and the look on his face seemed as if he were thinking the very same thing.

"OR HOW ABOUT this one: *To get away from hairy apes, ladies jump from fire escapes. Burma-Shave.* I think that one is so funny," Jeff chortled as the others joined him, enjoying his antics. Vivian had soon found out that Burma-Shave signs and their witty sayings were one of the boy's many hobbies – and he had a never-ending supply of them memorized.

"Here's another one: *The Bearded Lady tried a jar – she's now a famous movie star. Burma-Shave.*" The family laughed at that one as well; each member at the table leisurely eating what had turned out to be a delicious Sunday dinner. As promised, there were scrumptious venison steaks, fluffy mashed potatoes and brown gravy, corn on the cob, and an assortment of trimmings. Mrs. Banks cautioned that they must all save room for the chocolate cake she had baked – in celebration of her oldest son's long-awaited visit.

Vivian forked another bite of delicious mashed potatoes smothered in gravy into her mouth and allowed her gaze to roam the faces at the table. She had noticed right away that all four of Gene's brothers and sisters had their mother's green eyes. No one had his gorgeous sky blue eyes, or his dark hair. What Gene had told her when they'd first met popped into her head. *'I'm the odd one. Pop used to tease Mom that she'd had a fling with a traveling salesman and I was the result.'* Now, of course, the reason for his looks was clear.

Gene's dad, John, was in his mid-fifties, with silver hair and wire-rimmed glasses. His build was stockier than Gene's and he was a few inches shorter, with brown eyes and a pleasant smile.

Phyllis was also in her fifties, with straight, light-brown hair, a lovely, smooth complexion, and cheerful green eyes. She was everything a "Mom" should be – generous, loving, caring, gracious. In the forty minutes since Vivian had arrived, Phyllis had already managed to make her feel completely comfortable and at home.

Gene's brother, Jack, was an intense man of twenty-three, with light brown hair like his mother and he had her vivid eyes. He was quiet, though not unfriendly. He just seemed like he had a lot on his mind. Viv could only speculate, and she wondered if the brothers had ever hashed everything out after the "incident".

Laura and Julie were also quiet and sweet. Laura, 21, was a bit on the plain side, her hair was a lighter shade than her mother's and her eyes more pastel, and her teeth were a bit crooked. But, Vivian would class her as "pleasant looking." Julie, who was 19, more closely resembled Mrs. Banks, and was girl-next-door cute, with a beautiful smile and two charming dimples. She wore her hair, which was a bit darker than her mother's, long and wavy – it reached past her shoulders, and she kept it tied back with a white ribbon.

Lastly was Jeff. A bright, precocious youngster, he was small for his age, and wore wire-rimmed glasses like his father. But he was full of life and energy, and his mind seemed to run 100 miles-an-hour. Phyllis periodically admonished him, with gentle persuasion, to eat his food, as he tended to get off on a subject and forget.

"*Said Juliet to Romeo – if you won't shave, go homeo. Burma-Shave,*" Jeff rattled off another rhyme.

Gene swallowed a bite of food and exchanged glances with Vivian as he rolled his eyes, whispering, "He's on a roll now. He might not stop 'till this time next week."

"Sshh," Viv admonished softly and reached under the table to give him a playful swat on his knee.

"If you think she likes your bristles, walk bare-footed through some thistles. Burma-Shave."

John, who was light-heartedly laughing, leaned toward his youngest and warned, "All right, you've had your fun young man, now *eat.*"

"Aww Pop, I'm just gettin' warmed up!" the boy whined, even as he took a bite of his meat and quickly washed it down with a drink from his glass of milk.

"Here's one for you, Mom. *Does your husband misbehave, grunt and grumble, rant and rave? Shoot the brute some Burma-Shave!"* the boy quoted teasingly, a giggle escaping as his father reached to aim a playful swat at his head, which he missed, on purpose.

"Where did you find all of those, Jeff? Those are some really good ones," Vivian complimented.

"Oh, I don't know – here and there. There's a man at church that's a long-haul trucker and he writes 'em down for me when he sees a new one. I've been collectin' 'em for years," the boy answered with a big grin. He was obviously pleased that she was enjoying his recitation – and he was relishing her attention.

"And we've been hearing them for years," Jack contributed. "Let's see... *He played a sax, had no B.O., but his whiskers scratched – so she let him go – Burma-Shave."*

"I've always loved this one: *Mug and brush, Old Adam had 'em. Is your husband like Adam, Madam? Burma-Shave,"* Laura recited with a laugh. "That one gets me every time."

"My favorite has always been, *Whiskers long made Samson strong, but Samson's gal, she done him wrong. Burma-Shave,"* Julie giggled.

"What's your favorite Mom?" Jeff chuckled as everyone continued to erupt in giggles at the silly game.

Phyllis thought for a moment. "Well, I never forgot: *His tenor voice she thought divine, till whiskers scratched Sweet Adeline. Burma-*

Shave."

"Miss Vivian? How about you? Do you know any?" Jeff queried, obviously not wishing to let the game stop.

Vivian pursed her lips as she tried to remember one a customer at the bank had told her several days before. "Um...I heard this the other day and thought it was funny...*College Cutie, Pigskin Hero, Bristly kiss, Hero-zero. Burma-Shave."*

Everyone burst out laughing at the rhyme and the cute, sing-song way she had said it, and with a perfect delivery. Gene looked over at her as he laughed with the others, his eyes sparkling.

"Okay, I'll bite," Gene relented, wiping his mouth with his napkin and clearing his throat in preparation. He raised his fist and made as if smacking the air past his chin and recited in a perfect buccaneer's brogue, *"Shiver me timbers said Captain Mack. We're ten knots out but we're turnin' back — I forgot me Burma-Shave."* The room erupted in boisterous guffaws.

Vivian put one hand on his arm and another on her stomach as she tried to hold back her mirth, but couldn't stop giggling as tears of giddiness filled her eyes. She couldn't remember when she had had more fun during a meal — her parents were always so quiet and formal at dinner.

"Oh oh! I almost forgot this one!" Jeff burst out as he readied his audience for another Burma-Shave rhyme.

"OH MRS. BANKS, that was absolutely delicious. But I wish I hadn't eaten that second piece of cake!" Vivian playfully groaned as she rubbed her stomach. She was sitting on the couch next to Gene, while the girls, Laura and Julie, were in the kitchen cleaning up. They had adamantly refused her help. Jack had gone outside to do some chores, taking Jeff with him on the pretext of needing his help. Gene knew he was purposely trying to make it easier for him to have a conversation with their parents.

"Man, I didn't think about it, but, where's Emma?" Gene had asked his brother as he had reached the door.

Jack smiled as he thought about his wife. "Her sister had a baby, she lives in Owensboro, so she's there helping out," he answered, meeting Gene's eyes. "Listen Geebee," he began, using the nickname he used to call Gene when they were kids. "I've said it before, but…I'm sorry for the way I…"

Gene shook his head. "Don't worry about it." He had given his brother a bear hug, brother style, and then the younger man had headed out the door.

Now, the confident sergeant looked across at his father, settled in his over-stuffed chair, and his mother in her high-backed wooden rocker, and he felt dread coming over him again. He was torn between wanting to know more and not wanting to stir up ill feelings – for any of them.

Viv, as if she sensed what he was feeling, reached over and laid her hand on his arm in silent support. He turned his head and gave her a small smile.

"So…it's been a long time since we saw you…I mean, since Jack and Emma's wedding…" Phyllis began.

John cleared his throat in the suddenly awkward atmosphere. "Yeah, did Jack tell you we fixed up the old cabin at the base of the south hill for them?"

"Yeah, he did, actually. I think that's swell for a first home…give them some privacy," Gene also cleared his throat. Vivian squeezed his arm again, wishing she could help.

Finally, he ventured, "Listen, I don't know quite what to say…"

Phyllis suddenly leaned forward and reached across for his hand. He took it, and she smiled at him through misty eyes. "Eugene, honey…we know now that we were wrong not to tell you. Ask us anything you need to know, and if we know the answer, we'll share it."

Gene drew in a deep breath, picking through his thoughts and deciding what to ask first. He finally murmured, "Do you know who my parents were?"

John and Phyllis exchanged a look. John offered, "Your mo...the woman who gave you birth, worked as a cook in the house of one of the oil field owners. Her husband...your real...*father*," John faltered at that word and stopped briefly to press his lips together. "He was killed in the Great War. The oil field manager, Mr. Carriker, well, he promised her that he would find a good home for you. It all happened quickly. One day your mom and I were childless, and the next, we had a tiny, precious new son," his voice choked and he took his glasses off to wipe his eyes with a handkerchief.

"We love you so much, Eugene," Phyllis urged as she held tight to Gene's hand. "Right from the first, you were *our* baby, *our* little boy. We didn't actually *plan* at first to keep it from you. It just never seemed the right time – first you were too young to understand, then the other children came along, and then you started school. Matter of fact, the conversation that your brother overheard, we were discussing that fact. A little girl at school that week had asked you why you didn't resemble the rest of your family, and you'd come home and asked me..."

She turned her head and her eyes met those of her husband again. When she turned back, her eyes were full, and one tear spilled over to run down her cheek. "You're our son, honey. You're a Banks. And we love you and worry over you just as much as your brothers and sisters. There has *never* been any difference in our hearts."

Gene sniffed and gave his mother's hand a squeeze, then let go so that he could reach into his pocket and retrieve his own handkerchief. "I know Mom...Pop...it was just..." he hesitated.

"Just *what*, honey?" His mom prompted, glancing at Vivian, who was blinking through her own tears.

Gene scrambled for how to share his heart without hurting his parents. "I'd always thought both of you were...straight up…"

"Eugene," John began, leaning forward much like his wife and met his son's eyes. "Keeping that secret from you was the hardest thing I've ever done. And I'll tell you right now, before God, it's the only thing I'm ashamed of. In every other way and every other thing, I've always been honest, just like I've always taught you kids to be. I'm sorry that we hurt you, son. That was the *last* thing we wanted to do."

"Can you forgive us, honey?" Phyllis whispered.

Suddenly, the room was full of crying members of the Banks family. Laura and Julie had finished up the dishes and had been hovering nearby, when they suddenly launched themselves at their brother. He rose to receive their embrace. The floodgates opened and everyone was hugging and sniffling. The girls told their older brother, over and over, how proud they were of him and how much they loved him. Julie added that they wouldn't trade him for all of the "brothers in China." That got a laugh out of everyone, and the tension started to recede.

Gene turned, holding a hand out to Viv who stood and went to him instantly as he pulled her against his side. He was so glad now that he had heeded this special woman's urging and come back home. She'd been right – it was long overdue.

Now, he hoped that hovering feeling of the "unknown" that had dogged him his whole life would begin to fade away.

CHAPTER 14

VIVIAN HAD NEVER been happier. She had found her Prince Charming, and every day getting to know her blue-eyed sergeant just got sweeter and sweeter. The days slid into weeks, with the happy couple sharing the occasional phone call or note, anxiously waiting for the weekends to arrive so that they could spend time together.

During that time, Gene took the tests for promotion to the rank of first sergeant, had met with the panel of twelve officers, passing both with flying colors, and received his new stripes and a pay increase of twenty dollars a month.

Tired of depending on friends or the bus, the first thing he did was purchase some transportation – a 1932 Ford Sedan, black on black. It didn't look like much, kind of rusty and had a dented fender, but it ran well. He and Vivian celebrated the milestone by going on a picnic with his friends Vic and Louise Matthews.

It was a sweltering July day. Once Gene and Viv picked the other couple up at their apartment, they all decided to take off down River Road until they found a good spot to pull over and enjoy the view of the river. They were all fanning themselves in the hot car by the time Gene pulled off the pavement and set the brake.

"How about here?" he asked his passengers. As one, they agreed it was a good choice. Down below was a small area with a soft cushion of fallen leaves, with trees and bushes all around.

The foursome collected the picnic basket and old quilts and headed down the incline.

"Oh, it's so beautiful here," Vivian gushed as they neared the water. The river was shallower than usual, due to the low amount of rainfall that summer, but the view of Indiana half a mile across the expanse of slow-moving water was lovely – green trees, hills, wild shrubbery, and a one-lane road meandering next to the water.

They spread the quilts out side by side and settled down, with the girls in the middle, and the guys sitting on the outside. The air was much cooler there, coming off the water and in the shade. It was peaceful, with the gentle lapping of the small waves and the river breeze.

"Oh, this is so wonderful. I really needed this. It was a hard week at work, the building is so hot now," Louise sighed, reaching to gather her hair and tie it up off her neck. She looked fetching in her sleeveless bandana shirt and Bermuda shorts.

Vivian settled comfortably on the blanket and stretched her slender legs out, hoping Gene was looking – she was wearing a pair of Bermuda shorts as well, with a light blue sleeveless top. She slipped off her shoes and cast a look at the other woman. "Where do you work, Louise?"

"At the American Tobacco Company plant at Thirtieth and Madison. I work on a four-person cigar rolling machine."

Viv whistled, impressed. "Wow, I can't imagine – that sounds complicated..."

Louise laughed softly. "In a way, it is. Takes a while to learn. But, I could roll cigars in my sleep now."

"Sometimes, you do," Vic teased, laughing when she swatted him on the arm with a gasped, "Victor Herbert!" Louise's face was red, and not from the heat.

"What? I didn't mean anything bad," Vic professed, pasting an innocent look on his face. She swatted him again.

Vic chuckled and propped himself up on his hands to watch a

boater sailing down the river. He looked around at the surrounding trees and then glanced over at Gene.

"Isn't this about where we found that mule carcass up in the tree?"

"What? Ew!" the ladies squealed simultaneously, causing the fellows to laugh again.

Gene flashed his friend a wry smile as he yanked apart his tie and unbuttoned his uniform shirt so that he could peel it off. He left on his white tee shirt, which he pulled out of his trousers for comfort. Leaning forward to unlace his shoes, he grinned at the girls. "He means after the flood. We were coming back from delivering some supplies in a truck and we came across the ghastly sight. Made me about lose my lunch."

"Green Gene," Vic laughed, catching Gene's flung shirt and flinging it right back. "And you're a first sergeant now? How'd you swing that with such a delicate stomach?"

"By being good at my job, you knucklehead," Gene shot back. Vivian eyed them, making sure they were still only ribbing each other. They were, their eyes were sparkling without malice as both men were grinning like fools and snickering.

Vic laid back and linked his hands under his head. "That reminds me, did you ever find out the answer to that problem you hinted at when we went to the movies a few months back?"

Gene lay down on his side, facing the others. Images of the incident in question swam before his mind's eye. The visitor who had brought him the final piece of information…The moment when he and several MP's opened up the warehouse door and caught the perpetrator in the act of loading boxes of parts into a jeep…The look of anger and hatred on the face of the guilty man as he glared at Gene for discovering his operation.

Giving his head a shake, he focused again on his companions. "Yep. I guess I can talk about it now, since the perps are behind bars. Viv, you probably won't be surprised, but…Hendricks was caught red-handed in a smuggling racket."

Vivian's eyes rounded. "Oh my goodness!"

"Yep," Gene tilted his head in the affirmative.

"Who's Hendricks?" Vic asked, his interest more than piqued by Vivian's reaction.

"Would you believe, my *roommate?* Staff Sergeant Blake Hendricks."

Vivian turned to Louise and shuddered. "Eww, he's an awful man. Remind me to tell you sometime about *my* experience with him." She reached out to Gene and grasped his hand, picturing the moment when he had punched the vile scoundrel in the mouth in defense of her honor.

Gene winked at her and continued, "Seems he had recruited a couple of civilians, one of them a nurse who must have needed extra money or something. I'm not sure what her part was, maybe medical stuff. Anyway, they had somebody at the landfill and somebody in the warehouse and they were cleaning up used parts and switching out boxes of new ones when they came in, then selling the new ones on the sly. Seems he'd done that at the last post he was at, but when the heat got too close, he put in for a transfer to Knox. The brass at the other post never knew he was behind the scheme. The thing is I should have figured it out because of other things I caught him at. He was never without a jeep anytime he wanted one, and out at Knox right now, captains and majors get first dibs on them."

"People like that really irk me. Why don't they put their energies into honest work instead of illegal shenanigans?" Vivian groused, catching a long look exchanged between Vic and Louise. She wondered what that was all about.

"Yeah, I know," Gene agreed. "Oh, and Vic, I can't believe I forgot to tell you, but a corporal in one of the other motor pools is the one who blew the whistle. He actually came to me and clued me in on where to catch them because he knew I knew you – and guess who it was?"

Vic sat up, his attention fully on Gene. "Who?"

Gene grinned and wiggled his eyebrows. "A real nice light-skinned black fella. Said he was in the C's with you. Name is Floyd Grimes?"

Vic and Louise both laughed out loud. "Floyd?"

"Good ol' Floyd!"

"Yes, we know him. He saved Vic's life when they were serving in the C's together," Louise explained. "He was one of Vic's closest friends – and we just saw him not long ago."

"He never mentioned anything…"

Gene shrugged. "Well, he was probably told to keep it under his cap, at least until all of the t's are crossed and the i's dotted."

"Makes sense."

Gene turned to Viv and caressed her arm. "Oh, and I found out something else. Remember we kept wondering why Hendricks acted like he had a personal grudge against me?"

"Yes – did you find out?"

"Yeah…well, in a way. I went to the lockup and had it out with him, and he 'reminded' me of seeing him steal something back in high school and turning him in. I told him I had no idea what he was talking about, but he just sneered at me and turned his back. Wouldn't say anything else. So, it's still a bit of a mystery."

"Where'd the jerk go to high school?" Vic asked.

Gene's eyebrows furrowed as he searched his mind, but then gave a small shrug. "Someplace up in Indiana, I think."

Changing the subject, Gene leaned over and whacked Vic's leg. "Hey pal, I need to talk to you about something. Take a walk with me?"

He stood, and then leaned down to give Vivian a good, long kiss that left them both tingling. When he pulled back, he whispered, "Be back in a few. Miss me."

"You know I will," she innocently purred back, giving his lips a final smooch and caressing his smooth, warm face with one hand. Her eyes shimmered with happiness; his gleaming with desire.

Vic, not to be outdone, grabbed his wife and plunged her back over his arm in a move that would make Valentino look like an amateur, kissed her thoroughly, and set her up again.

All four erupted in peals of laughter as he parted with, "Don't sit under the apple tree with nobody else while I'm gone, babe."

VIVIAN WATCHED THE men saunter down to the edge of the water, deep in a friendly conversation. She sighed softly as she watched the man she loved, he was so handsome, so sweet, kind, and generous – not to mention romantic! That kiss, oh my! Sometimes she couldn't believe she had found someone so perfect.

"So, when's the big date?" Louise playfully bated, watching Viv watch her soldier.

Vivian turned her head and smiled at her new friend. "Don't have one yet…but I think he's working up his nerve to ask me. Matter of fact," she added with sparkles in her vivacious honey eyes, "I'm hoping he's asking Vic to be his best man right about now."

"Mmm, in that case, I'll worm the information out of a certain brown-eyed fellow," Louise declared, causing both girls to lean against each other and dissolve into giggles.

Spent with cheer, they turned to the business of emptying the basket of its food and setting up for lunch, figuring their men would be hungry when they returned. Viv sighed again, feeling as if she would burst if any more joy tried to pour into her heart.

"Oh Louise, I'm so happy. I've found the perfect man – he's everything I've ever dreamed of. I'm wondering how I got so lucky."

Louise chuckled, leaning a bit to watch the two men who were about a hundred yards away now, lingering along the shore still deep in conversation. At that moment, Vic turned his head and caught her looking. She sent him a wave and he waved back.

"I feel the same way. You probably don't know this, but...I was married before, and I have a son by that man. But Vic was always my first love, and he was always in my heart. We had a terrible fight and a stupid misunderstanding that broke us up. But, I'm so blessed to be married to him now."

Viv had stopped her movements and met her friend's eyes. "Wow, Louise, I had no idea."

"I figured you probably didn't. I'm telling you this because...I know how fast things can happen. A silly misunderstanding, and wham, it's like a bomb goes off and everything is wrecked." She paused, placing a hand on Viv's arm and catching her lip between her teeth as if she were trying to choose her words carefully. Finally, she added, "Gene's a good guy, I've known him for years...but he's a *man*, you know? Don't put him up on a pedestal..." At Viv's startled look, Louise went on, "I just mean he's human...subject to mistakes or bad choices. Just...don't let any misunderstandings happen between you two, okay? A pastor friend of ours named Doc Latham always says that sometimes when two people fall in love...it's like it stirs up the devil or something, and he sets out to see if he can ruin it so they don't get married..."

Viv felt a chill sweep over her body at Louise's warning. It was as if she knew something Viv didn't.

Before she could ask, the guys came jogging up the bank.

"Hey ladies, we're hoping you've got the food ready, cause we're a couple of hungry males and we just might take a bite out of you!" Gene jokingly called out before he flopped down next to Viv, wrapped her in his arms, and zoomed in to nibble her neck with a mischevous growl.

She responded with a squeal and playfully pushed him away, forcing a piece of fried chicken into his hand as he came at her again.

"Here, Sergeant, chew on *this*!"

Once again, the four dissolved into laughter as they resumed their leisurely afternoon together.

Viv did her best to put Louise's ominous warning out of her mind...

THE FOLLOWING WEEKEND, Gene finished getting ready for his liberty. He had some important errands to run in town before the regular dance that night. He also had plans for Sunday – big plans. Plans that involved asking a certain older gentleman for permission regarding said gentleman's daughter. Gene shook his head at himself that he was a bit nervous about the asking part. He wanted it to be a moment neither he nor Viv would ever forget – a memory that they would cherish for the rest of their lives.

As the door opened, he turned to smile at his replacement roommate – a newly promoted staff sergeant named Bob Sells.

"Hey Bob," Gene greeted as he finished tying his shoes. "Hope that phone call wasn't bad news or anything."

"No, it wasn't. I'm glad I caught you before you headed out, though. Got a favor to ask."

Gene glanced over as he sorted out necessary things to put in the pockets of his clean uniform. "What's that, buddy?"

"My grandmother lives across the river, in Jeffersonville, and she wants me to come and stay with her this weekend. Problem is, I don't have any way to get there. Sure, I could take a bus into Louisville, but...then what? Would you mind playing chauffeur?"

"I could take you over there, no problem," Gene answered in his usual, carefree manner.

"Thanks, man," the other man replied. "She wants me to pick up my cousin on the way, too, and she don't drive. Is that all right? And – don't worry about Sunday night, I'll catch a ride back on the bus, even if I have to walk over the bridge," he added with a laugh.

"No problem," Gene returned with a grin and a friendly pat on the back as they exited the room and closed the door behind them.

"What are roommates for, huh?"

THIRTY-FIVE MILES NORTH, Viv and her parents were eating breakfast. Viv was slowly leafing through a copy of *Bride's Magazine*. She sighed as she came to a picture of a dress she particularly liked, but it looked like it would be way too much money.

Her father looked at her from his newspaper, and over the top of his spectacles. "You got something you should be telling your mother and me, pumpkin?" he asked waggishly.

Viv look at him, smiling impishly. "Not yet. You'll be the first…well *second* to know when I do."

Her father expressed his mirth with the situation and smiled at Viv's mom as he reached for his coffee cup. He looked at Viv again. "Listen, I don't suppose you'd want to go run some errands with your old dad, like you used to when you were a kid, hmm?"

Viv's face showed her delight at the invitation and she put the magazine down. "I'd love to, Daddy. I miss doing things with my favorite guy."

Her father raised his eyebrows and teased, "Oh now, I don't think I rate *that* moniker anymore, but I'm willing to share that spot – provided the guy deserves it."

Her smile grew even wider and she got up to give his cheek a kiss. "Oh, he does, Daddy. He does. I'll be ready in a jiffy."

She hurried on to her room, a smile on her face as she heard her beloved father chuckle.

Two hours later, Viv and her father were coming back from an errand he'd had to run over in Indiana for his job as a machinist for the railroad. Although gasoline was rationed, and he normally got just enough to go back and forth to work and not much else, he'd been given an extra few ration stamps by his boss to do this particular job.

It was hot out, over ninety degrees, and before they got on the road to pay their toll and cross the bridge back into Kentucky, they stopped at a corner grocery in Jeffersonville for something cold to drink.

"I'll get it, Daddy. What would you like?" Viv asked as she climbed out of the car and leaned in the window.

"Get me one of those Grapette's you like, I'll give that a try," he said, feeling content.

"Two Grapette's, coming right up," she chirped cheerfully. Practically skipping, she made her way up to the store, which was actually a converted house of modest size. There was an extra room built onto the back for storage and who knows what else. From the looks of it, the owners lived upstairs.

As Vivian walked up to the door, she noticed a black '32 Ford Sedan parked near the entrance. *Hmm, isn't that odd – that looks just like Gene's car. There's probably a million of them running around. It's a Ford, after all.* She knew it couldn't be Gene's, as she was sure he was still at the base.

With a shrug, she opened the door and went inside. She wandered around the two aisles, looking at different things, nodded to a tall red-haired woman wearing bright red lipstick, and finally stepped up to the cooler and rummaged around until she found what she was looking for. As she turned to go up front and pay, she ran smack into a hard chest.

"Oh! Excuse me, I'm sor..." she stopped dead, gasping for

breath as she came face to face with her favorite pair of sky blue eyes.

"Gene! What are *you* doing here?"

Not giving him time to answer, she rushed on, "I didn't know you'd be over in Indiana today." Juggling the ice-cold bottles, she put her arms around him. "I've missed you this week," she murmured against his neck. Vaguely wondering why he hadn't taken her in his arms and kissed her yet, she explained, "I'm out running errands with Daddy."

She pulled back, beaming up into his face. Wiggling her eyebrows, she flirted, "Well, soldier? Aren't you going to kiss me?" When he didn't move, but merely stared at her as if stupefied, she added, "Are you that shocked to see me, or are you waiting for *me* to make the first move?"

"I..." he began, when suddenly, a high-pitched voice yelled from behind Viv, "Hey, you hussy! Get your filthy hands off my boyfriend!"

The red-haired woman came charging up and rudely grasped hold of Vivian's arm, jerking it hard and causing her to drop both of the bottles. They crashed onto the scarred hardwood floor, the glass shattering and splashing purple liquid all over Viv's legs. "I said get your hands *off* him!" the woman growled.

He glared at the woman, while she, in turn, looked down at Viv's purple stained legs and started to laugh and point. "I hope I ruined your only pair of stockin's."

"Shut up, Roxy," He grumbled at her, then shifted his eyes back to Viv, his expression one of sympathy.

Viv's heart dropped to the floor and tears immediately sprang to her eyes. *Oh my gosh. It's happened again...just like with Walter! It's happened again!!*

With a cry, she put her hand up to her mouth and turned to run out of the store. When she got to the door, the woman behind the counter yelled, "Hey you! Where's my money for the two bottles you just broke?"

Viv stopped, tears blinding her eyes as she fumbled in her pocket for the money. Shaking uncontrollably, she slammed it down on the counter and pushed through the door without looking back at the two still by the cooler.

She had never felt so humiliated in her life. This time around, it felt even worse than it had when she'd caught Walter in the arms of another girl.

This time, her heart was crushed beyond repair.

CHAPTER 15

G ENE PARKED HIS car along the street in front of the club
and climbed out, whistling happily. It had been a produc-
tive day. He'd taken his roommate over to Indiana, picked up the
cousin, dropped them both off at their grandmother's, stopped at
a jewelry store he happened to see on the way back – and found
the perfect item he'd been searching for at just the right price, and
then had finished all of the other errands he had planned. He'd
hoped to get done before now, but at least he had completed his
mission.

With a jaunty step, he took the stairs at the front of the building two at a time and whipped through the door, his quarter
ready.

The girl at the table looked at him with a frown, and without
saying a word, merely took his quarter. She didn't even wish him a
good time.

He thought that was a bit odd, but with a simple shrug, he
continued inside. Once again, Johnny Burkhart's Orchestra was
playing, *I've Got a Feeling I'm Falling,* and he quickened his pace,
wishing he'd gotten there just a bit sooner, so that he could be
dancing with Viv. That was *their* song!

He stepped into the room and searched over the sea of dancers for that special head of wavy honey-blonde hair. But, he didn't
see her anywhere. *Hmm, maybe she's in the ladies' room or something. Or
maybe she just couldn't make herself dance with anyone else for this song.* He

154

grinned to himself at that thought and scanned the walls and tables, but couldn't catch sight of her anywhere. Finally, he wandered over to the refreshment corner to request a Dr. Pepper. The woman behind the counter was a different one than was usually there, but she smiled in a friendly way and gave him his drink. He thanked her and moved over to where he could see the whole ballroom, and waited for Viv to appear.

Fifteen minutes went by and no Viv. He was beginning to become concerned and hoped nothing had happened to her – could she be sick? *Would she have stayed home and not gotten word to me?* Just then, he spotted her friend, Mary June, across the room dancing with a tall merchant marine. Gene waved and tried to catch her eye, but she didn't look his way. After half the song had run its course, he finally gave up and walked over to the table where he and Viv had sat together several times before, thinking he would wait until either Viv showed up or Mary June took a break.

Forty-five minutes later, Mary June and a sailor made their way toward the refreshment corner. The girl came to a halt when she saw Gene smiling and attempting to flag her down from a table nearby, but then she raised her nose in the air and kept on walking as if he weren't there. As she reached his side, he put out a hand and stopped her.

"Mary June? Hey, I've been waiting for you to take a break for an hour. You've got some stamina there, girl."

She turned slowly, shooting daggers at him with her eyes. He was instantly taken aback.

"What…what's wrong? I've been waiting for Viv, but haven't seen her…" he paused, and a sinking feeling began in the pit of his stomach. Something wasn't right. "Do you know where she is?"

"You're a piece of work, you know that – *Sergeant Banks?* You rip a girl's heart to shreds and then have the gall to act like you've done nothing wrong. Who do you think you are? Why, if I were a man, I'd let you have it, mister. Viv's my best friend, and you…"

"Hold up," Gene interrupted, rising to his feet to face the irate girl that had just unloaded on him. The sailor was hovering at her elbow, both fists clenched at the ready, in case she needed him to do bodily harm to the army sergeant. He looked like he would relish the opportunity.

"What in the Sam Hill do you mean I ripped her heart to shreds? I haven't seen her since last Sunday night, but I've talked to her twice this week and she was fine." He stared at her, but she just stood still with her arms crossed over her chest, tapping her foot and looking at him through squinted eyes. Her mouth was pursed as if she'd eaten something sour. "You gonna tell me what I'm supposed to have done?"

"Huh!" Mary June snorted. "As *if* you didn't know!" Then, she turned on her heel, grabbed the sailor's hand and growled, "I'm not thirsty anymore, Harold. Let's go dance."

"Mary June, wait!" Gene hollered, extending his hand to try and lasso her arm, but she slipped just beyond his reach and kept right on going.

Good Lord, what is going on? What is it I'm supposed to have done?

Shaking his head to clear out the confusion, he stalked his way to the door and found the girl at the entry table.

"Excuse me, Miss. Do you know Vivian Powell?"

She gave him an icy glare. "I do."

Gene's eyes flared. *Does everyone know about this but me?* He tried to calm his racing heart and soften his voice. "Is she here somewhere? I've *got* to talk to her. It seems there's been some kind of mistake or misunderstanding, but I can't find out what it is…please, will you help me?"

The girl looked into his eyes, and then forced Gene to wait while she welcomed several newcomers to the dance before she looked back at him. Something in his countenance must have gotten through, because she thawed a bit and said, "She didn't come tonight."

Gene let out a breath, knowing where his next stop would be. "Thank you," he said to the girl.

She just stared after him as he ran out the door.

"I DON'T KNOW why you felt you could come here tonight and bother my daughter, but you'd better get yourself on away from here before I do something we'll both regret," Vivian's father declared, holding the front door to the house only about six inches open.

Gene twisted his cap in his hands; his heart was hammering in his chest so hard it was downright painful. "Please, Mr. Powell. I've got to talk to her. Something's not right. Can you tell her I'm here? Please?"

"She knows you're here, *Sergeant,*" Mr. Powell sneered. The use of his rank instead of his name, and in such a tone of voice, hit Gene like a fist in the gut. Viv's father had been calling him *Gene,* or *son,* for weeks. "When she heard your car drive up, she told me she doesn't want to see you. She told me to tell you to go away and not bother her again."

"But...*why?* What have I *done?*" Gene demanded, his voice catching on the last word. His patience was at an end. How could he defend himself if they wouldn't tell him what he needed to defend *against?*

Mr. Powell lifted an arm and pointed behind him, into the house. "Because my little girl is in her room right now, cryin' her eyes out – over YOU – *that's* why!" he shouted, nearly spitting the words, his face red with anger. "And if you think I'm gonna let you anywhere NEAR her after what you did today, *you're crazy.* I think you've got to be crazy *anyway* to do what you did to a sweet, wonderful young woman like my Viv!" He brought himself to a halt for a moment, gulping in air as he tried to calm down. Gene could hear a woman's voice on the other side of the door, probably Viv's mother, cautioning him to remember his blood pressure and urging him to shut the door. Mr. Powell pointed a blunt finger in Gene's face. "If I wasn't a Christian man, or if I was a bit younger, I'd come out of this door and whip the tar out of you for hurting my little girl like that – army sergeant or not. Now you *go on,*" he flung his hand toward Gene's car. "Get back to your *girlfriend,* and stay away from my daughter!" With that, he slammed the door in Gene's face so hard the glass rattled, near to shattering.

Gene stumbled back a few steps, so shocked he could hardly breathe. His hand went to his forehead. *Girlfriend?* What in the world? Had everyone gone crazy??

He backed up a few more steps, trying to remember which room was Viv's. Seeing a light on in a window on the far side, he staggered over to it and banged on the glass. "Viv! Viv, honey, open the window! Talk to me! Tell me what it is you think I've done! Sweetheart! Viv, please!!"

The curtain moved and Gene saw her mother's face with tears in her grave eyes, glaring at him like an enraged mother bear. Her father came to the edge of the front porch.

"Sergeant!"

Gene tried one more time, his warm palms pressed against the glass leaving steamy handprints. "Viv, what about your promise? You said you would stand by your man no matter what. Remember?"

Her father stepped down off the porch with a baseball bat in his hands. "Leave my property *right now* Sergeant Banks, or so help me, I'll call the cops, or the Army, or Fort Knox, or *someone,* and have you forcibly removed!"

People in the house next door were coming out on their porch to watch the spectacle.

Defeated, Gene's shoulders sagged and he let out his breath. There was nothing else he could do – tonight. He'd have to leave. Getting arrested wouldn't help anything – and he could tell Viv's father was dead serious on that account.

He shuffled to his car and stumbled in. Looking up at the porch, and the seething man standing there still brandishing the bat in his hands, Gene started the engine and backed up to turn around. An image of the girl he loved crying her eyes out over something she believed he had done tore him up inside. He wanted to go to her, comfort her, and tell her that this betrayal she was so positive he was guilty of, wasn't true!

With no other options, he shut his eyes and prayed.

Oh dear Lord, help me sort this out. And...comfort Viv...my sweet Viv. Let her know I love her... Please Jesus...

A tear rolled down his face, but he didn't feel any better. Slowly, he pulled out of their driveway and down the road. He could barely see where he was going; it was as if his eyes and his whole face were numb. And where *would* he go? No way was he driving back to the base tonight. Back to the club... He had no place else to go...

There was nothing for it but to come back tomorrow and try again. And they could be sure he would.

An idea swam through the misery and he headed his car in that direction. Maybe someone separated from the situation, a friend on his side, would help him see things clearly.

Someone's got to help him out of this nightmare!

He wiped his face and drove on toward his friend Vic's home.

VIVIAN GRABBED ANOTHER hanky, having filled up two others with tears that wouldn't stop, as she heard her father screaming at Gene. *Oh, what a mess! What an awful mess! I can't believe he actually came here to the house! What is he thinking?*

When she had come running out of the store in tears, sticky grape soda all over her stockings and her dress, her father had demanded to know what had happened. Not wanting to cause a

LINDA ELLEN

scene, and only wishing to get as far away from Gene and his
girlfriend...that word made her heart spasm – as she could, she had
told her father she was just embarrassed at having dropped the
two bottles in front of strangers who had laughed. She had
begged him to drive on home.

Before long, however, she couldn't contain it anymore and
had burst into sobs. They'd crossed over the 2nd Street bridge by
then and her father had immediately pulled to the side of the road
and tugged her into his arms, pleading with her to tell him what
was wrong. So, she had. And oh my, did the fur fly.

Furious, her father had turned the car around, and gone *back*
over the bridge, paying the toll *again,* and driven at breakneck
speed to the little store – only to find that the black Ford was
gone. He threw the car into park and went inside anyway, but
neither Gene nor the girl were anywhere around. With no further
recourse, they had turned back around and gone home.

Vivian had run to her room and thrown herself on the bed.
Her heart hurt so much from Gene's betrayal, she could barely
breathe. Her mother had hovered over her frantically, trying to
console her, but no words made any difference. It was Walter all
over again, only ten times worse.

Mary June had called to ask if she could borrow a dress for
the dance, and her mother had told her the whole story.

Now, after six hours and a warm relaxing bath, and with no
sign of appetite for lunch or supper, she had heard *his* car in the
driveway and had dissolved into tears again.

In her room with the door shut, she could hear her father's
voice clearly – and she could hear Gene's too. He sounded so
sincere, like he had no idea what he had done. *Why? Oh WHY is he
doing this? Can he be that cold hearted? Could he possibly think he could
have me, and that...that red-headed floozy too?* She had told him about
Walter's deception with another girl, and he had sworn to her that
he would never EVER do anything like that. He had even joked
that he would go after Walter if she wanted and take a bullwhip to

160

his "sorry hide."

So…*why???*

Viv sniffled and then pressed the hanky over her mouth as she heard Gene knock on her window and beg her to talk to him. Her mother mumbled something along the lines that he should be ashamed of himself as she pushed the curtain aside and glared at the offender. *How can he sound so sincere? Did I ever really know him? He must be crazy — but why did I never see it before? He really had me fooled. Well, no more. What's that old saying? Fool me once, shame on you. Fool me twice, shame on me. Never again, Eugene Banks. Never again.*

Viv put her hands over her ears, but it wasn't enough to stop her from registering Gene's voice asking about her promise, and her father's threats as well. Oh, how she wished this night were over.

It was the worst night of her life.

CHAPTER 16

THE NEXT MORNING when Vivian woke up, everything somehow seemed... *better.*

Perhaps it was the bright sunshine streaming in her window...or perhaps it was the vivid dreams she'd had the night before. She'd dreamt crazy dreams, about the *Sabotage* movie she and Gene had seen – Barry Kane running from the police, declaring his innocence, while Pat stubbornly declared him guilty. Somehow, though, the face in the images was Gene instead of the actor.

Now, as she broke free into the waking world, Gene's friends Vic and Louise came to her mind – and Louise's warning about misunderstandings. She remembered Gene's words at the window the evening before, begging her to remember her promise to *stand by her man.*

Could this be a bizarre misunderstanding? But...*how?* She had come face to face with him, and another woman calling him her *boyfriend!* Somehow, she felt as if the Lord were urging her to let him explain.

Viv put her hands up to her face and scrubbed the thoughts away. Mechanically, she rose and performed her morning rituals, dressed, and nibbled some breakfast. Her parents questioned if she felt up to going to church.

"Yes, I'm fine," she sent them a tiny smile. Then she went to them both and embraced them. "Thank you for loving me."

Her father hugged her in response, murmuring, "Honey, you're *easy* to love."

His words gave Viv strength and fortified her resolve to open the door of *What If* and see what was on the other side.

GENE PULLED UP in front of the church. He was late, having overslept after a night of tossing and turning far into the wee hours of morning. Having driven to Vic and Louise's place, he had poured his heart out to his wise friend. Vic had advised him to do everything he could to get to the bottom of the mystery. Then finally, Gene had crashed on their couch, and this morning they'd been kind enough to feed him some breakfast and send him on his mission.

Louise had offered to try and talk with Viv if Gene thought it would do any good, but he had declined. Deep down, he felt he had to make Viv see the truth on his own merit. He knew if she doubted his veracity at every pothole along the road, and needed the intervention of others to get them back on course, their relationship would be torpedoed before it even got underway.

Now, checking his watch and realizing the service was almost over, he decided to wait in the car and try to talk to Viv in the parking lot.

Twenty gut-twisting minutes later, during which Gene spent begging God to soften Viv's heart and make her listen, the doors to the church opened and the parishioners began to disperse. He watched them tarry at the door, shaking hands with Pastor Rodgers. Gene climbed out of his car, scanning the people and waiting, his pulse pounding with a mixture of trepidation and hope.

When Viv and her parents emerged, Gene immediately moved forward.

"Viv."

She looked his way, and he couldn't tell what she was thinking. Her parents bracketed her on either side as if prepared for battle.

He came closer anyway, braving the wrath of Mama and Papa Bear.

"Viv, I've got to talk to you. Please. Just…just give me five minutes. After that, if you still want me to leave you alone, I will."

Gene held out one hand, praying she would give him hers. His heart pounded as the seconds ticked by, but he kept his gaze locked on Viv's face, ignoring the throng of the departing congregation who had lollygagged in an effort to watch.

Finally, she moved a bit and placed her hand in his. When their fingers touched, he felt the same zinging tingles he did every time. Judging by the way her eyes flared for a brief second, he knew that she felt them too. He just *had* to make her listen!

Holding on to her hand, he gently tugged her over to the car. They stopped by the door and he turned her so that her back was to the disapproving stares of her parents.

"Viv…honey…I'm not sure what happened, but I want to get to the bottom of it," he began. Vic had advised him to lay all his cards on the table and go for broke, so he took a deep breath and plunged ahead. "This wasn't how I pictured saying the words the first time, but…Viv…*I love you.* I love you more than anyone or anything in the *world.* I've never been in love before, but I fell in love with you the first time we met. I…" he drew in another breath. "I kind of figured you knew how I felt…and I kind of thought you felt the same way. Please…tell me what that was about last night?"

Vivian's eyes misted, but she didn't pull away. He wished he knew what she was thinking. She seemed to be fighting to control her emotions. Finally, she gave a little. "That *girl*, Gene. She called you her boyfriend, and you didn't argue with her…"

Gene shook his head, totally at a loss. "*What girl*, Viv?"

Exasperated, Viv flung an arm in the general direction of

Indiana and snapped, "At that little store over in Jeffersonville, Gene – yesterday at about 11:00? *That* girl? I *saw* you with her. How can you say 'What girl'? You both laughed when she made me drop the bottles and get grape soda all over my brand new pair of stockings!"

What in the world?? Gene grasped both of Vivian's hands and looked her straight in the eyes. "Viv, I admit I was in Jeffersonville yesterday – about 9:30 in the morning. I dropped my roommate and his cousin off at his grandmother's house, and then I stopped…at another store," he paused for a moment, knowing that probably sounded guilty, "but then, I headed straight back over the bridge. I was in Louisville at 11:00. I swear it on my honor as a sergeant in the army of the United States – *and* as a gentleman." He waited, searching her eyes. "How could I be in two places at once? You've *got* to believe me – I'm telling you the *truth!*"

Viv's eyes filled with tears, and the sight of them sank claws into Gene's heart. "How *can* I believe you, Gene? It was *you.* I ran right into you, don't you remember? I was as close to you as we are now. Your eyes stared into mine. I even asked you to kiss me – until the girl came around the aisle and ordered me to *get my hands off her boyfriend,*" she added heatedly.

Gene stared at her, wondering how in the world they would get past this. He could tell Viv was sure of what or whom she saw.

Determined, he declared, "Well, I must have a double out there, then. I heard once that every person has a double somewhere, but I never believed it. But that's the only explanation that makes any sense. I'm getting to the bottom of this. *Right now.* And you're coming with me."

She opened her mouth as if to argue, but then clamped it shut and searched his eyes as if trying to tell if he was just blowing smoke or if he meant what he said. Hope flared to life in his heart as he could see she was striving to believe him, in spite of the insurmountable odds. Finally, she turned to her parents, who had moved a bit closer, ready to spring to her aid. "I'm going with Gene. We'll be back later."

The looks they exchanged spoke volumes. Her father stepped a few paces closer and raised one hand to point straight at Gene. "If you hurt my daughter in any way, I'll make you wish for the ground to open up and swallow you whole." Gene's line of sight held ground with the man and he nodded acceptance. Then, Viv's father shifted his eyes to her and said, "We'll be at home all day, Vivvie. You need me to come get you, you call me – you hear?"

Vivian sniffed back tears and nodded softly. She touched her fingers to her lips and blew her father a kiss. Then, she allowed Gene to walk her around to the passenger door and put her inside. As he walked to the driver's side, Gene sent a respectful salute to Viv's father, in thanks for the man not stopping them.

They didn't speak the whole trip through town, over the 2nd Street Bridge, and all the way to the Mom and Pop store. Viv sat practically on top of the passenger door, staring out the window, her arms crossed over her chest.

When Gene pulled the car to a stop, they could tell the store was closed for the day; it was Sunday, after all. However, he hoped the windows upstairs were the owner's living quarters.

"Is this the right place?" he asked Viv as he turned his head to look at her.

"You know it is," she answered, but the fire had left her tone.

He nodded and turned the car off. Getting out, he rounded the front and opened her door, taking her hand and pulling her out after him, mumbling, "C'mon."

They walked up to the front door, but of course, it was locked. A cardboard "Closed" sign hung on the other side of the glass. Determined, Gene led her around to the back door that looked like it led to the second floor. He knocked, hard.

No answer. He knocked again.

They exchanged glances. Neither one had a clue what to do if no one came to the door. Where would they go to find answers?

Finally, they could hear footsteps clomping down the inside stairs. The door creaked open about three inches, and a woman's voice said, "Yeah? What do you want? The store's closed today."

"I'm sorry, ma'am, but could we ask you a couple of questions? It'll only take a few minutes," Gene asked politely.

The woman opened the door a bit more, giving him the once over, and then doing the same to Viv. She had a hard look on her face beneath the curlers in her hair. "What questions?" she asked.

Gene looked at Viv and then back to the woman. "Have you seen us before?"

The woman squinted at Viv and indicated with a tilt of her head that she had, and then her eyes met Gene's. "Yeah, sure I have. Her I saw yesterday when you made her drop the sodas, but you come in all the time, Corporal. What's this all about?"

"You've seen me before?" Gene couldn't believe his ears.

"That's what I said." She looked him up and down. "You look a little more put together today, but yeah. You're usually with that red head, though...or did you mean what you said to her after this one here ran out?"

"What do you mean?"

"Don't you remember? You yelled at the red head and told her to get...well," she stopped and cleared her throat. "You used a few *colorful* words, called her a few names, and you left."

"Do you know my name, ma'am?" Gene asked, feeling as if he were walking around in a nightmare from which he desperately wished he could wake up.

The woman shrugged a shoulder. "Corporal Wheeler."

"Look close, ma'am. My nametag says Banks. And I'm a sergeant, see?" he angled his arm to show her the stripes on his sleeve.

"Stripes don't mean nothing to me, can't ever keep 'em straight."

Gene was about at the end of his rope. He opened his mouth

to ask another question, when Vivian spoke up.

"Do you know where Corporal Wheeler is stationed?"

The woman laughed and shook her head. "You mean he won't tell you, hon? He's stationed out at the Charlestown Ammo plant, right down the road about fifteen miles, or at least that's what he said once. If he's two-timing you with that red head, you're better off without him," she huffed.

"Do you know his first name?" Vivian added, and Gene could feel in her grip that she was believing him. There *had* to be a double.

"I think the red head called him Steve."

Vivian smiled for the first time that day and turned to Gene. "I think I know our next destination."

They thanked the woman and ran to the car together, linked up tight. The woman's voice followed them as she hollered, "Don't take any wooden nickels from him, honey! Men – they're all alike!"

Once inside, Viv was actually excited and it showed in her smile and in the way her eyes dazzled when she looked at him. "I believe you now, Gene. I've heard of this before. I think this man is your doppelganger. And believe me, he's your double in every way. Except..." she broke off, searching her memory. "Except that he smelled of cigarettes...and beer...and his hair is a bit shorter than you wear yours...and his eyes don't sparkle like yours do..."

Gene chuckled and pulled her into his arms, his lips connecting with hers for the first time in what seemed like eons. She melted into him, kissing him back just as eagerly. As with other times in which their lips had merged, they both got lost in the effervescent glow of their union, and they forgot all time and location. It was a kiss of dedication and trust – forgiveness – and passion. Their lips melded and moved together as Gene deepened the kiss with more ardor than ever before. They were reconnecting their hearts and re-establishing the bond that had been so cruelly ripped apart the day before.

Finally, he broke their connection enough to open his eyes and peer into hers. Her eyes were full of love and desire, as well as a hint of shame. "I love you, Vivian Powell," his words caressed her lips.

"And *I* love *you*. Oh Gene, I'm so ashamed of myself for the way I acted – the way I treated you! I should have known you were telling the truth!" Viv whispered. "Here I had insulted that Pat character in the *Sabotage* movie for not believing Barry, I swore to you that I would 'stand by my man', and then the first challenge that came along, I tossed you out the window! I'm so ashamed."

"Honey, there's no way you could have known I have a doppelganger. Who'd have thought? I mean, I've heard of that phenomenon, too, but I guess I'd always thought the stories were just made up or exaggerated. But from what that woman just said – and from what you've said – he looks just like me. I, for one, can't wait to see this fella for myself!"

"Okay then, let's get to the bottom of this and go meet your dead ringer," Viv declared, sitting up and smoothing her hair as she sent a sassy wink his way.

Gene shivered, "Ew, don't say it like that!"

They laughed as he turned to start the engine.

GENE HAD HEARD of the Indiana Army Ammunition Plant, of course. The Army's brand new government-owned, contractor-operated facility was located in Charlestown, Indiana – sixteen miles north of Louisville – and had been his second choice of assignment. It was touted as the world's largest smokeless powder plant, and construction on the buildings had begun in September of 1940. Situated on land close to the Ohio River, it was to eventually consist of three separate, but adjacent operations – the

Indiana Ordnance Works Plant #1, the first line of which had been put into production in April of '41 producing smokeless powder. The Hoosier Ordnance Plant had opened in September of '41 to manufacture and load propellant charge bags. Finally, the Indiana Ordnance Works Plant #2, which would produce rocket propellant, was to be built at a later date. It was a massive undertaking, and was quite the would-be prey for saboteurs – hence the army detail stationed there.

At the gate to the compound, which was completely surrounded by a massive electrified fence, Gene pulled the car to a stop and handed the guard his military I.D.

"I'd like to speak to the commanding officer, please."

"Your name, sir?" the guard asked after giving Gene an odd look and checking the card with a double take. Gene figured the guard knew this Cpl. Wheeler personally.

"First Sergeant Eugene Banks."

Still looking at Gene in total puzzlement, he mumbled, "Just a minute," and went inside the guard shack. They could see him nodding as he made a telephone call. Gene and Viv exchanged uncomfortable expressions. Then the guard hung up the receiver and came back to the car, handing Gene's I.D. back to him.

"Major Lewis is the commander of this complex. He will see you in his office," he said, pointing to the left and what looked like a large administration building for the vast 10,000-acre site.

When they arrived at the newly built structure, they walked together into the outer office, where a harried private sat at a desk. His eyes widened a bit when he looked at Gene, and numbly waved them on into the inner office. Gene figured he had answered the call that a Sgt. Banks wished to see the commander.

When the major looked up from his paperwork with his eyebrows raised, he stopped dead and gawked at the sergeant in front of him.

Gene saluted and held it until the stunned major returned the military gesture. "I'm First Sergeant Eugene Banks, Major Lewis, and this is Vivian Powell. We would like to ask you some questions about Corporal Steve Wheeler."

The major's slack-jawed expression turned into an amused smile. "I imagine you *would.*"

"Do you know if he's here in the complex at the moment? And if so, could we speak with him?"

The major cleared his throat and relaxed back against his chair. His gaze ran over Vivian and then met Gene's again. "Yes, he's here, but he's on duty. Might I ask what this pertains to?"

Gene turned and met Viv's eyes and she inclined her head in a nod. Gene looked back at the major and cleared his own throat. "You're not going to believe this, but…"

The major grinned. "Knowing Corporal Wheeler? Try me."

Gene laid out everything he knew about the other man, with the major bobbing his head the whole time. Finally, he motioned for them to take a seat. "Let me send for Wheeler," he said simply, picking up the phone and issuing the order. When he hung up, he looked at Gene and winked. "This should be interesting."

Five minutes later, a knock sounded at the door and the major bid the person to enter. The door opened – and there stood the man Vivian had seen two times before. He was wearing the same uniform she had seen on both occasions. He, then, saluted and waited for his commander to acknowledge, and then walked a few paces inside.

"You wanted to see me, sir?"

Gene stood up and turned to face him, and the man froze in place, his mouth dropping open.

There they stood, as identical as two people could be – the same eyes, the same nose, the same ears, the same chin, even the same hair. Doppelgangers to end all doppelgangers! Finally, after a few moments, Cpl. Wheeler shook his head and allowed his lips to curl up in a half smile. Addressing Gene, he quipped, "Hey Sergeant – where'd you get my face?"

That broke the ice and everyone laughed.

Gene stepped forward and extended a hand, which the corporal took and they shook heartily. When their hands touched, however, both men instantly knew a surprisingly profound sense of rightness, familiarity, and kinship – as if they had known one another all their lives. The sensation startled them both.

"Sergeant Eugene Banks," Gene let the words fall from his lips.

"Corporal Steve Wheeler," the other man offered, his expression alive with wonder. Then, his eyes flicked to Vivian and recognition shone in their sparkling sky blue depths. He inclined his head in her direction. "Ahh, I get it now. Yesterday. In Hankins's store. You thought I was *him*."

Vivian hadn't said a word, but just stared at Gene's double. Now, she gave a dumbfounded nod and whispered, "Yes."

"Yeah, and I caught the brunt of it," Gene put in.

Cpl. Wheeler good-heartedly smirked. "Sorry, man," he aimed at Gene. Then, as his eyes connected with Vivian's, he added, "Sorry, Miss. I must say, though…you really threw me for a loop. It's not everyday a beautiful woman throws herself in my arms and asks me to kiss her."

Vivian blushed bright red and lowered her eyes, but Gene just chuckled.

The major hadn't said a word, but his expression said he was enjoying the show as he sat tilted back in his chair, observing. However, army business always had a way of interfering with life. His telephone rang. Before he answered it, he lifted a hand and indicated they were dismissed. "Take the day off, Corporal." Gene and the corporal saluted and the three quit the office.

Once the door was shut, with the private staring at them both in open-mouthed wonder, Gene quipped, "You busy, Wheeler? Can we go somewhere and talk?"

The corporal replaced his cap and smiled. "Can't think of anything I'd like better. I know a place. Let's go."

Simultaneously, the two men offered their elbows to Viv, one on each side. She giggled and slid her hands in, noting that even the size of their biceps matched.

"Two handsome soldiers for the price of one. A girl can't beat that!"

The sound of their joined laughter followed them out the door as the private sat scratching his head.

TOGETHER, THEY SETTLED in a circular booth in a cozy little restaurant on the outskirts of Charlestown. The waitress took their orders, her eyes flicking from one man to the other, and then mumbled, "I'll be right back with your drinks."

Cpl. Wheeler watched her walk away, and then chuckled. "Okay, Sergeant. Where do we go from here?"

Gene took off his cap and laid it on the table. He then moved closer to Viv where she sat between the two of them and grasped her hand.

"Tell me about yourself, Steve. And…call me Gene."

Wheeler cocked his head to the side. "Okay. Gene. Well…I'm twenty-five, I was raised in Carmel, Indiana – that's just north of Indianapolis, I've been in the army since January…my Pop's dead, my mom's living with her sister, and I don't have any brothers or sisters."

Gene raised an eyebrow. "You've been in just since January and you're already a Corporal?"

Wheeler shrugged and waited for the waitress to set their order – one iced tea and two Dr. Peppers – on the table, and then said, "Yeah, well, I was in the CCC for a full run. Had a pretty good record. So, they put me in as Private 1st Class and just bumped me up to Corporal a month ago. What about you?"

Viv was staring at Gene, watching him swallow before he took a long drink of his Dr. Pepper. She had noticed both men ordered the same soft drink, not to mention, she had just realized, they had both purchased the same make and model car – a black 1932 Ford Sedan. The coincidences were mind-boggling.

"Okay…I'm twenty-five, I was raised in Elizabethtown, Kentucky – which is just south of Louisville, I've been in the army since January, but as a CCC alumni of two years plus one, I went in as a technical sergeant, my Dad and Mom…" he paused, "live on a farm in E-town, and I have two brothers and two sisters."

"I don't know about you two, but I've got goose bumps!" Viv laughed.

Wheeler agreed. "Yeah, me too. This is like, out of this world."

Gene took a swig of his drink, and then snapped his fingers with a wide grin. "You grew up in Indiana…tell me something – in high school, did you ever catch a guy stealing and turn him in, only he didn't know your name, just what you looked like?"

Wheeler thought for a moment and began to nod. "Yeah, junior year, caught some dirt bag stealing sh.." he stopped himself from finishing the curse word and quickly looked at Vivian. "Sorry, stealing some *stuff* out of a locker that belonged to a friend of mine. So I turned him in. How'd you know that?"

Gene and Vivian exchanged excited glances and laughed. Gene chuckled, "I've been catching crap for *that*, too!" He couldn't help but laugh as he shook his head in amazement.

After a moment, he grew thoughtful. A suspicion had germinated in his mind and had grown quickly as they talked. Pressing his lips together, he swung from Viv's face then back to Wheeler. "What do you know about your parents?"

Wheeler curled into his half grin and took a mouthful of his drink. He swallowed slowly, his eyes alive with wonder. "You mean – were they my real parents? The answer is no. I'm adopted. And…" he wavered, two sets of blue eyes holding. "And so were you – right?"

Gene nodded. Wheeler stared.

Wheeler narrowed his eyes and leaned closer across the table. "State your date of birth, soldier."

"3 February of '17," they both said at the same time.

Vivian drew in a gasp. "Oh my word, I hadn't even *thought* of that! You're identical twins!"

The twins affirmed the pronouncement in unison, as their hearts had known the truth the moment they shook hands.

THE THREESOME STAYED in the restaurant for hours, talking, getting to know one another, laughing, and even getting choked up on a few occasions. At Vivian's declaration on the subject, Gene had met her eyes and then switched back to his never-before-met identical twin.

"Now I can say it. I've *always* felt like there was something…missing. Like…"

"A part of you that should have been there, but wasn't?" Steve finished for him. Once they had made the connection and realized they were, indeed, twins, they had been finishing one another's sentences and practically reading each other's minds. It was as if all restraints had disintegrated and now their "twin-ness" had been unleashed.

"Yes. Exactly. But, I've never told anyone." Gene shook his head with a snort. "I figured they'd think I was crazy. After I found out Mom and Pop had adopted me, I really started to wonder. But – I had nowhere to start to look. And truly, being a *twin* never really occurred to me, at least not in so many words. I just thought I was missing…well, my folks…my *real* family. Ahh," he added with a grimace, "I hate to say it like that. I love my folks, and I'd do anything for my brothers and sisters…" He met his twin's eyes again, seeing within their depths total understanding.

"I found out I was adopted when I was about eight," Steve commented. "My folks knocked about the oil fields in Texas until one day Pop was killed in an explosion. After that, Mom went kind of crazy, she told me they'd adopted me and that she'd always hated it in Texas, on those 'dirty, nasty oil fields', and she packed us up and we moved to Carmel, where she'd grown up. Can't say I had a good upbringing. Things like clothes and food always seemed to be in short supply. So, at eighteen, I went in the C's and stayed till they booted me out. Been living on my own since then, 'till January."

Gene focused on his brother – *his twin!* – and shook his head sympathetically. "Steve, it hurts me to think about you having it so rough. And to think...we grew up less than two hours apart from one another."

"Aw, I did all right. I survived," Steve grinned.

Vivian held up a hand. "So...that oil field manager, Mr. Carriker, was it? He *must* have known you were twins, but he let you be adopted separately! That's awful!"

"Yeah," Gene agreed. "But maybe he had his reasons. That was 1917, the world was a different place then."

"I'd sure like to get my hands on that old geezer and shake the truth out of him," Steve grumbled.

"You and me both, brother. You and me both," Gene declared.

"Well..." Viv began, the corners of her mouth curling at her identical tablemates. "Perhaps we *can*."

The men turned as one and looked at her, and then identical grins slowly took over their faces.

"I don't know about you guys, but I think God's had a hand in getting you two back together. I'm sure He can help you find the answers you need..."

Gene agreed, his eyes twinkling happily, but they both noticed that Steve didn't affirm or disagree; he merely gave a small smile.

For the next thirty minutes, they discussed ideas on how they would try and locate the man who had split them up. They realized it could prove quite difficult to achieve, after all these years. In addition, there were restrictions on travel since the US was in the middle of wartime, and both Gene and Steve were on active duty.

Finally, Viv looked at her watch. "Oh goodness, my parents are probably frantic." She gingerly tugged at Gene's sleeve. "I need to get home. But..." she looked at Steve and held out a hand to him. He took it in his and gently squeezed as she gripped Gene's with her free hand. Looking between the two, she practically sing-songed, "I think this momentous event calls for a celebration – don't you boys?"

"I'm up for that," Steve happily went along over Gene's laughter.

"Somewhere with elegance, wonderful service, and beauty..." Viv hinted.

Gene wiggled his eyebrows as an idea dropped into his head. "Okay, how about we celebrate at the Brown Hotel in Louisville, next Saturday night?"

"The Brown...whew...that's kind of pricey..." Steve began, but Gene interrupted him. "My treat."

Steve flashed his identical smile. "Brother, I ain't one to ever look a gift horse in the mouth. You're on. But...that joint's a little formal. I'd need a date and..." he hesitated and pointedly looked at Vivian with twinkling eyes. "I kind of ditched my *girlfriend* after that little incident at Hankins'."

Viv looked at Gene and they beamed at each other conspiratorially as she revealed, "I think I can do something about finding you a dinner companion."

Steve groaned, remembering times in the past when he'd been set up with a date that had turned south in a hurry. "Oh honey, have mercy."

Gene laughed and slipped an arm around his lady. "Don't you worry, Brother. I promise, you will have a...roaring good time."

With that, the three got up from the table, Gene tossed some money down for the bill, and they walked to his car, making firm plans along the way for a night they would never forget.

They didn't have a clue what was just around the corner...

CHAPTER 17

T HE WEEK WENT by like the speed of sound.

Gene placed long-distance telephone calls to his twin several times during the week, on the pretext of checking on details or simply to tell him "something", but really it was just the absolute thrill of finding out about one another after twenty-five years of wondering. Hearing his voice in the receiver, which sounded so much like his own, was still something of an awe-inspiring experience. He couldn't quite get over that initial shock.

Vivian was nearly as excited as Gene. Sunday evening, she couldn't wait to tell her parents all about the wonderful news that – not only was Gene telling the truth – he had met the twin brother he had never known! She also called her loyal and amazing friend Mary June to let her in on the revelation. On the heels of that conversation, when Mary June stated offhandedly, "I'd sure like to meet that guy," Vivian smiled secretively. "Your wish is my command. How would you like to get all dressed up and go to the Brown Hotel with us to celebrate? You can be Steve's date."

"Steve, huh? Nice name," her friend replied. "And he looks just like Gene?" Only taking a few seconds to think about it, she gushed, "Heck yeah, I'll go – who in their right mind would pass up an invitation to eat dinner at the Brown?"

The girls laughed together, and then Mary June added, "Two questions – is Gene paying, and can I get a Hot Brown?"

Vivian giggled in sheer joy and nodded, even though she knew her friend couldn't see her. "Yes and yes. I've got to run, we'll talk about it tomorrow, all right?"

"You bet!"

The girls rang off with high expectations of an evening "on the town." All week, they planned and chatted about the big night. On Friday, payday, they went together to the Lerner's on Fourth Street and splurged on dresses that were not only very becoming on them, but also on a nice mark-down. Viv's was a pale green; it looked fetching on her and she knew Gene would like it. Mary June's was dark blue and she looked stunning in it. They couldn't wait for Saturday night; their anticipation could hardly be contained.

The fellows picked Vivian up first and then Mary June in Gene's car...or was it Steve's? The girls couldn't tell since the vehicles were as identical as their owners. Vivian laughed and smacked at Gene's arm as he teased her, claiming he didn't know whose car it was. That caused a chuckle. The men were wearing their dress uniforms, and the girls were more than impressed with their escorts. Excitement and anticipation seemed to crackle in the air. Vivian was sure her Sir Galahad would pop the big question on this magical evening – would he get down on one knee right there in the restaurant? Effervescent tingles zipped through her body at the thought.

All the way downtown, the conversation was lively, with the men sharing other similarities they had discovered during the week – parallel likes and dislikes of food, music, movies, and even subjects in school.

"I've never known identical twins personally before. It's so fascinating and exciting," Mary June commented, casting the words in the direction of Gene's twin. Steve was sitting relaxed against the back cushion, one arm thrown casually behind his date.

He grinned and sent her a wink. "Me either. I'm still pinching myself that I have a *brother* after flying solo all this time."

"Well, I'm also excited about getting to dine at the Brown," Vivian giggled. "And with two handsome soldiers in dress uniforms. Every girl's dream," she added, her eyes twinkling up at Gene as she scooted closer on the front seat.

"I've been hearing about their food. Can't wait to try the Hot Brown," Gene agreed, reaching for her hand and bringing it to his lips for a kiss.

"Me either," chorused three other voices. All four could feel exhilaration in the air, as if something unexplainably monumental was about to occur. Gene thought of the object he had stashed in his pocket and pictured a moment during the evening when he would feel the time was right to spring a certain question on the woman seated at his side.

"I've heard that Hollywood celebrities frequent the Brown, but the newspaper always reports on it *after* the fact. Maybe we'll see someone famous tonight..." Mary June gushed, her eyes alive with star struck anticipation. "John Wayne...Betty Grable...Henry Fonda..."

"Not good old Henry," Steve caught her eye and grinned. "Didn't you hear he's serving overseas?" At her expression of surprise, he added, "Yep. He joined the Navy. I heard they put him in as Quartermaster on one of the destroyers."

"Gracious," Mary June whispered. "Well, anyway, I've got a good feeling about this night."

The others murmured their agreement.

NONE OF THEM had taken into consideration the fact that SO many soldiers would be in town – each one intending to dine at the Brown at the same time. Gene hadn't given one thought to making a reservation. He wanted to kick his own rear end. All of his plans seemed to be on the verge of unraveling.

"I'm sorry, sir," the maître d' said as the four stood together at the doors to the Bluegrass Room. "There are no more tables, and the wait will be at least an hour, possibly more. Perhaps you could try one of the Brown's other fine dining establishments?"

They'd already tried the English Grille and the Thoroughbred Room in the hotel, but they were full, as well.

Gene sheepishly turned to his companions and raised his shoulders in an abashed shrug as they moved over out of the way of people approaching the maître d' with actual reservations.

Before he could say a word, however, Mary June's eyes and mouth rounded into O's as she watched someone get off the elevator. Shaking herself, she leaned closer and hissed, "Shut my mouth and don't look now – but I think Elizabeth Taylor's coming this way!"

The other three immediately whipped their heads around and stared, but when the woman in question got close enough, they could see she was not Ms. Taylor – although she did bear quite a resemblance to the actress. Gene, Viv, and Steve all burst out laughing, but immediately clamped hands over their mouths in embarrassment. The woman, in a mink and laced in diamonds, cast them a ruffled glance as she glided by on the arm of a well-dressed man.

Mary June scowled and crossed her arms in an exaggerated pout. "Oh, all right, so I was wrong. But, it sure looked like her."

Viv leaned over and put an arm around her friend. "I thought the same thing when I first saw her – no harm done."

Mary June chuckled ruefully. "You know, I heard that Bing Crosby and Bob Hope have stayed here lots of times, and Claudette Colbert and Lana Turner. Maybe if we stand here a little longer, we'll see *someone*," she whined. The men ribbed each other and shook their heads at her celebrity fetish.

"Maybe we'll see Victor Mature!" she continued, on a roll. "Did you guys know that before he became a famous movie star, he grew up here in Louisville and he worked as an elevator operator right here at the Brown?" The others exchanged brief looks and rolled their eyes at her exuberance, but she went right on. "They say he was a mischievous teen and he was madly in love with a girl who, one evening, was at a dance up on the roof garden. Well, he couldn't get off that night, so he would put the 'Out of Order' sign out, run the elevator up to the Roof Garden, have a dance with the girl, and run it back down, hide his coat, and operate the elevator for a while. Then later, he'd do it again. It worked like a charm all evening, except the last time he was dancing with her, he saw the manager across the room carrying the 'Out of Order' sign – and that was the end of his career at the Brown Hotel," she finished with a giggle, surveying the large foyer as if she expected to see Mature himself striding toward them with his dark good looks and signature bravado.

"Well, gang. I don't think management will like it very much if we spend the evening standing around hoping to star gaze," Gene sighed. The magnificently elegant foyer of the hotel was teaming with people coming and going. All of the plush seats were taken; there was absolutely no place to sit and relax to wait for a table. Guests dressed to the nines were mingling alongside servicemen in various types of uniforms.

"So, that means we're going to have to pick another place. I don't know about you three, but I'm *hungry*. There's always Blue Boar, or Kunz's The Dutchman, I've heard their food is great. We could…try the Seelbach. Or maybe even just go to the club dance…"

The girls had been nodding along to his suggestions until the last one, at which they immediately balked. The indignant expressions on their faces made the guys laugh.

"Hey, you guys don't know what that's like for us girls – be-bopping all evening with dead hoofers – and I'm wearing high heels tonight, so no thank y…" Mary June stopped mid-word to once again stare toward the elevators with rounded eyes and an open mouth.

Entertained by her complaining over having to dance with lousy dancers, Steve noticed Mary June's expression and grinned. "Oh no, not again. Who is it *this* time, babe? John Wayne? Clark Gable? Jimmy Stewart? Or maybe Winston Churchill?" He snickered when she didn't move or breathe, just continued to stare. Then, shaking her head in the negative, she wordlessly raised a hand and pointed at something past the shoulders of the other three as he quipped, "The President?"

Gene and Viv, with their heads together, had been trying to discuss where to go when they noticed Mary June's fascination, as well. They looked questioningly at Steve before all three gave a shrug.

"Okay, I'll bite," the sergeant teased. "Who do you think it is *this* time?"

The three of them turned around and froze on the spot – eyes round as saucers.

Threading their way toward them through the crowd in the lobby were two men, dressed in fine clothing, one older, one younger.

What had arrested Mary June's gaze was the fact that the younger man's features were *identical* to those of Gene and Steve. The only difference at all was that he wasn't in uniform.

The soldiers were instantly struck dumb as Vivian gasped in shock.

Mary June recovered first, with a whispered, "Heavens to Betsy! How many of you *are* there?"

VIVIAN COULDN'T BELIEVE her eyes as goose flesh broke out on her arms.

Just as Mary June had uttered those words, the two men heading their way saw Gene and Steve. Separated by about twenty feet, they stopped mid-stride and balked – the younger one in apparent fascination and shock – but the older one with an expression of dread.

The six of them stood frozen.

Oblivious, other patrons walked between the two men and the party of four, but the stares didn't break.

Then, finally, the older man made a move. A thought went through Vivian's mind that he seemed to wilt before their eyes. He turned his head and looked toward the younger man, leaned to say something to him, and the two slowly came forward.

Vivian moved a bit closer to Gene and looked up at his face, but he didn't meet her eyes. His attention was riveted on the man who so precisely resembled he and his twin. *A doppelganger this time?*

When they approached, the older gentleman raised his top hat, and in a cultured voice, he said, "My name is Gareth B. Tucker. This is…my son, Gareth, Jr." Politely meeting the eyes of the girls first, he then turned to the two in uniform as he added, "May I invite all of you up to our suite? I…believe we have much to…discuss."

Numbly, the four nodded, feeling as if they had been plunged into some kind of dream world or nightmare from which they hoped they would soon wake up. The girls grasped onto their dates' quivering arms, and the six walked together to the elevator as if in a daze. Viv and Mary June kept surreptitiously examining the guys' faces, only to receive quick, unsure glimpses in return.

It was an awkward ride. The operator of the conveyance couldn't stop shooting peeks from one to the other of the young men. The older gentleman stood silently, staring at the floor, while the younger glared straight ahead at the closed elevator door, his jaw tightly clamped. Gene and Steve kept making eye contact, eyebrows raised. The girls didn't know where to look.

At their floor, Mr. Tucker unlocked the door to their suite and stood back to allow the others to enter. Once everyone was inside and he'd shut the door, his son rounded on him, his eyes angry.

Viv jumped as he barked, "What *is* this, Father? What's going on?"

Mr. Tucker released a tired, resigned sigh as he motioned for everyone to take seats in the connecting parlor of the two-bedroom suite. "Let's sit down, son. I'll explain – something I should have told you long ago."

Vivian rubbed the goose bumps on her arms and moved to one of the sofas, with Gene sitting down next to her. She immediately scooted close and entwined her fingers around his arm. He didn't acknowledge her nearness, but kept his attention on the two men, his gaze shifting from one to the other. She wondered what he was thinking.

Steve and Mary June sat on another couch directly across from them, while Mr. Tucker sat in an adjacent chair. However, his son remained standing, stubbornly refusing to sit as he aimed his eyes first at Gene and then Steve. He was obviously upset and it made the atmosphere in the room that much more uncomfortable.

The old man met each pair of eyes in the room and cleared his throat as he began.

"I have both dreaded and longed for this day for the past twenty-five years. At times, I prayed it would happen…and other times, I prayed it never would," he admitted, shaking his head in wonder as he viewed the twins. "I'm sure you have a great many questions. Let me tell you the story, and then we will talk – if that is agreeable?"

Gene and Steve shrugged at one another. Viv wondered if Gene was having as much trouble holding himself back as she was. She moistened her lips and looked at Mary June, noticing her friend's wide-eyed, deer-in-the-headlights look echoed her own.

Mr. Tucker sat back in his chair as the younger man paced.

"As you all have no doubt realized…the three of you are identical triplets."

Although that had been the foregone conclusion from their first sight of the younger man, the girls gasped as the words were spoken aloud. Vivian was filled with the distinct sense that none of this was mere coincidence; she knew deep down inside – it was meant to happen. As if God, in His infinite wisdom, mercy, and care had arranged the encounter.

"What I'm about to tell you now is known only to a few people, and several of those are dead." Mr. Tucker paused and looked to his son, but he continued to pace, occasionally running one hand back through his hair, his mouth clamped tight. Viv watched him, speculating at his obvious anger. She wondered why he seemed to be feeling something different than Gene and Steve were…

With a sigh, the older man continued.

"I'll start by explaining that my wife and I – she has passed on…her name was Felicity – we'd had so much trouble trying to have children. My dear, sweet, beautiful Felicity was a delicate woman…delicate in features as well as stamina. She was never suited to the hot, miserable climate of Texas. The large bugs, the snakes, the armadillos. I regretted that I ever took her there. She stayed mostly in the house. She…she miscarried three babies before she became in the family way with…our son." He hesitated at Viv and Mary June's intake of breath and Mary June covered her mouth with one hand as she swiveled her gaze to Steve's face. Did that mean he was their father?

Before the soldiers could even react, Mr. Tucker held up a hand, "No – I know what you're thinking. I wish I could say I was your father, but… Let me go on…"

The girls could hardly sustain but forced themselves to stay silent. Gene and Steve sat still, their faces carefully blank as they waited for the man to continue. Occasionally, they would glance at their despondent brother, but he seemed in a state of semi-shock and his hot anger hadn't lessened.

"When we realized Felicity was once again expecting, we did

everything we could to try and prevent another baby being lost. She stayed abed the last four months of her term. Everything seemed fine, except that she was weak and nervous...flighty – but then, she was that way quite often, it was just her nature.

"Finally, the day came when the baby was ready to come. We sent for the doctor at once, of course, and he arrived and began her care. I thought it would be over in a matter of hours, but...her labor went on and on...more than thirty-six hours passed, and still no baby."

He stopped for a moment as he relived those trying times in his mind and heart. Taking a deep breath, he went on, "When our baby was finally born...he was...not breathing. The doctor said he was *stillborn*. My wife was barely hanging on to life, the trauma just too much. I...I thought I would lose them both that night," his voice trembled as he reached into a pocket to remove a handkerchief and dab at his moist eyes.

Viv's own eyes had begun to sting as he had related his sorrow. She sniffed back a tear and tried to tamp down her own reactions, utterly concerned with how this was affecting the man she loved. She could feel the tension in his body where her hands rested on his arm.

After Mr. Tucker collected himself, he went on, "She stayed like that, in limbo, for two days and nights. The doctor said her constitution was just so fragile, he couldn't guarantee that she would live..." he cleared his throat. "Well, anyway, what happened next is what you are waiting for," he sent them a weak smile. "We had live-in servants. Our cook was with child at the same time as my wife. She had gotten rather large with her pregnancy, very quickly, and the last two months, we had taken her off her duties and hired a temporary cook."

Viv heard Gene swallow and turned to look at him. His eyes were squinted and he seemed to be almost holding his breath. She knew he was fighting to control his emotions as he heard, for the first time in his life, the events that had occurred the night of his birth. "You okay?" she whispered, and he squeezed her hands and shot her a quick nod as Mr. Tucker continued relating his story.

"Three nights after my wife gave birth, a terrible storm came up. The rain was so fierce, the wind so strong, we wondered if the house would stand. Cook had held on until three weeks from when the doctor had predicted she was due, but during the midst of that storm, she went into early labor. I sent one of the hired help for the doctor, and he came immediately – and worked through the night to deliver...the three of you. That was February 3rd, 1917..." he paused again, his expression pained.

The very air in the room seemed charged with emotion.

Extremely affected, Steve could take the suspense no longer and heatedly spoke up. "So...*what?* Why were we separated? Why did we not know about each other all these years?!"

Mr. Tucker held up a hand, but met Steve's accusing glare with compassion. "Let me explain," he said softly.

Steve clamped his mouth shut with a huff and exchanged frustrated looks with Gene.

IT WAS ALL Gene could do to remain seated. Emotions and thoughts were zipping through his mind like bullets from every direction. *I've just begun to become accustomed to the reality that I'm a twin...and now I find out I'm a triplet!* He looked toward his brother, *Gareth,* still pacing, and felt an immediate kinship with him. Unconsciously, he yearned to reach out and offer comfort, support...something. But for now, he held back. The whole situation was still so... so unbelievable... so amazing... so miraculous... and yet, so awkward.

He could sense Viv gripping his arm, and he knew she was feeling nearly as much emotion as he was. He also knew she wanted badly to find a way to give him support, and that knowledge warmed him, and helped to keep his mind from spinning off into a tangent. With difficulty, he directed his attention to Mr. Tucker.

"You were all so tiny, and the doctor had his hands full trying to take care of you three and your mother, as well, as she was hemorrhaging terribly." Gene winced at those words, for the first time thinking of his birth mother as a real person, with feelings and pain. "The doctor summoned the other servants to help and I went back and forth from my wife's sickbed to Cook's room, trying to assist, but I could do nothing to help either of them. I was also trying to deal with my own grief from having lost my son…" he wavered, casting a longing look at the triplet still pacing, but the younger didn't respond.

Gene nearly said something to the brother, but again he held back, although he looked toward Steve again, recognizing the same sentiment in his eyes. They were both thinking, *What's wrong with him?*

The man sighed and then resumed. Gene prepared himself to hear what he knew was coming. "Your mother was very weak, of course, and frightened, and when she sent one of the servants for me, I came to her bedside." The man met each brother's gaze, adding as if he needed to explain his actions, "She had been with us for years and had been a faithful employee and dare I say, as much a friend as two from different classes could be. When she took my hand and told me she knew she was going to die and she wanted me to find homes for her babies, she made me give her my word of honor…" his breath shuddered as he remembered, "To find you *good* homes…but to not let anyone know you were triplets."

It was as if a rocket went off in Gene's head. Emotions burst forth with no chance of containment.

He and Steve shot to their feet at once, each bursting out, *"What?" "Why?"*

The old man merely pressed his lips together, his eyes cheerless with memories and regret. His words sounded tired and worn, indeed from many years of carrying the burden. "Because she was convinced if prospective parents knew there were three of you, they wouldn't take you as a unit, or any at all, as they wouldn't want to be the ones to separate you."

Gene felt as if he were about to hyperventilate. His own *mother* had been the one to deny them knowledge of each other?

Mr. Tucker looked around at the shocked, disgusted faces, held up a hand again, and nodded. "I *know*. I know exactly what you're all thinking – and you're *right*. For her to insist upon such a thing was absolutely wrong. She was not in her right mind – but then, neither was I. I gave her my solemn word. She…she smiled and thanked me, still squeezing my hand…and then within a minute, she was gone."

The fight evaporated right out of Gene's body and he lowered himself back down to the sofa. Hearing the details for the first time, it was as if he had only just then lost his mother – before he ever had a chance to know her… Swallowing dryly, he turned his head and met his brother's eyes. They were moist with grief, and he seemed to be lost in his own feelings about the revelations.

Steve sank back down in his seat, and Gene watched Mary June whisper something and lay a hand on his arm in an attempt at comfort.

Mr. Tucker drew in another deep breath and seemed to shrink a bit farther in his chair. "I was part owner of one of the first oil wells in Texas. I had plenty of money. Anything I wanted, I could buy. Anything, that is…except for the health of my wife and child. What I did next, I am ashamed to admit. But at the time, boys, I truly thought it was for the best. *I don't now.* Please believe me."

VIVIAN GLANCED AT Gene. He and Steve had both been sitting forward with their attention riveted on Mr. Tucker, forearms on knees, hands clasped together in front so firmly their knuckles were white. Both men had shot to their feet in reaction to the admissions about their mother. Viv had sucked in a startled breath and swapped looks with Mary June, shaking her head at the incredibleness of it all. To find out there were three of them, and then to learn that their own mother had been the one to order they be separated!

Her heart went out to each of the triplets, but Gene especially, and she longed to comfort him. Reaching over, she laid a hand on his arm as he sat back down and relinquished a sad smile before turning his attention back to their host. She knew he was trying to convey that he was grateful for her presence and her concern.

"Doctor Ross had never delivered triplets before," the old man continued. "But he took it upon himself to do everything humanly possible to insure success. He'd read some literature that advised to keep them warm and try to get them to nurse. The next morning, he sent one of the servants to find women who could serve as wet nurses, and he found two who were willing. I don't know what went on about that, I'm afraid. I made myself scarce. However, I know my gardener rigged up a way to keep the bassinet warm, using bricks heated in the fireplace, I believe. All of us were determined to do everything we could to assure your survival."

Wiping his eyes with his handkerchief again, Mr. Tucker went on, "My wife had awakened and although she was extremely weak, she was aware of what had happened – and she was grieving terribly. She wanted a baby so badly; I thought it would drive her mad. Weeks went by. Day after day, she wouldn't eat. All she could seem to do was cry, or stare out the window. The doctor wouldn't let her get out of bed. Finally, in desperation, I made the decision to keep one of you boys and adopt out the other two."

Viv felt nauseous hearing the words. They seemed so heartless. As if he were talking about a litter of puppies. Incredulously, they all listened as he continued.

"Our company employed a very efficient Oil Field Manager by the name of Carriker." The four indicated they were quite familiar with that name. "I sent for him. When he arrived, I explained the situation and I asked him to find good homes for the babies. Please understand – at first, he balked at the idea. But I convinced him, somehow, that it was for the best and it had been...your mother's specific request. He, being the loyal employee that he was, agreed to carry out my orders. Also, I made him sign a paper swearing that he would never reveal there were three of you.

"The household had kept up the vigil of your twenty-four hour care for four weeks, until each of you seemed to be gaining weight and stabilizing. Once I made my decision, I went to Cook's room and stood there looking at you, sharing space in one big bassinet," he murmured.

Viv had the impression, as his eyes rested on each one of the triplets, now grown, that he was remembering them as newborns.

"You were all so small, just four pounds each, but you were healthy. Gareth was the only one with a problem...his right leg had been twisted during those weeks in the womb, but the doctor said with care and exercise, it might straighten out, which it eventually did," he chuckled softly, remembering. "I reached out and laid a hand on each of you in turn...and Gareth..." he turned and looked at his son. "Gareth, you latched on to my finger with one of your tiny hands. You captured my heart. So, I chose you."

The old man, who seemed to have aged ten years in the time he had been telling the story, wiped his eyes again. He met the gaze of the other two. "I would have kept all three of you. Please know that. My decision wasn't a rejection of either of *you*. It was only that my wife was so fragile...I was afraid the responsibility of rearing three rambunctious boys would wear her out. I know now that I was wrong, of course. We could have hired nannies. My only excuse is that I wasn't thinking right. I wasn't thinking of the future, only the immediate moment."

Viv watched as Gene and Steve gave each other a long look, then both of them turned and observed their brother, as he had yet to react. The third triplet seemed to be holding his emotions under fierce control...as if he were a pressure cooker slowly gaining steam. Viv hoped he wouldn't blow his lid.

Mr. Tucker further explained, "Carriker went home to get his wife to help him. Together, they bundled up the two of you," he indicated Gene and Steve, "and left the house. I charged them with being very careful to choose the right families – and to let neither family know that the baby they received was a multiple. When he returned after a week, he assured me he had found two very deserving couples and was sure that you two boys would be raised well."

"Why didn't the other servants in your home, or the doctor, or Mrs. Carriker give the secret away?" Vivian wondered aloud.

Mr. Tucker smiled sadly. "The doctor, of course, is bound by the doctor/patient oath. Mrs. Carriker, I presume, obeyed her husband's authority. The servants...well, I suppose because they had each given their solemn word to their deceased fellow servant and friend that they would honor her wishes. I know that there must have been times, especially when Gareth was young, that they found it hard to hold their tongues. However, each one was of good stock, loyal and trustworthy."

Mary June spoke up for the first time, uttering a question that had been brooding in Viv's own heart. "Didn't you ever want to find the other boys? Make sure they were okay?"

The old man nodded soberly, his eyes beginning to drip. "On Gareth's fourth birthday, we were celebrating, trying to get him to laugh...he was always such a quiet, serious child...and my wife said to me that she wished we could have given Gareth a brother or sister. We had kept the secret, incredible as that sounds, even from her. My conscience stabbed me in the heart, but I couldn't tell her the truth; that I had, in essence, booted his two brothers out of our home. I did, however, send Carriker to investigate the families he had allowed to adopt you…to check up on your lives. He found the couple named Banks, and he saw the triplet happy and healthy, and that he had a brother and a sister by then. The parents seemed to truly love the boy."

Vivian squeezed Gene's hand and he gave her a warm yet sad smile.

"Then, he searched for the other family, but eventually found out that they had left the immediate area and he couldn't nail down where they had gone. Unfortunately, on his way back to report to me, he had an automobile accident and shattered his leg. It was months before he could walk again. I never asked him to go on any more fact-finding missions." He discontinued once more, and then took in a quaking breath. "My wife…when Gareth was six, came down with pneumonia and…we lost her. It's been Gareth and me, alone, ever since."

Everyone in the room was silent, ruminating on the boatload of information they had just been dropped in their laps. So many emotions and thoughts were roiling around in Viv's mind, first and foremost, she wondered how this would affect the man she loved. Would it change him at all? Would knowing he was one of triplets make him happy? Or would it make him angry that he had missed out on so much and leave him brooding over the injustice of it all?

Softly, Mr. Tucker added one more thing. "This day, this meeting, is like an answer to prayer…"

Suddenly, Gareth reached his limit. He pounded on the back of a chair with an anguished cry.

He glared accusingly at his father. "I can't believe you have kept this from me my whole life! Don't you know how lonely and miserable I was growing up alone? Do you know how I longed for brothers or sisters to share my life with?" he demanded, his tone a mixture of agony and grief.

The others in the room held their breath as Mr. Tucker stared at him in shock. Then, the four of them watched as the old man broke down in tears. "Yes, my son," he sobbed. "I do. All I can do now is ask you to forgive me."

"*Forgive you?!*" the miserable young man yelled incredulously, both hands grasping his head as if he couldn't believe what his father had said.

Instantly, his brothers were on their feet and rounding the couches to get to him from both sides.

"Hey hey, hold on, now," Gene admonished, reaching out with one hand to firmly grip his brother's shoulder. Steve reached Gareth at the same time, clamping a hand gently on the back of his neck. "It's okay, Gar'. Don't be so hard on the old man…"

The three stood there together, and it was astoundingly obvious to the girls, as well as Mr. Tucker, that they were already bonding. Viv watched with tears dripping down her cheeks. It was as if the years were melting away as the triplets communicated with one another in short pieces of sentences and soft words, cajoling and comforting, until Gareth calmed down and perceived his siblings, each in turn. His eyes were pools of sky blue, matching those of his brothers. So familiar, and yet the sensation was so new.

Viv could barely see through her tears now as she and Mary June stood huddled together, their arms around one another, watching the amazing spectacle unfold right before their eyes. Vivian knew she had never seen anything so touching in her life. She looked over at Mr. Tucker, not surprised to see tears slowly streaming down his face, his lips trembling as he watched the wonder of their connection.

"I used to dream of you…" Gareth whispered to his brothers as he sniffed back tears, seemingly embarrassed by his outburst now. "I thought of you as my pretend playmates. Probably sounds lame, but sometimes I would talk to you, and try to imagine what you would say in return. I'd picture having brothers to do things with, climb trees, stomp through mud puddles…but in my mind, their faces looked like mine…" he paused and let out a shaky snort as his newfound brothers showed how fully they understood, and their audience somehow knew they had each experienced the same thing. "I never told anybody. I knew they'd think I was crazy. Sometimes I wondered that myself…"

Gene's eyes as well as Steve's had grown misty, and neither one could seem to find their voices to reply, the emotion was far too overwhelming.

For the first time since they had been separated at birth, the brothers grasped one another in a fierce hug.

Then, they broke down and wept for the lost years they had been forced to spend apart.

CHAPTER 18

NINETY MINUTES LATER, after dining on a scrumptious meal delivered by room service, the six sat digesting the food and the information.

Gene was immensely relieved that Gareth, or "Gary" as he insisted his brothers call him, had calmed down and reconciled with his father. Now, the three searched their hearts for questions.

Steve glanced at his brothers, and then at Mr. Tucker. "Sir? What was our mother's name?"

The old man smiled. Turning towards Viv, he cleared his throat. "Her name was Vivian, and she was as sweet and beautiful as this young lady."

Viv gasped and Gene turned to her with startled eyes, reaching for her hand. However, he wasn't surprised that he had fallen in love with a woman by the same name as the one he had never known, but had brought him into this world. Viv was such a huge part of his life now. To him, that made perfect sense.

"And...our father?" he asked when he turned back to Mr. Tucker.

"Your father's name was Charles Arville Tabor. He was born in Texas and was called up to serve in the Great War. He was twenty-nine when he was killed," Mr. Tucker responded. "I only saw him a handful of times. Vivian had been with us for several years as a single woman. She met and married him in a whirlwind,

I even gave her away at their wedding," he remembered with a sweet chuckle. "They had one week of honeymoon together, and he shipped out the following week. He was killed in the first battle in which he fought, and she found out a month before her babies…before *you three*, were born. As far as I could ever find out, he had no living relatives – and neither did she."

Gene and his brothers were nodding as they absorbed this, repeating their father's name in their minds and trying to imagine him. "And by the way, you inherited your looks from him. He was tall with dark hair and blue eyes. I remember hearing your mother talking about his 'sky blue eyes' and how they had completely swept her off her feet from the first moment they met." The guys checked each other like reflections in a mirror, laughing as Mr. Tucker added, "I wish I had photographs of your parents to show you, but your mother never had any made of herself, and she didn't have one of your father. Not even of their wedding. I'm sorry."

Though sobering news, Gene was able to take comfort in the fact that something of their father survived in him and his siblings. They gave each other the once over again, identical smirks on their faces as Vivian leaned to bat her eyes at Gene and coo, "I can totally understand and sympathize with your mother. Those eyes of yours are what hooked *me*, too." Everyone laughed as Gene leaned close and playfully wiggled his eyebrows at her like a philandering Lothario.

Steve then sat back and eyed this man who had played such a huge role in all of their lives, either directly or indirectly. Picking up his glass of wine, which Mr. Tucker had ordered along with their meal, Steve swirled the liquid around and took a sip before casually asking, "What line of work are you in, Mr. Tucker?"

Senior and Junior glanced at one another and Gary grinned at his brother. Wiping his mouth on his napkin, he offered, "Father owns Tucker Manufacturing in Dallas. We, well, the company, manufactures machines for various mining industries, and now that the war is on, we landed a government contract and have begun producing parts for diesel motors, such as fuel pumps and injectors, among many other things. We..." he waited as he noticed Gene beginning to stifle his mirth.

Viv knew why he had found that amusing, but the others looked at him oddly, and he waved an apology. "I'm not laughing at that. Remind me sometime to tell you about the rather involved plot I helped uncover regarding a certain pain in the neck and boxes of used injectors masquerading as new."

Gareth Senior and Junior could only stare quizzically at one another, the older man with a raised eyebrow.

"I'm sorry," Gene apologized. "You were saying?"

"Oh, well, just that we came in on the train last week to secure a deal to open a plant here in Louisville, and I'm to be the overseer."

"That's great, Gary," Gene praised as Steve echoed the sentiment.

"Gareth earned degrees in Mechanical Engineering and Business Administration at Texas A&M," his father bragged, obviously proud.

"But Mr. Tucker...didn't you say you owned one of the oil wells in Texas?" Mary June asked.

"That I did, young lady," the older gentleman replied, smiling at the girl. "But when Gareth...Gary, was ten, I found myself tired of the dog-eat-dog competitiveness of oil rigging. I sold my half of the business to my partner and with part of that money I started Tucker Manufacturing. I've been much happier since."

"Do you still live in Texas?" Viv queried.

"Yes, I do, although I was born and raised in New York. My dear wife...God rest her soul...was from Massachusetts. I met her on holiday when I was a young man and she, very quickly, hooked me," he added light-heartedly at his play on Vivian's earlier comment. Everyone laughed with him.

A HALF HOUR had passed and the girls were sitting together, watching the triplets interacting, laughing and teasing as if they had grown up with one another. Turning to Mary June with an unspoken question, to which her friend nodded, Viv cleared her throat.

"Gene…"

He immediately swung around and crossed to her, sitting down and taking her hand. "I'm sorry, sweetheart. I'm afraid I've been ignoring you. It's just that…"

She interrupted, placing a gentle hand up to his cheek. "I understand, there's no reason to apologize. I just wanted to ask if you could take Mary June and me home now…"

He nodded, "Of course!"

The girls gathered their wraps and bid the brothers goodbye, and then turned to Mr. Tucker.

"Thank you for the lovely dinner, Mr. Tucker. I hope we shall see each other again," Viv politely acknowledged.

The elder gentleman took Viv's hand and raised it to his lips. "The pleasure was all mine, young lady. And may I say…" he paused and cast a side glance at Gene, "That this young man had better not let *you* get away, or I just might give him a run for his money!" Everyone burst into happy laughter and Viv blushed at his compliment, knowing he was playfully teasing.

He kissed Mary June's hand, as well, and cast a look at Steve, who stood to the side, watching. "The same goes for *you*, young lady."

Mary June's face heated up and she flashed a quick gander at Steve before she said her goodbyes.

Gary gave his farewells and made assurances that they would definitely be seeing them again soon, and then Gene escorted the girls out into the hall.

When the door to the suite closed behind them, Mary June let out her breath in a huff, fluffing the hair on her forehead.

"Wow, what a night this has been!" she exclaimed in a whisper-shout. "It was such a coincidence – if I hadn't been in on this myself, I'd never have believed how it all came about!" She shook her head in wonder. "Three of you so identical it's impossible to tell you apart...and you never even knew about each other until fate decided to step in and shake things up a bit."

Viv immediately slid her arm through Gene's and gazed up at him. "Oh, they're identical, all right...but I wouldn't say it's *impossible* to tell them apart. I bet I could pick you out first time under any circumstances."

"Just for fun sometime, we might just put you to the test," Gene chuckled, his dimples pronounced and his eyes sparkling with happiness. Viv thought for a moment that he'd never seemed happier...it was as if he felt...well...*whole. Yes, that's it. He probably feels whole, now, for the first time in his life. What a wonderful thing.*

Out loud, with a grin, she remarked as they moved on down the hall, "I have a feeling that this whole evening was more than just incredible coincidence. I think it was arranged by an 'Invisible Force'."

The others murmured, "Me, too."

"And I'm so very glad that Mr. Tucker told all of you the truth tonight," she added. "He could have just hurried Gary on or found an excuse to turn around, and not acknowledge you..."

"And I'm glad that Gary forgave him...for a while there, I was starting to wonder," the other girl added.

"Gary's been through a lot," Gene immediately took up for his sibling. "You know...of all of us, I think *he* had the hardest time of it growing up – in spite of their money. Steve grew up on the streets for the most part, so he learned to be tough, plus he had lots of friends. I had the best situation, because I had two parents who were great role models, plus four brothers and sisters to play with, get in trouble with, confide in…but, Gary missed out on all that. I was never alone from the time Jack was born, and that was before I was two." He paused, his expression reflecting his affection for his natural brothers. "I feel a bit sorry for Gary…"

Mary June took Gene's other arm as they left the building and walked down the street to his Ford. "Oh, I wouldn't worry about him. If he's anything like you and Steve – and I'm betting he is – he'll be just fine. He has you two now, and that will never change."

Gene smiled as he mused over her words and nodded. "That's true. Like you said – what a night this has been!"

ONCE THEY DROPPED Mary June off at her house, Gene drove slowly, wishing to prolong his time with Viv before they reached her home.

"I'm so glad you've found your brothers, Gene – and I'm still in awe that God had a hand in this and worked everything out to get you back together. It's almost a miracle the way it all happened."

"Yes, I thought so, too. Starting with the incident that almost tore us apart," he reminded her with a grimace, referring to her bumping into Steve and thinking it was he. Then, thinking of what she had said earlier about telling them apart, he couldn't resist kidding her, "Hmm, what was that about how you could tell us apart under any circumstances?"

She pressed her lips together and batted at his arm. "Oh you. That was *before* I knew about Steve and Gary. I wasn't expecting you to have duplicates!"

They laughed together at that, although Viv scooted a bit closer to his side as she remembered that awful night and how she had made up her mind to never see him again. Turning to look at his profile in the moonlight streaming through the windshield, she sighed softly. "I'm so glad you came back Sunday and tried again – and made me listen. I…I'm still a bit ashamed of how I acted about it all…and how my father yelled at you…"

He glanced from the road to her face and sent her a grin and a wink. "No, I totally understand why you both reacted like you did. The way you'd been treated before, you were gun shy. And you're the apple of your father's eye and he was defending you. Makes perfect sense."

Viv smiled and leaned her head against his shoulder with another soft sigh. "Did I tell you lately how wonderful I think you are?"

"Hmm," he hummed and tightened his arm around her. "No, but I'm willing to listen if you'd care to expound."

Viv giggled at that. "No, you might let all that praise go to your head. That would be awful!"

Snuggled close, they couldn't help but feel overflowing with joyfulness.

Minutes later, Gene pulled up in front of Viv's house and switched off the motor.

Swiveling to her, he drew her into his arms for a thorough and quite stimulating kiss. She melted into his embrace like always, wishing they'd never have to part, and loving the feel of his smooth, warm lips exploring hers.

When they finally pulled back, both breathless, Gene touched his forehead to hers as he dialed himself down.

"I love you so much, Vivian Powell," he whispered.

"And I love you, First Sergeant Eugene Banks. Very, very much," she answered with a contented exhale.

"I have something to ask you…" he stilled and Viv's heart kicked into overdrive. "Right now, I'm going back to spend time with my brothers,…but I want you to go with me on a very important outing tomorrow, so don't make any plans that don't include me, hmm?"

She grinned up at him, their eyes inches away from each other's.

"Yes, sir, Sergeant."

Chuckling again, Gene gave her one more long, scintillatingly wonderful kiss, and then walked her up to her door.

Touching her lips with his one more gentle time, he gave her a playful salute, whispering, "See you tomorrow, my sweet Vivian," and turned to go back to his car.

She watched him back the Ford out and drive on, and then closed the door, resting back against it with a hopeful sigh.

I hope that outing tomorrow is for the purpose I think it is...

With a delicious shiver, she wrapped her hands over her arms and made her way to her room.

GENE DROVE BACK down to The Brown and spent several more hours in the company of his brothers and Mr. Tucker.

As one would expect, none of them wanted to go their separate ways now that they'd finally become aware of one another. Twenty-five years was a lot of ground to cover, and the triplets wanted to share everything that had ever happened in their lives. At one point, Mr. Tucker laughed and pointed out that they would have the rest of their lives, God willing, to catch up. It didn't need to be completed in one night.

Around midnight, Mr. Tucker – or *Dad Tucker*, as he'd told Gene and Steve they could call him – yawned and announced that he was going to bed. Indeed, it had been an emotionally taxing evening for him as well.

As he stood up to take his leave, the brothers stood as a unit, and as one, embraced the older man. Stepping back, each wore identical silly grins on their faces. It seemed the more time they spent together, the more alike they became.

Gareth Senior took one last glimpse at all three, standing

together shoulder to shoulder – his Gareth in the center – and his eyes misted.

"Boys...I'm so profoundly ashamed that I separated you twenty-five years ago..." When three mouths opened to argue his comment, he held up a hand and shook his head. "I know...I thank you for forgiving me. But..." he halted and then laid one hand on Gene's shoulder and the other on Steve's.

"I want to make amends, and I want you boys to believe me...my door will always be open to you. If you ever need something and I can help, please allow me. I want to be involved in your lives from now on...if you'll have me. You'll make an old man's burden feel a bit lighter if you do."

Steve and Gene exchanged a quick brotherly meeting of eyes and Gene spoke for them both. "Dad Tucker, we would be honored to have you in our lives. You are our honorary dad from now on. And...I thank God for you."

The old man clamped his lips, trying to keep them from trembling. He cleared his throat and met their eyes once more. "Boys, none of us knows how long this war will last or what is going to happen, but...once it's over, and if you don't decide to make the army your careers, you'll always have places at Tucker Manufacturing. You'll never be in want, as long as I have anything to say about it." He smiled then, and added with gentle humor. "But, from what I already know of you – you probably won't even need my help."

He bid them goodnight and the triplets watched him walk to the door of his room and close it behind him.

They turned to one another and with wide grins, slapped each other on the back.

"Well, brothers, should we call it a night?" Gary asked.

Steve let out a guffaw and called his brother a few risqué names.

The three of them burst out in laughter and with that, they continued their chat. They still had quite a few years to cover.

THE NEXT DAY, Gene, once again late to church, waited in his car for the service to let out. *I've got to get myself back in the church habit.* He and his brothers had stayed up most of the night and had fallen asleep sometime before dawn.

Now, he yawned and stretched, checked his pocket once again, and straightened his somewhat wrinkled uniform. He cringed when he looked down at his pants and saw the absence of their customary crease. Then, he let out a snort as he remembered something good-naturedly sarcastic Steve that had said regarding his penchant for neatness.

Gene shook his head. *Those brothers of mine.* He marveled at how familiar they seemed to him after having known one another such a short time.

He had told his siblings of his plans for the day and amid some friendly ribbing, they had come up with some ideas to add to his agenda that he thought were quite brilliant.

Even at that moment, they were seeing to some last-minute particulars.

Suddenly, his attention was jerked back to the present as the door to the church opened, and his palms began to sweat as he waited for the woman he loved to emerge with her parents. After just a few moments, there she was – wearing a dress he hadn't seen on her before – a lovely black and white plaid creation with a full gathered skirt and a wide off-the-shoulder collar.

With a beautiful smile, she waved and ran toward his car. He climbed out and caught her in his arms and to his surprise, was the recipient of quite a boisterous kiss.

Jubilantly, they waved to her parents and then climbed into the vehicle. Unable to squelch a sneaky grin, he started the engine and immediately headed toward the destination he had planned.

"So, how long did you stay with your brothers last night, and what time did you finally get to bed? Dawn?" she asked, cocking her head and perusing his face. His surprised expression made her laugh out loud.

"How could you know that?"

She rolled her eyes and tossed her head with a silly smirk, then let the passing scenery claim her attention. "Oh, I just know you, that's all."

He let out a guffaw, thinking how much he loved this woman. The previous night, he knew it was her loving, sympathetic presence at his side that helped him plow through the myriad of intense emotions as Dad Tucker had revealed his mountain of secret revelations. In a smaller way, Mary June had steadied Steve. Gene knew, in his heart, that Gary's very "aloneness" had been one reason he had reacted so forcefully to the news. He knew, too, how lucky he was to have found the woman sitting at his side.

Patting his pocket, he began to whistle happily as he pressed his foot down a bit more on the accelerator; anxious to make it to the spot his brother, Steve, had told him about. *Lord, let all of the plans come together…help me knock her socks off!*

Twenty-five minutes later, he turned the car into the entrance to Iroquois Park and headed off to the left. Although he had never visited their ultimate destination before, he knew that Iroquois Park was one of ten magnificent city parks Frederick Law Olmstead had designed in Louisville, and that it, with its sprawling 739 acres, was considered a "scenic reservation" for all to enjoy. As the Ford rolled along, he readily agreed.

Eagerness was about to get the better of him.

TURNING HER HEAD, her brows furrowed, Viv asked, "Where are we going, Gene?"

He just flashed that white dimpled grin. "You'll see, babe."

She watched him, noticing his eyes seemed to be twinkling extra bright, as if he were holding back mirth. With mystery masking his countenance, he resumed his whistling and her heart thumped in expectation. She forced herself to pay attention to the lovely scenery the park had to offer as the car slowly rolled along the narrow paved lane under the continuous canopy of trees. It was a hot day, but passing under those marvelous leaf covered branches, the air seemed magically cool and comfortable, a bit like a cave.

Occasionally, they would see a car parked to the side and the people nearby would wave as they passed. Viv waved back, thinking how nice the people of her hometown were. Everyone seemed so happy...

Ten minutes later, following the winding path that took them to the top of a high hill, Gene pulled the car to a stop at the parking area of the scenic overlook, touted as the highest point in the city. A large flag hung on a tall pole in the center of a rounded area.

Whistling the tune to *I've Got a Feeling I'm Falling*, Gene exited the car and jogged around to Vivian's door. With the flourish of the doorman at The Brown, he opened it and helped her out.

"This is lovely, Gene, but...why..." she began, but he met her eyes with an innocent face.

"I just thought you might enjoy the view from the lookout. I hear it's the most beautiful spot in the city. Have you ever been up here before?"

She shook her head. "No..."

He flashed that boyish half-grin at her and wiggled his eyebrows. "Come on, then."

They approached the low rock wall that surrounded a paved sixty-foot diameter area, with the flagpole in the middle and the 368 feet high vista of the city's finest natural panorama spreading out beyond.

One could literally see for miles, east to north to west, and the view was breathtakingly gorgeous. Down below were acres upon acres of trees and greenery of every hue, dotted by the occasional house and ribboned throughout with narrow roads, although they were too far up to hear the cars. It was mesmerizingly quiet way up there. Straight ahead, far in the distance, they could see a long line of hills on the horizon – the "Floyd's Knobs" of Indiana.

Viv breathed in the magic of the picturesque scene. Everything was flawlessly wonderful, including the fact that she was in the arms of such an amazingly thoughtful man. A clear turquoise blue sky, the same shade as Gene's eyes, swelled above them. The temperature was ideal and the gentle breeze was just enough to fluff tendrils of her hair. It waved the flag on the pole above them and caused a few leaves to rustle in the trees at the edges of the cliff sides.

"Oh Gene, this is magnificent," Viv murmured as they stood together, their arms around one another, taking in the panoramic view.

"Yeah," Gene concurred, equally awed. "Steve told me about this place. It's incredible – the view just goes on and on. Never-ending, huh?"

"Mmm," she nodded slowly, in full agreement.

"Kind of like my love for you," he observed quietly, his arms drawing her in a bit tighter.

She smiled languorously and laid her head against his chest.

He gently cleared his throat. "And speaking of that, my sweet, wonderful Viv…"

Letting go of her with one hand, he reached into his pocket and withdrew a small, dark blue velvet-covered box. Turning toward her, he urged her to sit down on the flat top of the two-feet thick wall, and then he sank down on one knee in front of her.

Viv's mouth dropped open. She had hoped and dreamed of this moment, but now…it was actually happening!

Taking her hands in his, Gene gazed up at her, no pretense in his eyes. And what she saw in them took her breath away. Her eyes began to sting and glisten.

"Vivian Powell, I love you with all my heart and soul," he began softly. "I fell in love with you the first moment I saw you – when I stood there in the club, watching you as you took a big swallow of your drink, closed your eyes, let your head drop back, and sighed in pleasure. When you opened your eyes and they met mine, I felt an electric shock fire through my whole body."

Viv nodded, tears rimming her lashes as she remembered that exact moment and the fact that she had felt the very same thing. "So did I," she whispered.

He smiled tenderly. "I knew then that I wanted to spend the rest of my life with you. Viv, I promise I will never let you down and I'll love you for eternity." He let go of her hands and opened the box. Inside was the loveliest engagement ring she'd ever seen – a European cut diamond, set in a square, white gold fitting and accented with two small illustrious diamonds on each side.

He looked back up at her, his expression hopeful, earnest, and kind of shy.

"Will you marry me...and make me the happiest man on earth?"

She didn't have to think or wait. "Yes! Oh yes, Gene, I'll marry you!" she exclaimed as a single tear spilled from each eye and trickled onto her cheek. He grinned as if he'd just been given the keys to Buckingham Palace and took hold of her left hand, sliding the ring onto her finger. It fit perfectly.

Then, he climbed to his feet and drew her up with him, before he leaned down and captured her lips with his. When he did...such a chorus of whistles, yells, and catcalls arose, it caused the birds in the trees down the hill to squawk and take off flying.

Viv broke off the kiss in total surprise, looking to the right and discovering that they had an audience. And what an audience!

Her eyes fell on her parents' faces, so full of love and hope. Gene's entire family along with Mary June were clapping and cheering next to Vic and Louise, who had brought their boys. Even Mr. Tucker, sandwiched between Gene's brothers, Gary and Steve were in high spirits celebrating with everyone else. They had all snuck in close enough to hear, but had somehow stayed out of Viv's line of sight. Something else she didn't know, was that the brothers had fixed it so that the couple would have the overlook to themselves for the amount of time it took Gene to perform the deed.

Gene turned with her in his arms, pumping his fist in the air as he called out, "She said yes!"

The group hurried over and Steve clapped his brother on the back. "Good job, bro! I couldn't have done it better myself!"

Giggling with delight, Gene and Viv turned back toward one another. Viv lifted her arms and draped them over his shoulders, peering up at him with a look of such absolute adoration it took his breath away. He smiled blissfully down into her lovely face, and there was no mistaking the depths of his feelings for her.

"This is the start of our life together, Viv. From now on, I promise – it'll be smooth terrain. I'd say we need to thank good old Warden Warren and the USO for helping us find each other, don't you?"

Viv smiled up into those sky-blue eyes she loved so much. "Amen, my blue-eyed sergeant. Amen."

The couple leaned toward one another, and as their audience "awed" and their lips met, their adventure began.

~THE END~

Coming soon – Book 2 – *Her Blue-Eyed Corporal*
(which will be Steve and Mary June).

Dear reader – did you enjoy Gene and Viv's story? If so, PLEASE consider leaving a review on the Amazon page. Reviews are the lifeblood of a book's success. (But, please no spoilers about our wonderful triplets!) Also, if a friend or a family member would enjoy this book, please recommend it. This author would be forever grateful. Thank you!

If you enjoyed this book, please check out the Christian Indie Author Readers Group on Facebook. You will find clean & Christian Books in multiple genres. Opportunities abound to find other clean or Christian Authors and learn about new releases, sales, and free books.
facebook.com/groups/291215317668431

Another opportunity to find good, clean books to add to your collection is the Clean Indie Reads website. cleanindiereads.com It's the home of Flinch Free Fiction of every genre. Check it out today!

Dedications

I have so many people to thank for helping to make this work of fiction happen. First of all, **Jesus my Savior**, Who helped with ideas and inspiration every step of the way. Next would be my husband and best friend, **Steve**, who is my biggest fan and is always full of encouragement and wonderful help. Countless times, I have gone to him needing help or clarity, or information about something within his realm of expertise, and with his wisdom and common sense always helped me find the right path. My beta readers and friends, **Judy Glenn, Liz Austin,** and **Barbara Goss,** helped tremendously with ironing out the flow and small details, and letting me know things they hated or loved. Thanks also to the many friendly and helpful members of the Facebook group *Clean Indie Reads*, for their encouragement, knowledge, and helpfulness. My friends at the office, **Mary June, Verna, Kathryn, Sherry, and Terry**, who were more inspiration than they know, always interested and asking how much more on the story I had written over the weekends. Their genuine interest means the world to me. I thank God for you guys! Special thanks goes to **Verna Powell,** who was my inspiration for Vivian – especially when I found out Verna had been to dances at the Louisville USO club! Verna inspires me in so many ways, and I'm blessed to call her friend. Thanks goes to my wonderful editor, **Venessa Vargas**, for fitting me into her busy schedule to polish, tone, and cull out my many repeats and stumbles; my cover artist, **Samantha Fury**, for her many hours of scanning photo sites for just the right faces and backgrounds, plus her incredible talent for taking a piece here and a piece there and bringing it all together into a magnificent cover; and my dear friend and co-worker, **Kathryn Lockwood**, for her final combing of the manuscript. A special shout out goes to **Miss Terri Drake**, manager of the gift shop at the Patton Museum at Fort Knox, who on a busy Saturday, went above and beyond the call of duty to find me much-needed information, and even put me in touch with her dad, **Command Sgt. Major H.C. Richie**, who is 87 and was for many years commander of that post. Their input was invaluable in understanding specific terminology of ranks and day-to-day operations of Fort Knox during the War. Thanks also to my cousin, **Robert Sells,** for his invaluable help, making himself available to answer my dumb "army" questions and explain the workings of the Army, and especially Ft. Knox. And last, but not least, thank you to **Judy Hayes Fischer, Charles Conn, and Peggy Shofner Ray**, of the Facebook group *Louisville's Past*, for their tireless help in researching obscure details of how things were back then. I couldn't have done it without each of you! Thank you all!

About the Author

Linda Ellen lives in Louisville, Kentucky with her husband of thirty-five years. A lifelong avid reader, and after encouragement from her family and friends, she tried her hand at writing in 2009 and never looked back. Prior to the release of her debut novel *Once in a While* (fashioned from the real-life story of her parents' romance), she wrote articles for a local newspaper, *The Southwest Reporter.* Linda keeps very busy with her work in her church's prison ministry and writing every spare moment she gets. Many more plans are under way for books and series, both historical and modern day. To keep up with the latest news on her books, including trailers, cover reveals, release dates, and book signings, visit and "like" her Facebook page, *Linda Ellen – Author.* Also, if you "Follow" her on her Amazon Author Page, you will be notified when she publishes her next book. And another way to contact Linda is through her new website! Link below.

For a special treat, go to her Pinterest page to see many pictures related to all of her stories:
www.pinterest.com/linda4him59

Linda loves to hear from readers.
You can contact her in any of these ways:

Email:
LindaEllenBooks@gmail.com

Website:
lindaellenbooks.weebly.com

Twitter:
@LindaEllen54

Facebook:
facebook.com/LindaEllen.Author

Follow her on her Amazon Author Page:
http://goo.gl/rFj5Ci

Other works by Linda Ellen

The Cherished Memories Series
Book one – Once in a While
Book two – The Bold Venture
Book three – Almost as Much

www.ingramcontent.com/pod-product-compliance
Lightning Source LLC
Chambersburg PA
CBHW051247250626
47155CB00009B/3192